KARAN

Also by B. Wongar

WALG (novel)

THE TRACK TO BRALGU (short stories)

BARBARU (short stories)

BILMA (poems)

B. WONGAR

KARAN

DODD, MEAD & COMPANY
New York

5292

FIRST EDITION

Library of Congress Cataloging in Publication Data

Wongar, B.
Karan.

1. *Australian aborigines—Fiction.*   I. *Title.*
PR9619.3.W62K3 1985   *823*   *85-6769*
ISBN 0-396-08722-1

To the unknown tribesman,
victim of nuclear testing in Australia

What times are these
when a poem about a flower is a sin,
because of so many silences
about so many sins.

Bertolt Brecht

They wander about forever
men of Blood Gum Tree
men of Ghost Gum Tree

clan of *karan*
lost in bush

(Tribal chant from Australia)

PREFACE

This book is fiction. However, in the 1950s and 1960s the British carried out nuclear testing on tribal areas of South Australia. It was revealed to the Royal Commission, set up in 1984 by the Australian government to inquire into this activity, that the testing, which lasted for about a decade, had a lethal effect on Aboriginal tribal man and his culture. The testing preceded a severe drought.

The author acknowledges receiving a Senior Writer's Fellowship grant from the Literature Board of the Australia Council, which made this book possible.

INTRODUCTION

I might never have thought how it would be to enter the Nuclear Age with a stone ax and a boomerang had it not been for old Miru. The day I met him north of the Musgrave Ranges he was smoothing a newly made wooden spear with *kanti,* a stone adzing flake. With him he had a small chiseling tool made from a piece of discarded metal, the lighter end of which had been rasped with stone, thus fashioning a blade. The handle consisted of a much heavier part that twisted in a bend ended with a lump—most likely melted away from a larger metal structure; he called it *karupa.* It bothered me later where the strange metal piece had come from; that evening while we rested by the fire at a dry creek bed I worried about scorpions seen creeping about. "Pungal, they are the ones to fear," he told me.

The following day as we drove south toward the ranges in search of his wife and *idi,* child, he told me that in mythological times two strangers had wandered into his tribal country in the desert of Central Australia. They knew nothing of the bush and were just about dying of thirst. One of the Pungal stumbled on a *gabi,* a small waterhole and, after having a drink, covered the place with dry weeds. His companion, Ninya, growing desperately thirsty, opened a vein in one of his legs and drank his own blood. Not long after he died, his spirit followed *wonambi,* the serpent, and squeezed through the crevices into a deep cave. On reaching a cold subterreanean place, Ninya turned into a frost man. His companion, Pungal, crossed the Musgrave Ranges and traveled farther south to search for a new country on the vast desert plain. I was told by Miru that Ninya people still live in subterranean ice caves and come out only now and then to look for food and female companions. It was then I noticed that below his left temple Miru had an open wound that looked like an un-healed scar, partly hidden by a soft leaf stuck on to keep off flies and dust. He never scratched the old wound, but his head often tilted that way and now and then his left ear twitched.

He was taking me to his country somewhere south of the Mus-graves, where we were to look for his wife and the child, *idi*. I expected him to chat about them when we pulled up for a rest in the shade of an old gum tree, but instead he explained how the Ninya used to scatter the country with flakes of quartz. Squatting on the sand, he showed me the sole of one foot; there were deep cracks across the hardened skin, caused by walking over the glassy chips during frosty mornings. As for the Pungal, I was told these people were farther south still, but they litter the bush with pieces of steel instead of stone flakes. "That's how it all began," he told me.

I wanted to ask about how he had lost his family, but watching his left ear twitching I reminded myself that life in an Aboriginal tribe begins with a myth and knew Miru would eventually come around to his own story, however hard it might be to tell.

Some camps after we reached the Musgraves I was told it would be wiser to leave behind my old car and walk, so as not to drag a long serpent of dust behind, which would give away our arrival. If his wife saw us traveling in a car, she would run away. It dawned on me then that we were near a prohibited area where for years the British had carried out their nuclear tests. This test area, greater in size than England but with rather ill-defined boundaries, oc-cupied about one third of South Australia, where scores of tribes had lived for about two thousand generations. As we headed that way, Miru kept telling me how his old country had been inundated with the Pungal and the best way to dodge them was to travel when the shadows were long. I felt confused about where tribal myths end and life begins, for I, too, found it more comforting to believe in the traditional tale than the lethal nuclear presence. Later on that day when we stopped for camp, I watched Miru using his metal *karupa* to burrow under the roots of a wattle tree and dig up some witchetty grubs. I watched his fingers grip the metal lump of the handle and wondered how long it had been since he had collected that tool from the nuclear testing site.

It was while he gathered the food that I realized how much his sight had deteriorated; he had to find grubs in the wood by feeling with his fingers, then thrusting his metal tool against the hard soil and roots. I tried to help by scooping out the loose soil and root chips from the hole while constantly taking care not to be stabbed by his *karupa*. His eyes were wet and red and must have irritated him, for he rubbed them often with the back of his hand. Some witchetty grubs slipped out through his fingers and he had to search for them with his hands. Gathering the grubs should be a young wife's job, and Miru cursed both the Pungal and Ninya for her absence. According to my companion, the Ninya are male people only. When out from the ground, they try to seize any woman who happens to be about. The entrance to their underground world of ice is on a small island in the middle of a salty lake, north of the ranges. No tribal man has ever been there, and only a few women of those seized have succeeded in running away. They come out of the ground through crevices in the ranges, for the Ninya, with the help of the *wonambi,* serpent, are tunneling to spread farther south to the Pungal, the country of the fearful metal people. It was there that Miru hoped to find his wife and *idi.*

How bad his eyes were I saw again later on, when by the campfire he tried to tell me how many waterholes it would take us to reach his tribal country. He placed a row of pebbles on the ground in front of him, then touched the ground with his fingers to make sure each of the little stones was there. Some years earlier, when the British began their nuclear testing in Central Australia, the local tribesmen, many of whom had never seen a white man before, were rounded up in the bush and removed from the area to be confined in government camps, thousands of kilometers away from their tribal country. I felt uneasy about asking what happened to Miru's wife and *idi* and tried to believe they could be captives of the Ninya people and would eventually spring out from the ground through crevices in the rocks. I was told that the Pungal were tough little giants; when moving about they rattle lakes, can split boulders, flatten mountains, blast immense holes in the ground, and do much more to hold the Ninya people from advancing through the tunnels from the north. Some days later while resting by a waterhole south of the Musgraves, he told me that he had seen the Pungal blasting the country and the tunnels below; the ground popped up in the air very high, it banged against the canopy of sky, and then a cloud bounced back, made of red dust, which rolled across the bush. The cloud engulfed the sun and turned the sky into a "rolling mist" storm, which swept from one country to another, tumbling leaves, birds, trees, and anything else that stood in the way.

I stayed at the waterhole for days while Miru went farther into the plain to search for his family. Looking at that plain, I wondered how far away man had to be to survive a nuclear blast. The boulders and some of the trees were still there, although no human appeared. Like Miru, I tried to believe that people could rise through the crevices into a country of sand and dust; they could even come out through holes left in the ground from the blast. He thought we should come back once again to the scarred country. He knew of a *gabi-bulka,* a big waterhole, farther away on the plain and felt his family might be there. How far it was, I could not tell. At night when we camped, I saw a greenish smear glowing below the horizon; it looked like a distant country town though there was no settlement for hundreds of miles around.

Some years later I met old Miru again in one of the government camps while I was working on *Karan,* the second volume of my nuclear trilogy. He came this time with his dingo dog and squatted next to me only hours after I had arrived at the place. "I like to see my country," he said. He had a spear and a boomerang at hand, but I doubted if he could have used either of them. The people at the camp called him Sandy Blight Mick, sandy blight being for trachoma, commonly seen in the eyes of the camp inmates. Although he still moved about just as he did years ago.

We sneaked out from the camp unnoticed and headed again toward the nuclear test area. At first I worried that with him being blind it would be left to me to follow the track. But led by his dingo dog, Idi, he moved a few spears ahead. When the day warmed up, we stopped under a mulga tree with hardly any leaves on it. "There should be better shade about," suggested Miru. The dingo led us down the track and halted at a large kurrajong laden with foliage. Later as we moved on, I watched Idi walking closely beside her master, directing him to dodge bushes and clumps of spinifex. We carried no water bag, and the flat, dry country around promised nothing to quench our thirst. At the end of the day, I began to think of returning; Miru must have followed my thought and, led by the dingo, walked down a gully—I tried to tell him the ground was too hard, it had not seen rain for years; but he came out with a handful of bulbs. He crushed one of them in his palm, taking care that no drop was spilled, and ate the juicy pulp. He squashed another even harder and let Idi mop up the juice from his palm with her lolling tongue. The bulbs tasted bitter but gave us strength to keep on. In the afternoon of the following day, as we reached a dry creek, the dingo grew alert and suddenly rushed into the bush. I thought that a wandering bird or an animal must be about, but Idi halted under a gum tree laden with flowers. Miru picked a bunch, sucked a handful of them, and passed some to the dingo to do the same. The two of them hardly seemed to notice having different shapes and being species apart. That evening I reminded myself that the tribesmen believe the dingo is one of their dead relatives reborn, as I watched Idi licking Miru's wound, which looked almost healed now with young tender skin covering the temple. The dingo had kept the wound clean by licking it whenever we sat down for a rest, and I thought that Idi must know that to heal an open cancer one would need endurance as much as will. "She's fond of you," I remarked. The old man wiped his eyes. "It's my daughter, why else would she hold on to me?"

It was much to Miru's comfort to have Idi with him, for we journeyed during the middle of winter with long frosty nights. "Six dogs nights," he often repeated, meaning that so many dogs would be needed to keep a man warm.

We always stopped for camp beside a boulder, and at night he would lie on bare sand with his back against a rock, which kept some warmth from the previous day, while Idi curled up on top of him. Miru often muttered in his sleep, but that hardly concerned Idi, even though he was cursing the Pungal. Actually, it was only in his dreams now that I heard him mentioning them. On reaching *gabi-bulka,* however, he spoke of the Ninya, for during the night the frost was heavier than ever before. As the morning broke, quivering by the fire, we watched through the misty haze surrounding the sandhills hanging down from the sky; the trees hung down too; even a pair of grazing kangaroos appeared upside down. Only twice before had I seen a cold desert mirage, but this time a whole country hung suspended from the sky. "The Ninya are about," I was told. The old man looked toward the horizon and uttered some words of a chant for the trees to be put back into their proper places on the ground. It helped; the mirage faded away, and soon after, as the morning sun broke through the mist, Miru left the camp and did not come back for several days. When he did return, he told me of two skeletons he found in a crater where the Pungal had blasted the ground. I never got around to asking if the remains he found were those of his wife and child, for he left soon after and walked some distance from the camp and sat on the sand. I wanted to go and comfort him, but reminded myself that he had come to his country to die and I should not take that away from him.

Idi stayed away for several days, curled up on Miru long after the body of her master had cooled, still trying to lick his wound. After coming back to camp, the dingo went hunting and brought back a lizard. I had never seen a two-headed reptile before and persuaded Idi to free her quarry. That day, after leaving *gabi-bulka,* we stopped at a boulder to camp, and as I stretched on the sand for a rest, the dingo curled up on me. We slept for a while, and when I woke I found her staring out into the dark toward the glowing smear on the horizon. The light came from a crater at the nuclear testing site and, I told myself, would be there for generations, glowing long after humans and dingoes had gone.

Some years later Miru came to me in my dreams, still rubbing his milky eyes. "Look around for *karan* of my wife: it could be wandering about," he whispered. I wondered whether to remind him that when a soul leaves a human body and wanders into the bush, only a tribal medicine man could be able to catch it. "Those Pungal people: are they whites?" The wound on his temple looked as if it had healed long ago, leaving hardly a mark to show where it had been. He asked me about Idi, the dingo, and I thought the nights must be cold in that spirit world they sent him to.

Some years later, when entering a clinic for a cancer operation, I wondered just how cold that world Miru had gone to was, for I, too, had been caught in the Pungal and Ninya conflict—I was told that I also suffered from cancer. I felt sad, not because I shared the fate of many others affected by nuclear dirt, but because I was not in the bush and did not have Idi, the dingo, to lick my wound.

KARAN

PART ONE

CHAPTER 1

He must have spent quite a turbulent night, though when he woke, the Reverend Anawari Mallee remembered little except for a few dark tribal faces still lingering in his mind. His visitors were elders, ceremonial and serious—men he doubted if he had ever seen before.

Anawari put his hand under the bedclothes and slid his fingers across his chest. "Oh hell! They got me," he thought. A network of newly cicatrized lines stretched from one shoulder to the other, and extended toward his abdomen to cover almost the entire skin surface. The incised marks should reveal some tribal identification—Anawari threw off the blanket and jumped out of bed to examine them more closely. The lines he saw in the mirror spiraled outward in the form of a coil resembling the spring of a discarded clock. They meant little to him; he had never seen such marks on an Aboriginal skin.

There was an eerie feeling that someone had just left the house. Still in only his shorts, Anawari rushed to the edge of the veranda and stared down the empty, dusty road toward the settlement, for it was too early for even the dogs to be out of their night nests. Then it occurred to Anawari that stealthy night visitors would, more likely, come from the opposite direction—from the open scrub behind his house, from "the bush," the word with which he and all his white friends condemned everything beyond the doorsteps of the settlement. This stretched from the fence around Anawari's garden to the plain of red dust, spinifex, and scrub, extended far toward the horizon, and faded into unknown vastness. This house was the last in a row jutting out from the clustering settlement and stood at the very end of the road. The position was certainly isolated, but Anawari had never considered that to be a disadvantage until now; he was aware, nonetheless, that the house had been given to him because none of his white neighbors cared to live without a buffer space between their yards and the harsh, intimidating bushland.

Shivering slightly in the early morning chill, Anawari moved back inside the house. He was quite alone. For a moment he wished that Ann, his fiancée, were there to advise him. Ann normally stayed in the house, and often, as they lay in bed, she and Anawari would talk over all their secrets and worries; she was almost addicted to advising him, and seemed to know everything happening not only on the earth, but on the moon as well. But Ann had left a week ago to visit relatives down south and was not expected back for a month—if evil spirits were after Anawari, they could not have chosen a better time to strike.

Perhaps he ought to report the matter to his boss, Superintendent Hunt, or maybe have a word with Dr. Tinto down at the hospital. The sharp cry of a bush parrot broke in suddenly and echoed through the empty house, sending a chain of shivers down Anawari's spine—better to be discreet about this, he told himself.

Anawari hurriedly locked the back door and drew the curtains without knowing exactly what he feared. Do the whites have any gadgets to intrude on a man's dreams? Anawari wondered. Though he had never heard of any such device, he suspected a whole world of secret means and ways to read the black man's mind. He had no proof, but down at the new hospital that housed the Tribal Research and Assimilation Centre (T.R.A.C.) there were perhaps a hundred rooms, and he had been in only five of them. There were secrets there of which Ann knew, certainly, for not long ago she had told him: "Don't try anything foolish; we have ways of seeing everything." Why did they name the hospital Wilberforce? It is not an Aboriginal name.

A veranda window had been left open and Anawari rushed to lock it. . . . What would happen if the whites should find out that he, in some strange way, had been initiated? It had been done without his consent, but certainly the whites would give him no chance to explain that, and if they distrusted him, he would lose his job at the Centre. They would not let him use the canteen; they would kick him out of the club; he would have to clear out of the house as well. Anawari almost panicked at the thought that if all his privileges were taken away, he would have to go into the bush and search for food as did any other Aborigine.

He must be an Englishman, that Wilberforce, thought Anawari, while leaning his head against the glass of the locked window; the sun was about to rise and was spreading red across the eastern sky. The settlement rested, still, but several columns of smoke smudged the tops of the mulga trees, pinpointing the exact position of each Aboriginal tribal camp around the township. If they reclassified him as a tribal Aborigine, to which of the four camps would he be sent? Every local black man belonged to one of the four groups—Para, Tjuta, Pipalia, or Yalpiri. To be accepted by any one these, however, Anawari knew that his cicatrized marks must be identical to those of his fellow tribesmen, and he was convinced that not one Aborigine bore tribal patterns to match his own.

The machine could be of help, he thought suddenly—it was a computer installed at the Tribal Research and Assimilation Centre and programmed to decode tribal signs and symbols. Anawari had seldom felt the need to draw on mechanical assistance in the past, not only because he bore an inherent mistrust of a machine handling tribal affairs, but because the tribal marks and signs that he had encountered to date could be successfully classifed into one of four categories, without any need for scientific guidance. "Well, let's go and see who really are my mob," Anawari thought aloud, and he grabbed a shirt to put on, but quickly realized that its open neck would show part of his chest and expose the tribal marks.

5

Perhaps he should wear a high-necked jumper . . . no! His clerical outfit would be perfect for the job, he realized, and for a moment or two he felt confident that, with a bit of luck and some help from the computer, the trouble would all be sorted out before the whites at the hospital knew anything about it. That Wilberforce . . . ? He thought for a moment that it could be the name of a scientist who had something to do with the nuclear testing that took place across tribal countries farther south. Who else would they glorify in this wilderness?

Anawari did not have far to go—the hospital lay in the center of the settlement hardly five minutes' walk from his home. It was a three-story building erected in a Y-shape—the T.R.A.C. occupying the ground floor of the left fork, while the same space on the opposite wing served as a police station. The triangular yard between these two blocks had a tall concrete wall isolating the area from outside, and creating the jail compound. Dr. Tinto and his nurses, including Ann, had control of the rest of the building, but Anawari did not have much to do with them as he had been instructed to reach his office only by way of the main entrance and the long corridor through the medical section. He had never asked why such a roundabout route was necessary, but sometimes felt subconsciously that his coming and going was observed.

On this particular morning, though, Anawari deliberately avoided the main entrance and walked, instead, along the left-hand wall, hoping to sneak unseen into his office through the side entrance; it was a full hour before his usual starting time and he expected the building to be deserted. According to the tribal elders, no place is without *mamu,* the spooks.

"Well, well! Who did we bury during the night?" came a voice from overhead.

Anawari stopped and looked up to see Dr. Tinto at a window just above him. "Is there anything wrong with my clerical clothes?" he asked.

"Not at all, old fellow, but you're going to be terribly hot in that dark, stiff outfit." The doctor suggested an open-neck shirt

as more appropriate. Anawari explained about having an engagement later on during the day and felt joy in deceiving the
man above him. The doctor was Ann's boss; the whites in the
settlement admired him and spoke of him only with respect and
gratitude. Anawari, on the other hand, always had a feeling that
he couldn't put into words, but he instinctively knew that if a
white man wears an overcoat the same color as his skin then it is
wise to keep out of his way.

The doctor remarked, "You look quite the professional."

What's the bastard after now? Anawari looked up expecting to
detect some trace of sarcasm in the white face. He did not like
others making a joke of his clerical title, although he himself often
chuckled at the knowledge that he had never yet finished reading
the Bible. His title of "Reverend" was purely honorary, an idea
hatched by someone in Canberra not to pay tribute to him as a
man, but to gain religious sympathy from the Aborigines by
promoting him as a "Christian" figurehead. No one had asked
for his consent; perhaps Anawari could have refused it, but he
was not in the mood to make an enemy of his employer. "The
whites would ordain even a kangaroo if they thought it might
convert a few boongs," he commented inwardly after the promotion, but took care not to make any public criticism. Now
feeling that he was being sneered at about his honorary title, which
benefited neither him nor his tribal people, he asked: "What's
brought you in so early, Doctor? I've never seen you here before
the cleaners."

"Dedication, Rev. You know, I've just been looking into the
history of our work. Since I joined the T.R.A.C. we've saved ten
tribes from extinction; that's about a quarter of your total race."

The doctor must have gone mad, thought Anawari. He pops
his head out of a window, like a snake from a hollow log, to tell
me what he's done for black people. "Our tribes numbered nearer
five hundred than forty."

"Come now! I'm surely not expected to have saved those tribes
already extinct; even good old Wilberforce did not manage that.
It was 'our,' you just said, was it . . . ?"

7

Anawari turned to walk away, but from behind him came the doctor's voice again, "We'll let you off this once, but next time make sure you use the main entrance." Anawari did not turn or answer, for there was a need to reach his office quickly, to get his hands on the computer while there were few people about, and to hope that the machine might be able to identify the newly inserted marks on his chest.

As he faced the side door Anawari realized that he had no key. He tried to appear calm; Dr. Tinto was probably watching him, and he wished neither to go home nor to use the main entrance. He walked, slowly, farther along the building, turned the corner, and then dashed to one of the windows. Anawari had always hated the air-conditioned atmosphere within the building—an inaccessible system that was operated from somewhere in the heart of the building; no independent control mechanism had been installed, and he had often found himself irritated and headachy from the acid taste of stale air, but he had no way of opening a window or of cutting off the airflow inside. Recently, however, a dust storm had swept through the settlement, smashing a pane in one of the back windows and solving the air problem—Anawari took care to remove all traces of broken glass, replaced the fly mesh, and subsequently had enjoyed fresh air circulating in and out of his office.

This glassless window stood only a few yards from the ground, but Anawari made the mistake of squeezing through it head first. His hands stretched down the wall inside but fell short of reaching the floor, and on the way through his shoes had become caught in the window frame, leaving him suspended in midair. It was impossible to swing back again, and Anawari's hands could reach nothing but the plain wall.

His first thought was to call for help, but that was unlikely to bring results—no one else worked in this office, and the customers, the Aborigines, never called early at the Centre. Often no one called at all, early or late.

Someone must have approached on the outer side of the wall, for though Anawari heard no footsteps, his feet were gripped and lifted slightly, and he was lowered to the floor. "A bit of a strange way to get in, Rev.," said a voice from outside.

Anawari stood up and faced the police sergeant. "Thanks for getting me off the hook, Sarge."

"The whites are prosecuted for entering premises that way— in the old days some fellows were even hung for it."

"You'd better come in through the door then." Anawari pretended to have misunderstood the warning and hurried himself to the side entrance and let the sergeant in.

"You're to come with me. We've got a job to do; just the two of us."

"But I've got plenty to do here, Sergeant."

"Look Rev., it's an emergency. We've got to get one of your fellows in from away out in the desert."

"What about the trackers?" There were two of the trackers at the sergeant's disposal. Anawari remembered neither of the names but he knew their tribal leader, Nupuru, fairly well.

"Both of them shot through to the bush. We have to rely on you—that's why you are . . ." The Sergeant searched for a right word. ". . . emancipated. You have to come with me."

It dawned on Anawari that the hospital must have been named after William Wilberforce; he felt uncertain whether the man was a politician or a clergyman, but knew he had a lot to do with the abolition of slavery about a century or more ago. Anawari would, however, have felt much happier had the hospital had the name of a nuclear scientist; to commemorate someone who at least had put his foot on Australia and seen something of the bush, whether for good or evil.

CHAPTER 2

Anawari had never before had the opportunity to see the layout of the settlement in such detail; the helicopter climbed slowly, providing the perfect opportunity to observe every tree and dwelling on the ground below. "William Wilberforce" hospital, occupying the central point of the township, had a flat concrete roof and two towers of roughly the same height—one of these being the incinerator chimney and the other the communications mast—and from above, the building resembled a huge, twin-funneled ship afloat in a sea of red sand. From this edifice jutted four dusty roads in four geometrically opposed directions, through the straggle of small houses and into the sparse scrub; each traveled for the same distance until each turned sharply to the right and ended at an Aboriginal tribal camp, forming a perfect cross pattern, which Anawari had not recognized before.

The street in which Anawari lived lay close to the center of the settlement, and was little more than a row of white painted houses and patches of green lawn, almost swamped by the surrounding red, dusty landscape. Away toward the desert sprawled the tribal camps, oozing untidily over the flat red earth like flood waters and seeming grotesquely large compared to the tiny township. Each camp was named after one of four prime ministers—Menzies, McMahon, Whitlam, and Fraser—and a stout concrete wall bearing a bronze plaque with the appropriate name stood at each of the four entrances.

The camp had few and scattered trees, so the most common shelter was fashioned from a sheet of corrugated iron partly buried in the sand at one end and propped aslant with a stick at the other, which served to shield a man and his family from the wind off the open desert. In the past Anawari had often been troubled by the comparison between the opulence of the immense hospital and the conditions suffered by the people forced to live by a camp fire under the open sky, without a single toilet or water tap in all the camp. Now, while in the air, he tried to mentally calculate how many simple huts could have been built with the great sum of money spent on the hospital. When Ann got back, he would talk to her about it. She could write a paper or maybe have a word with some of her friends down south. . . . Anawari's eyes closed as his mind dwelt on figures and plans for improving the Aboriginal settlement.

"Look down, Rev. We're over the gap now."

Below and ahead of the helicopter stretched a jagged line of ranges, half sunk in misty haze. As both his hands were occupied controlling the machine, the sergeant was jerking his head toward the ground below. "The ranges," he yelled. Anawari realized that he must have slept for a while, for the mountains lay deep in the desert and he wondered how much further they would fly, as the sergeant was making no sign of landing the helicopter. "Take some clothes off, you're sweating like a pig."

"I'll be all right," Anawari pretended, though the air in the cabin felt like hot ash.

"Don't be shy, Rev. Take your collar off, anyway, and that blooming monkey jacket. Father Namir, your predecessor, used to wrap himself up in clothes too."

"Not just now, thanks. I'll take them off later when . . ." Anawari looked around him, seeking a topic of conversation to distract the sergeant from his unsuitable clothing. An automatic rifle with a telescopic sight lay behind the seat, and with it a box of pint-sized metal containers—gas maybe, or some kind of bomb, Anawari guessed. There were sets of chains, nets, and ropes as well as the sergeant's usual hunting gear, but none of it seemed suitable to a comfortable chat. Jammed behind Anawari's seat were several buckets full of oranges. "You don't mind me having one of these?" he asked.

"Don't eat that, for God's sake; they are D-15." The sergeant sounded panicky.

"You mean you have to account for each orange in all fifteen buckets?"

"Well, in a way. We get those from the hospital; all injected stuff, you know what I mean."

Anawari didn't know. Looking at the buckets again he noticed the initials P or D and a number written on each, but it remained a mystery why the hospital must classify oranges under separate codes and . . . against what scourge does one inject fruit? But Anawari's desperate thirst was in no way assuaged by just looking at "classified" fruit.

The helicopter landed abruptly, raising a choking cloud of red dust, and Anawari jumped out after the sergeant, copying his stooping run under the rotor blades. When they stopped behind a boulder, Anawari thought it was to avoid the dust, but the policeman kicked the rock in anger. "That bloody bastard—he's got loose again."

Anawari suggested politely that the man might have gone for a walkabout and would probably be back.

The sergeant pulled at the piece of broken chain looped around the base of the rock. "They're like bloody dingoes you know— if they've escaped once you're hardly likely to catch them again."

"Why did you leave him behind yesterday?"

"I had a good catch and he was the one too many to take on board. I wonder if he broke the chain himself, or if someone helped him to get away."

Good luck to him, thought Anawari, for he could not but sympathize with a man left chained to a rock in the middle of a wasteland. He was about to speak his mind but realized in time how unwise that could be; an angry white man would remember such a suspicious remark when he needed a scapegoat for his own mistakes.

"We'd better get cracking after him while the track's still fresh."

"You'll be much better off if you have some of those trackers with you instead of me." Maybe Nupuru's cousins had fled into the bush and they too would be hunted. Anawari felt his throat growing stiff and said, "I hate to disappoint you but I've never tracked in my life."

The sergeant spit some sand out which had blown into his mouth. "Didn't the old man teach you?"

Anawari was silent; everyone in the settlement knew that he had been brought up by whites—they even joked that he was the only "European" with a black skin!

"You don't learn tracking from the holy brothers."

"I keep forgetting that you were brought up with us. Still, those wild bush fellows seem to mellow when they see your face and those monkey clothes. It's a blessing to have you about."

A thought began to irritate Anawari and his lips swelled with words: "Did Father Namir know how to track?"

The helicopter lost its grip on the air and slid down into an empty air pocket; then, finding a cushion of thicker air, it bounced up, jerking the sergeant from his seat. "He started well, actually, the lad almost made it, we all thought."

Anawari had rarely asked about his predecessor and felt uneasy at talking about not only the man himself, but the color of his skin as well, especially now, while hovering high above the desert. The words, however, like a spiteful infant were not obedient. "You raided together?"

"Occasionally, yes. He was properly ordained. He would have been about your age—he used to wear a collar about a size bigger than yours."

Down below, a willy-willy whirlpooled in an immense abyss of dust that for a while seemed to have sunk far below the surface of the earth. Staring at it, Anawari was going to ask, "Was he a full-blood black?" but he got hold of the unsaid words and mut-

13

tered instead, "He had the same background as me, I gather."

The sergeant wiped his sweating forehead with one of his arms. "A pity he slipped so badly before he left."

Ann used the same phrase when she was talking about Father Namir, though none of them had explained what had actually happened to the man. Glancing out, Anawari got a sudden impression that the machine was sliding down fast into an abyss in the dust and bit his lip to get rid of the imaginary fear.

Grapes of sweat gathered on the sergeant's forehead again. "Oh, we'll get the bastard soon. I've got plenty of gear on board here."

Hung on a panel inside the helicopter was a large map of the area showing scattered trees, the larger rocks, and dry creek beds. Small, colored stars were stuck on the map here and there, but there was no key to show what those might indicate, and while Anawari puzzled over the relationship between these and the topographical details, the sergeant enlightened him:

"Those're my scores; every star stands for an Abo I've caught. There should be ninety-eight altogether, and the catch after next will make 'ton-up.' That'll be worth celebrating, eh? You know, my total's twenty-five percent ahead of Dr. Tinto's."

Anawari tried not to let the disgust he felt show on his face. "It must be very exciting."

"Yes, it's quite a sport; I'm hoping to crack the national record this year."

"It's not only a two-way contest then, between you and the doc?"

"Oh no! The ladies are in it too, but their scores aren't very spectacular. They seem to lack tactics, and of course, mobility's essential out here in the bush."

What a gang! thought Anawari. Is Ann in this too, I wonder? Doubts that he had suppressed for months seemed inevitably headed for a public airing now.

"Listen, I can get you into this too, if you like."

"No! No thanks, all the same. I'm afraid I lack such a competitive spirit." It was lame, but the only excuse Anawari could immediately muster.

14

"I didn't mean that I could include you in our particular little group. You might not fit in too well anyway, but . . . listen, what if I lent you my patrol car and all the gear? You could drive out into the bush on your own. . . . The Abos would be less suspicious of you too!"

"I'm not the sporting type, really!"

"There's a good cut in it, Rev. What if you do it on a subcontract basis, paid by the head? We could work out a nice little deal."

"Who pays?"

"Ah well! You'll have to leave that one to me."

Anawari steeled himself not to show the revulsion he felt and smiled: "It sounds promising. I'll think it over and maybe have a word with Ann when she gets back."

"OK, but don't leave it too long. Abos are already getting scarce."

As the helicopter rose again, Anawari looked down. They were flying low along the course of a dry creek, and he searched for something to distract his mind from the sergeant's sporting offer. The country was suffering under a long dry spell, much of the scrub was leafless, and even the bark of the trees was dry and peeling in the intense heat.

"Grab those oranges, will you? Bucket D-15, thanks. That's right! Now drop them onto the ground, one at a time. One every several minutes."

Anawari did as he was told, though he was puzzled as to the purpose of the exercise. He knew that when a white man was lost in the bush the searchers dropped oranges from their Landrovers in a thirst-quenching trail for the lost man to follow back to camp, but the sergeant was after black men, unlikely to be led so easily by such bait. They flew along the valley still, and though water holes appeared below now and then, all were dry. In many places along the empty water course were heaps of sand dug from the creek bed, and Anawari realized that the last water in the area lay deep in the ground under the dry sand.

"There's not much to keep a man alive down there," he re-marked.

"Yeah! Not much water, but those tribal boongs are like snakes. It takes a lot to finish 'em off."

"Which tribe?"

Perhaps the sergeant was avoiding a direct answer. He glanced at Anawari, and then away again before he said: "Look, don't take P-15. That fixes those Abos for good, and I really want them alive."

"What do the labels mean, P and D?"

"P's for poison and D stands for drug—that one only knocks an Abo over till we get around to collecting him."

"Will they take it?"

"Of course. It's their only alternative to death or thirst or starvation."

Anawari hated the job but what else could he do? He had hardly ever said "No" to a white man; and now more than ever he must avoid trouble. The job didn't require much effort, after all; every several minutes an orange had to be rolled through a small shutter on the floor, which must have been specially installed as part of the man-hunting equipment. Anawari had never been into the bush on a similar expedition with the sergeant, and he wondered how long the practice had been going on—but judging by the worn paint on the shutter, tons of oranges must have passed through.

It was terribly hot, even in the air, and from time to time Anawari pushed his hand up under his shirt to let some air circulate, for none got past his tight collar and his skin was sticky with sweat. He prayed that supplies would run out quickly, either of oranges or machine fuel, but his hopes were in vain, for the sergeant had come well-prepared for a long chase and had ample supplies of both.

When they did occasionally touch down, it was mainly to sniff around for their quarry and not to rest, so that when, in the middle of the afternoon, the machine landed not far from a lonely gum tree, Anawari made a dash to sit in its thin shade. Halfway to his goal he stopped—there were the ashes of a campfire. At first Anawari thought the Aborigines must have left long ago, and that the fire was dead, but when he kicked a half-burnt stump, a piece of red coal broke away and spilled a few sparks on the ground.

Two curved oval wooden dishes of different sizes lay on the sand. "They call that *piti*," Anawari remembered, looking at the smaller container. It held a handful of roots crushed into a damp mass, but too dry even to produce a drop of liquid, and Anawari doubted if anyone had got a drink after all their effort. In the bottom of the other, larger dish, called *kanilypa,* lay a smudge of flour, which Anawari guessed had been made from *kaltu-kaltu,* the wild grass seeds. The Aborigines often talked about the way they made their *nyuma,* a damper cooked in the hot ashes of the campfire, and though he had often wished to see how it was done, the opportunity had never come his way. Several times though, Anawari had dreamed about a tribal woman, with pathetic skinny legs, making this food by a fire, and for several days afterward had been haunted by the smell of hot damper.

Anawari bent close to the earth and his nostrils caught again the scent from his dream—there, on the warm ashes, was a freshly made *nyuma.* Trying to memorize every detail of it, Anawari fingered the larger dish. It must have been in long use; on the outside, a layer of soot had gathered in the grooves made when it was fashioned with a stone ax. On the edge of . . . a sudden blow from the sergeant's boot sent the scrap of flour flying through the air and the dish rolling in the sand. "Steady now. Easy does it," Anawari warned himself, and kept looking at the same spot on the ground as before. Two grinding stones lay there, one round and smooth, called . . . Anawari tried to remember the proper Aboriginal name for it, but the word evaded him. As he took the stone and turned it in his palm, two of his fingers slid into a small depression on the surface that had been hollowed, over the ages, by the perpetual action of a human hand. Somewhere deep inside Anawari flickered a pleasant sensation of warmth and familiarity.

The small, blackened damper still lay on the ashes, where it was perhaps put to cool just before the raid—there must have been no time in which to eat it. Anawari snatched the *nyuma* quickly up and, holding it furtively against his trouser leg, moved away a few slow steps, then dodged behind a shelter made from a few scrubby branches. He had never eaten bread made from *kaltu-kaltu* grass, but he had, in one of the doctor's textbooks, read that it tasted bitter, and that fragments of the tough wild seed that had escaped the grinding process caused stomach ulcers that often developed into secondary cancer. This hampered research on contaminated Aborigines and could produce "misleading field results," according to the doctor. Why should the whites show so much concern about the contents of an Aboriginal belly, and so little about the conditions in which he lives and the loss of his tribal land?

The damper tasted . . . it reminded Anawari of biscuits he had once eaten, with crumbs of crushed peanut, which crunched pleasantly between his teeth. He finished the lot and wished for a few more dampers, and in a moment he had evolved a plan for collecting *kaltu-kaltu* seeds—not now, but secretly, some other time. Ann had left her car parked under Anawari's house and told him to make use of it; if he sneaked away early, no one in the settlement would notice his absence for a day or two, and by that time he could collect enough seed for scores of dampers, not only to eat in the bush but to bring home to have there now and then.

Only when he came out of his hiding place did Anawari realize that the sergeant was not close by; looking around, he saw him in the scrub some distance away, staring at the ground.

A naked child lay on the hot sand with his fingers clasped around a half-eaten orange, as though asleep, but making no sound or movement. Flies swarmed on the boy's face, trying to crawl into his nostrils and mouth. A trace of life still remained, for the child's limbs were not stiff and Anawari could feel a fluttering heartbeat, though so faint and weak that he thought each beat would be the last. One of the child's arms looked shorter, with fingers growing out from just under the elbow; four fingers only, with pointy nails that reminded Anawari of a lizard's claw. He ran to bring a water container from the helicopter, and was about to splash the child when the sergeant gripped his arm. "Don't waste good water on him; they're all doomed."

Anawari glanced up in anger.

"Look, he's going to die; even flies rot here. When that rot sets in, no one makes it through."

Anawari splashed some water over the child's body and backed away from the onslaught of flies that rose suddenly into the air. Why are they dying? There is no epidemic; no one at the hospital talks about it. He splashed some more water—the stunted fingers on the deformed hand sprang out as though trying to reach for the container. Patches of dead skin covered the child's body; sand was clinging to the sweating wounds. Poor little fellow, I should wash him.

"Come on, stop playing 'Jesus Our Savior,' Rev." The sergeant warned that they would run short of water if Anawari kept chucking it around. Anawari took no note, reminding himself that the epidemic seldom catches up with the people scattered in the bush. There's something lethal about, he told himself, splashing some more water on the child. This angered the sergeant. "I order you to take that container back to the chopper. Pull yourself together, Reverend."

Whatever that bright speck of defiance in his brain was telling him, it was impotent against all the years of obedience to the white man, and Anawari cursed himself for his lack of guts. He had never dared to stand up to his employers—he had never imagined there was enough strength in him to do so—but this time he had been close to rebellion. Close, yes. But not close enough. Twice, in the past, Anawari had dreamed that he had defied Dr. Tinto, dreamed that he had stood up to him and spoken his mind, and for days afterward was doubly obsequious to the whites for fear they could see into his secret thoughts . . . and Anawari was disgusted with himself.

Later that afternoon they found a woman lying in the scrub some distance from the camp. She, too, had eaten an orange, but had somehow crawled away into the shade of a mulga tree before losing consciousness. The sergeant dragged her closer to the tree, wrapped her arms around its trunk, and locked handcuffs around her wrists.

"Shouldn't we take her back to the settlement? She'd add another point to your score." Anawari hoped this way to bring an end to the hunt and let the fugitive get away.

"I want that other bastard, and I'm not giving up now."

"It'll be getting dark soon."

"You're going to stay here and keep an eye on her. I'll go to refuel, and come back."

Anawari didn't like the arrangement, but was given no choice. To be stuck in the middle of the desert alone, with nightfall approaching, did not appeal to him, but at least he would have the opportunity to take off his collar and shirt and expose his suffocating skin to the cool of the evening air.

Anawari couldn't remember ever having camped all alone before. He tramped about in the scrub looking for *kaltu-kaltu* grass, came back with a hatful of seeds, and though there were no stones with which to grind flour, found that the raw grains were no less tasty than the damper. At dusk, when the darkness began to close in on him, Anawari had the feeling that he had been abandoned forever there in the bush, and though the thought pleased him at first, a moment later he grew panicky and felt like yelling for help. As night fell he considered making a fire but, realizing that the light would reveal the position of his camp, decided that it was much safer to move a short distance away and hide in the scrub. If anyone came to rescue the woman, Anawari wanted to be well out of the way, and for reasons he avoided clarifying to himself, he decided that in the future he would remain neutral, and not allow himself to side either with white men or with blacks.

A clear patch of sand between clumps of spinifex provided a secure-enough resting place, but although worn out from the long and exhausting day, Anawari could not sleep, and whenever he moved, the sharp spinifex spines increased his wakefulness.

From time to time the woman's voice could be heard, and though Anawari considered moving farther into the bush out of

20

earshot of her nightmares, it was hard to leave his warm place in the sand and he feared becoming lost. Anawari knew all four of the local tribal dialects, but the woman's words were mostly unfamiliar to him, except the word *karan,* which she repeated twice. He had heard that word from Nupuru and also from some Tjuta, Blood Gum Tree people. He thought that perhaps it was her maiden dialect and then fell to wondering what language he spoke in his own nightmares. Ann often complained that he yelled in his dreams, but she had never said whether it was in English or . . . some tribal dialect.

It was no secret that Anawari had been taken from one of the tribes in the bush, but it had happened far earlier than his memory could reach, and he had hoped, all these years, that one day the whites would tell him, if not the name of the tribe, then at least the area from which he had been collected. The whites had shelves and cabinets of books, data, and records, and there was always a chance that Anawari's real origin had been written down in detail to be revealed to him at an appropriate time. Yet so much time had gone by that Anawari persuaded himself that the whites were keeping the information from him because it was too unpleasant for him to hear.

Now, turning restlessly among the prickly spinifex, Anawari found his hand again pressed against his chest, his fingers moving slowly across each tribal mark, while in his mind he saw an immense picture of that same tribal pattern reproduced on the distant horizon. Now, he felt, the time had come when he must dream the truth about his own tribal origin.

CHAPTER 3

Anawari dreamed, not about his tribe, but of being caught naked in the bush by the sergeant and chained in a spinifex clump.

The woman had recovered and must have been struggling for some time to break away from the tree, for the handcuffs had worn a groove in the bark of the trunk. "There's nothing I can do to help you," he apologized.

The woman did not seem terribly frightened, but rather calm, and behaved as though she knew Anawari already; he was depressed that he was unable to free her, and his imagination balked at what a night tied to a tree must be like. The front of the woman's body was scratched and bruised, and at her wrists blood colored the metal manacles. Patches of decaying skin covered her body; they looked like old burns from a campfire and appeared randomly on the upper arms and belly. She spoke some words but none of them held any meaning for Anawari—he expected her to be of the Pipalia, the local River Gum Tree tribe, but she spoke differently, with a nasal *r* evident in much of her speech.

"This must be your husband's *ngura?*" Anawari hoped to discover if the woman's tribal country was in the surrounding area.

She answered in Para, Ghost Gum Tree dialect: *"Tjamu ngura."* It was uncertain whether she meant "my father's country" or "the country of our spirit ancestors."

This sounded as if she were still unmarried, and though Anawari could not judge from the appearance of her body whether the woman had borne children, it seemed logical to deduce that she was the mother of the boy they had found dying at the camp site. Anawari thought of questioning her about the child, but hesitated to rub such salt into the fresh wound of her grief. "I'm glad your husband got away." He smiled. Her face brightened. "They didn't catch Gara then?"

"No, and let's hope he will stay free." Anawari felt there was something more he should say—a word or two of sympathy, or even a gesture that would express his sorrow—but he could say or do nothing, and only looked about helplessly before he sat down on the ground.

Two spinifex finches rose up from behind the bushes; they hovered against an air current for a moment, as if preparing for distant flight, but instead spiraled directly overhead before drifting downward to perch among the branches of a *pipalia* tree nearby, and behind them the pale sun struggled to break through the early morning mist into the open sky. Could the birds be the woman's kin? Anawari knew of a few local clans with the finch for their totem. One of the Para elders, an old man called Nupuru who used to come often to the Welfare Centre, had once told Anawari a story about his ancestor—a woman who changed from human shape into that of a finch. Every year, when nesting, she chose a site in a clump of spinifex, so inhospitable that nothing could approach to snatch her eggs—but neither could she roost among the thorns to raise the young. There was a moral to the story, Anawari was sure, and though he was never able to grasp it, he still found Nupuru's tale curiously rewarding. From the same old man Anawari had learned much about tribal custom as they wandered together in the bush, and if he was to be believed, what Anawari had just heard was all wrong—the Para, Ghost Gum people, never took their sons-in-law into their tribe. Customs that must have originated millennia ago, perhaps thirty thousand years or more, when their stone axes were new and two pieces of wood were first rubbed against each other to make fire, were all still

23

with them, so if a habit or custom should be abandoned, then the Para would be the last people on earth to do so. Anawari stared hard at the woman in front of him and asked softly, "Do many people live around here?"

He thought there might be more than one tribe in the area—that would explain the woman's confusing claim. She looked at the ground in silence and then repeated: *"Tjamu Ngura . . ."* Then she slipped back into the strange dialect of which Anawari comprehended so little, till the hard nasal *r* began to irritate him. She is no help, he thought, and watched her silently. Stones, pieces of broken wood, and decaying bark that covered the ground around the tree trunk had impressed their pattern on the skin of the woman's knees as she struggled to get to her feet, inching the handcuffs up the tree as she rose.

"What's your mother's mob?" asked Anawari.

The woman moved around the trunk. *"Tjuta,* same as yours." Her eyes were fixed on the tribal marks on his chest.

Anawari forced himself to be calm. "How far is it from here to our country?"

The woman made as if to raise her hand but could not, being shackled to the tree, so she sidled around the trunk until she reached the right position, then pointed with her chin toward the south: "Many, many waterholes away."

"Do you know the way?"

"No."

"Does Gara know?"

"Only the old people know."

Anawari was ashamed that he must talk to a woman who might well be his sister while she was tied to a tree and staring at him as though pleading to be freed. What would she do when she found out about the child? "Look, I'm going to try and set you free." Anawari grabbed a stone from the ground. It was too small and soft to make any impact on the tough steel of the handcuffs, but he kept smashing with it, unconscious of where or how the blows fell; the blood had rushed to his face and he felt his whole body and mind inflamed with a strange mixture of shame and anger. The stone hit the woman's wrist, tearing off some skin and drawing blood. "Rub the stone against the chain," she suggested.

Cutting the handcuffs that way might have taken a day or more, and Anawari needed to have it over before the helicopter showed up again; he rushed into the bush and found a bigger and harder stone, more effective against the steel, but then he devised a better use for the tool. The mulga trunk used to shackle the woman was a sapling, hardly thicker than a leg bone, and it occurred to Anawari that if he climbed the tree and, with the help of the stone, knocked off the branches and the thin crown, he could free the woman another way. Though it was extremely doubtful that Anawari's new idea would work, there was little choice of strategy, so he set his mind and muscles to the task till only the tree trunk was left standing in the air like a telegraph pole, then he bent to let the woman stand on his shoulders, forced himself upright and boosted her further up the tree trunk. In theory, she was to slide her arms over the crown of the tree and free herself, but she could not reach high enough to do so. Anawari pushed the woman as far up as he could, but she was unable to open her shackled arms wide enough to grip the tree trunk and climb higher, and then the handcuffs got caught on the stub of a branch. The woman hung there, stuck, and dangling from the middle of the tree, till Anawari hoisted her high enough to loosen the chain, and she slid back to the ground. "There has to be some way to free her," he told himself. "If I could bend that sapling and . . ." The sound of the approaching helicopter bisected his thoughts and as he tried to think of some excuse, the machine was already landing in a cloud of dust. "Huh! So they tried to free her," said the sergeant by way of a greeting.

"In a way, I suppose. Yes . . . I must have been asleep."

"It'd be her husband, for sure. . . . The bastard couldn't have got far. Come on! Let's get him."

As they were about to climb into the helicopter, Anawari looked at the woman still chained to the tree and then moved conspiratorially close to the sergeant. "Look Boss, I just had an idea. I'm no expert, so tell me if I'm wrong."

"Yes? Well, speak up."

"What if we let her go and then follow—maybe she'd lead us to him."

The sergeant tossed him the key without hesitation. "Here, let her loose."

They took off again, cruising about the area, but always swinging back to keep the woman in sight. Set free, she headed toward the camp, where she found the child in the scrub and carried it to the hut, cradled in her arms. She lay there in the shade of the tree, her body coiled in the pain of her grief.

There would be no one to comfort her in the whole world, thought Anawari. She might scream her agony loud enough to shatter the stars in the sky, but here, in this place, no one would hear. The immense vastness lapped all about, like a dead sea, under the persistent sun that had dried out the last fragment of life from man and insect and plant, and even if, by the one chance in a thousand, no, one in a million, *your* cry should be strong enough to bridge the shimmering distance between you and the cruel line of the horizon, there was no one to hear it. One was afloat on the drifting red sand, and the world beyond would never know that you had ever left your footprint there.

The sergeant kept a watch on the area for a while, then flew deeper into the desert, over the ranges and along a dry riverbed. A waterhole appeared, ringed by gum trees, and traces of camp fires could be seen, but judging by the whiteness of the ashes against the red of the dust, they were long extinct. The helicopter landed in the middle of the camp—a group of flimsy huts made by propping a few branches against a tree trunk and designed not as shelter from the rain that fell only a few times in a year if at all, but as a shield from the boiling sun. No one came out to meet the men and their craft. Even the dogs stayed still, as if under some magic spell, but as Anawari stepped over one of them, stretched out in the sun and hot dust, he realized that it, and its scores of counterparts, were carcasses, each buzzing with swarms of flies.

Why had no one buried them? An old couple sat in the shade of their hut, and as Anawari walked toward them, he smiled and mentally composed a cheerful and proper Pipalia greeting. . . . Hell! Both dead! And for quite some time, for their bodies had dehydrated into grotesque, dummylike shapes. Close to these two, a man sitting and resting his head on his knees had desiccated to a charcoal-colored carcass.

Anawari did not count the bodies, but there was not one camp fire without a dead inhabitant, and the scene so disgusted him that he was forced to look away into the distance. A tall blind woman moved slowly from behind a tree toward the waterhole. She had no hair, and an ugly, calloused scar covered half of her face and part of her shoulders. Her skin was stretched tight and transparent over protruding bones so raw and fleshless that they seemed scarcely able to hang together. The woman wore something around her waist—an old rag or *mawulyari,* perhaps the traditional cover?— it looked too dusty to tell. This scarred skeleton stepped through the ashes of a dead fire, tripped against a stump and fell. Anawari rushed to help her to her feet, and at his touch the woman pushed her hand under his shirt and moved her fingers slowly over his chest to identify the tribal marks on his skin. Her lips moved, and though the words she murmured were too faint to be heard, Anawari somehow felt that he had read the word *idi* in her mouthings. It means baby, he reminded himself.

"Don't touch her. You'll catch the Rot from that old wretch for sure," called the sergeant.

Anawari watched as the woman walked slowly away toward the waterhole, but she had not reached it when a willy-willy, a whirling wind, suddenly struck the camp. The spinning pillar of dust and ashes caught up the heaps of worn-out rags and bits of human hair, and spiraled them high into the shimmering air. The wind moved on as swiftly as it came, but when Anawari looked about, he could no longer see the woman.

He walked to the edge of the waterhole. On the calm surface

floated an old *mawulyari* belt. "What was that about the Rot sickness?"

"Quite a nasty brew, that: makes quite a mess of people. It's Dr. Tinto's department anyway. He has warned us people that the Rot could be contagious."

Anawari pretended. "Ah yes: it's a disease, isn't it?"

"Well, in a way, I suppose. He says when you blast a country with nuclear bombs, more evils hatch out than you can expect—there's no two ways about that." The sergeant leaned on the cabin of the helicopter and inserted a mark on the map, pinpointing a spot not far below the ranges. Only now did Anawari notice that a large plain locked within a circle of hills (he remembered seeing it from the air) was colored yellow, and that some distance away, deep in the desert, were several more patches of a matching shade. He stared at the map looking for some reference or code, but there was nothing to indicate why the areas were so marked. "It's sheer luck that we stumbled on this camp. I must let Dr. Tinto know straight away. He's obsessed with his research; there's going to be quite a job for him around here."

On the return journey the helicopter flew over the ranges again, and Anawari constantly kept one eye on the map and the other on the ground until he sighted the "yellow" area. A high valley—probably ten kilometers wide and perhaps three times as long—the place was well-sheltered from the drifting sand of the desert, giving it the character of a fertile patch surrounded by desolation. The trees and scrub had once grown thick and tall, but now only patches of green remained, in pockets here and there, on the edge of the valley. Most of the trees must have been dead some time, for they had shed both leaves and bark, and stood now as a forest of grotesque skeletons. In times long past this must have been a place for the hunter, for the valley of green would have attracted animals and birds from the surrounding areas of sand and rocks, not only in search of food but seeking the shelter, from the hot sun and from predators, that was provided by the canopy of leaves.

Anawari knew, however, that life is a chain of codes linking all those destined to share it in a mutual agreement between all species in or above the ground, to live together or not at all. When the time comes for one link in the chain to snap, then death is released like an avalanche of sand pouring down to bury the others as well. Humans are not excluded from the agreement, and if the tribal elders are to be believed, even rocks are part of the plan, for though they are so hard and outlast many men, still time, sun, and weather will grind them to sand.

As they flew deeper into the valley, the skeleton trees first thinned; they had no bark and few branches. Some of the trees lay uprooted; Anawari gazed for a while at a huge trunk pulled out from the ground, together with an immense clump of entangled roots, rocks, and soil that had been tossed in the air. Turned upside down, the tree rested against the severed trunk of another giant, while the immense clump mushroomed over both of them. What was left of the bush reminded Anawari of scattered telegraph poles covered with soot or charcoal—he could not tell. Then the trees disappeared, leaving nothing but red soil, without even the ubiquitous spinifex. The earth was flat and pitted like the bed of a dry lake, but Anawari's curious eyes noticed a smooth strip, the same color as the dusty plain that surrounded it and clearly prepared as a runway for landing aircraft.

"What a hell of a life a bloke would live down there," remarked the sergeant.

Anawari thought he sighted a wrecked aircraft but soon realized there ought to be more than one, for the ground below looked littered with thrown wings, blown parts of cockpits, and heaps of metal entangled beyond recognition. They flew over a pile of wrecks, striking out from which was the loose end of a large metal caterpillar. Two men from a parked Landrover were poking Geiger counter rods into the old wreck. Anawari assumed that the old military hardwear had been placed in the bush during the nuclear tests to register the impact of the blast. Unmanned equipment, he thought, suspecting that if any humans were there, they would have been puffed into smoke without leaving any trace behind. "Let's hope they'll not blast while we are about," he remarked.

Sweating, the sergeant wiped his forehead. "They're only mopping up; the testing is over, so they say."

Anawari asked how the men got so deep into the desert; then looking at the far end of the valley where the sergeant pointed, he saw an airstrip with a communication mast and a roof nearby revealing a camp. He looked around for humans, wondering what it would be like to live there, but the valley soon fell away and a chain of mesa-shaped hills appeared. Behind them a cloud billowed, looking . . . The cloud had already passed the infant mushroom shape as its whirlpooling gray mass rapidly engulfed the entire plain beyond the mesas. Ahead of the cloud a strong gale rolled a wall of red dust. "Hell, let's get out of here," yelled the sergeant.

Anawari remembered seeing a lightning flash earlier, while they were flying along the valley, but thought it to be a reflection from some object on the ground below and . . . The gust suddenly lashed the helicopter, the machine gripped the air, then was tossed away and plunged into the red mist. He waited for a while, seeing in his mind part of the machine, as well as part of his body blown out and then whirlpooling in the cloud. He was about to close his eyes but realized that because of the thick dust the machine tumbled through there was nothing to be seen except dark. When it was light again he saw the crushed limbs of newly uprooted trees hardly a few feet below them.

"That bloody dirt almost choked us," cursed the sergeant.

Not a word had ever been spoken in the settlement about any activities in that landlocked valley. The whites, some of whom Anawari knew very well, behaved as though the bush stretched uninhabited for a radius of a thousand kilometers, save for the scattered remains of the already-decimated and still-decreasing tribes. Aboriginal man had lived thereabouts for some forty thousand years, according to the textbooks, but all of these were written by white men and Anawari doubted their truth; he knew that his black ancestors had been around since time immemorial. The first man came into being at the same time as did the clouds, the rocks, the winds, the trees, and the ants. Man had, ever since the beginning, watched season follow season, and his world exchanging color for color as the wind ground the rocks into sand and strewed it across the landscape. That black man from the unknown whom the whites called the "desert beast" was far tougher than a hammer, though the white man thought he was a nut to be cracked easily. Such a man could dodge his hunters, ignore the oranges so cleverly left in the bush, and avoid drinking from poisoned waterholes, even withstand nuclear-blasted country where rocks have crumbled into dust—all for a time. But every road must finally lead to its end, and now . . . Anawari lost track of his thoughts, and found himself groping in the air as though the elusive words were some physical beings that had strayed from his mind, and that he could gather in his fingers.

The rattling of the helicopter hammered in his head, and only with great effort Anawari drew his thoughts back onto the duplicity of his white settlement friends. Yes, the whites liked to keep their secrets, and generally did so most efficiently; only occasionally had Anawari noticed that two plus two made five. Not long ago, for example, a small, dust-colored aircraft had landed at the settlement, causing suspiciously little comment, and Anawari had met the pilot that same evening at the staff club. The stranger coughed: "I called in for a checkup"; he had a slimy English accent. There was no sign of any injury—not even a bruise was visible; the man apparently was on his way north when his machine developed engine trouble, and he had been forced to come down. He looked exhausted, as though he was still recovering from the strain of the flight and the forced landing. Anawari almost believed the story except when he heard: "I flew through that bloody dust storm last Friday and the kite didn't let me down then—flew perfectly in fact."

Anawari remembered Friday's dust storm; it had taken off several roofs, broken the window of his office, and scattered corrugated iron sheets all over the settlement. No stranger, this fellow. Whoever he is, he comes from somewhere around here, Anawari had thought.

While still at school Anawari had read somewhere that the Aborigine possessed a highly developed extra sense, giving him the ability to detect another's dishonesty. In order to test the inheritance of that ability in himself, young Anawari had used the empty half of an old exercise book to record details of whenever he felt he was being deceived by whites. The evidence was impressive, and he might have filled the whole book had he not met Ann and lost interest in the project. Had that exercise book still been around, Anawari would have made a new entry to record his conversation with the pilot in the club—he never learned the man's proper name. Everyone seemed to make do with "you," except Ann, who chatted with the fellow most of the time and called him "Ranger." They had stayed on drinking for some time, Anawari drank far more than usual but in the haze between an empty and a full glass he could vaguely remember "Ranger" saying: "That Dr. Tinto must be sick of scratching our dirt. We sheeted the whole country with that nuclear muck, have shitted on your blacks and ourselves too," he coughed.

No . . . it was not in the club that he'd heard Ranger saying that. Anawari tried to sort out the sequence of events in his mind— it must have been much later, at home; Ann had become sleepy and, though obviously uneasy, had retired to bed leaving the two of them with the bottle of Bacardi.

The sound of the helicopter broke into Anawari's thoughts again as they came down to land in the jail compound, the noise of their arrival echoing and reechoing against the enclosing walls. Anawari cast a quick look at the sergeant. This man must know all about Ranger, he thought, as they touched the ground. The Bacardi bottle was empty when the sergeant had called, as day was breaking, to collect the pilot. There was talk of flying the chap to town, but the sergeant had headed the helicopter in the opposite direction, and as Anawari watched from his veranda, the twinkling rotor blade disappeared over the desert toward the ranges.

CHAPTER 4

t was midafternoon when they arrived back. Anawari would have gone home to shower and change, but to then come back, walking into the building when everyone else was on the way out, would have attracted too much attention—it was much safer to go straight to his office and shower there. Anawari intended to work for a while, then, as the others left, to lock his door until the building emptied; tomorrow, being Saturday, no one would be at work, and he hoped to have the whole building, except the police section, at his disposal. There should be time enough to sneak into all the rooms in the adjoining section and see what Dr. Tinto was up to.

Anawari was still showering when he realized that he was not alone—someone stood perhaps a meter away, throwing a shadow onto the shower curtain. Whoever had come sneaking unheard into the office had chosen the right moment, as the sound of falling water deafened Anawari to any other.

"Am I wanted on the telephone?" Anawari thought it must be someone from Dr. Tinto's staff. He repeated the question.

"No. But I've got a message for you," answered a female voice.

What is it that's so damned urgent? Anawari poked just his head out from behind the curtain, making sure his chest remained well concealed. "Has the world come to an end?"

"Phew, it stinks in here. Whatever have you been hunting, Rev., boars?" The girl standing there glanced at his clothes.

"We had quite a tough time out in the bush, the sarge and me!"

"A good catch?"

"Well, all the beasts are tamed. . . . Doomsday is not here yet—is that the message?" The girl stepped closer. "Ann rang yesterday and asked me to take care of you."

"Really? I'd be glad if you'd do some housework later today. Is that what she meant?"

"All she said was, 'Make sure he's all right.' "

The girl's name was Laura and she was more courteous than anyone else on Dr. Tinto's staff. Her little face, fringed with long hair, often smiled at work but Anawari never came close enough to find out if that smile was a kindhearted one or just a lure into a trap. "I'll see you at home, then."

Laura twitched the curtain: "You're not circumcised. They did it to Namir, you know—the tribal elders did it with a stone knife." She was in no hurry to leave. "I'm glad you're back safely."

"It was only a hounding excursion."

"Poor Namir was taken on a trip like that just before his trouble blew up. They broke him."

Before drawing the shower curtain Anawari glanced at Laura: There was much more behind that tiny face than the words—a warm corner was still hidden deep in her wounded heart. How long would she remember him? It was years since Father Namir had departed, but his memory still lingered in the settlement. Anawari reached for the tap to make the water run harder and muffle his words: "You'll have to tell me about him later."

Laura said something but her voice was drowned in the noise of the shower. Did he miss anything important? Anawari always liked to hear about his predecessor, so that he might learn what vice had trapped him, but now, against that ran the fear that the girl's presence could alert some of the bugging devices placed around. What was more, he needed to be alone. It would be another week before a similar opportunity arose for Anawari to pry into Dr. Tinto's rooms, and by that time something else might have happened to divert him from the plan, or . . . Ann might cut her holiday short and the chance to snoop would be lost forever.

Anawari was in the process of setting up the computer to decode the tribal marks on his chest, and the work needed his full attention. The actual system itself was quite simple—a copy of the tribal design had to be made, as accurately as possible, on a special sheet of paper ruled with numbered guidelines. The copy must then be fed into the computer—and the result should appear in a matter of seconds. Problems arose, however, in the transference of each line from skin to paper with absolute exactitude; even the tiny deviation of a single line, or the minute alteration of a shape, could set the machine on quite the wrong course. It would be much easier to stand before the camera's eye and allow it to copy the marks directly, but that process also recorded the tribesman's face and Anawari intended to stay anonymous.

Since he had first been employed at the Centre, Anawari had regarded the computer with a certain awe—it was almost a fear of the electronic beast that could not only process data but help gather information. On its keyboard the computer had scores of buttons of varying shapes and colors, each serving a specific function, and Anawari suspected that almost anything in the world could be achieved by pressing one or two of these buttons.

Aborigines from any of the four camps in need of food, clothes, or other human necessities came, sooner or later, to the Centre and, arriving through the side entrance, walked straight to the office counter. Anawari had a set procedure of inquiry into their names, tribes, areas of the bush they lived in, native food consumed, and other details listed in large letters on the standard questionnaire hidden on his side of the counter. At the conclusion of the interview he would present the caller with a handful of biscuits—each with a cross baked into the crust—or perhaps a blanket labeled Army Disposal. Two large baskets stood always by the counter, one marked "Freedom from Hunger" and full of lollies, and another marked "W.H.O." filled with oranges; the contents of the baskets were specifically for families with children. While Anawari kept his visitor busy at the counter, the computer, its electronic eyes and ears built into the bench top and sides, recorded in accurate detail every word spoken in any language or dialect, took photographs of the client, and carefully analyzed any tribal marks on his skin.

Utilizing the data was easy, as it went directly to the computer memory bank, while a reference number and interview summary were inserted automatically on an index card in the filing system.

Anawari had often thought that he must be the only man knowing the personal habits, beliefs, and origins of every tribal man in the area. "Doing your job," the sergeant would say. Ann, however, had a broader view: "Emancipating your skin brothers." Now it seemed that he might even learn his own secrets as well.

Leaning against the sash basin in the staff bathroom and peering in the mirror, Anawari had succeeded in copying the lines from the left side of his chest onto the paper, and had partly finished the other half when the interoffice telephone buzzer echoed from the hall. The nagger, he thought—his own name for the penetrating whir that distinguished a computer room call from the jangle of the public telephone. In normal circumstances the buzzer sounded several times a day and a cold, official voice requested specific data on individuals. Seldom was information sought on a tribe or a clan in general; Anawari assumed that the computer was connected directly to a central computer, but whether that was in the hospital building or even in Australia, he had no idea. The nagger had an unnerving habit of calling when one would least expect it, but there was no means, to Anawari's knowledge, by which he could make return contact with it himself.

Anawari ignored the buzzing, hoping it would stop, but instead it intensified until it was a persistent wailing like a siren. I should teach that mad electronic beast a lesson with a stick, thought Anawari, and rushed to prevent the terrible sound alerting the whole building.

"Give me the following data . . ." came the voice from the telephone receiver, but before he comprehended the rest of the sentence, Anawari's attention was suddenly attracted by words flashing on the computer screen: DO NOT, REPEAT, DO NOT IGNORE INTERNAL CALLS. THERE ARE WAYS TO PERSUADE YOU TO ANSWER.

"Jandjara . . . Jandjara . . . Jandjara . . ."

"Don't nag, I warn you; I'm the son of an unknown warrior," shouted Anawari.

"Jandjara . . . Jandjara . . . Jandjara . . ." the telephone voice repeated over and over again.

Anawari thought that the call must be prerecorded and that the tape had jammed, so he hung up the receiver to wait for a new call—but when it came, the voice was the same.

"Give me the data on Gara Jandjara. . . ."

Gara! Fugitive Gara! How the hell did they get his skin name? Anawari checked in the register index. "Sorry, nothing on *that* here." He carefully avoided relating the name to either sex. "Hey listen, sweetie, have you had any hot dreams lately?" he whispered.

"Personal requests are not admissible." The female voice did not alter its official tone even a fraction; for the years that he had been hearing that voice on the nagger every working day, Anawari had never guessed that it was not human but a machine.

It took Anawari several hours more to complete a copy of the tribal marks on his chest. He had to be confident that it was accurate in every line and mark, and at last he was ready to slot the diagram into the machine. Several days before, he would have been fully confident of a trustworthy result, but his experience lately had somehow replaced that confidence with the suspicion that, if necessary, the machine could twist its answers to satisfy its white masters.

"12,000 CAMELS, 12,000 CAMELS, 12,000 CAMELS . . ." The screen pulsated. Anawari shook the machine though he felt like smashing the screen.

"CAMELS, CAMELS, CAMELS . . ."

Anawari smashed his heel into the base of the computer. The machine rocked and shirred, and a moment later began pouring across its screen a flood of data: words, figures, and maps jostled

37

each other on the flickering rectangle, while Anawari gaped at the opportune madness he had created.

A map in progress of the nuclear development area appeared, shaded in dark colors. It grew rapidly, swallowing scores of tribal countries south of the Australian center. As the shadow expanded, a mounting tally of figures enumerated the total of tribespeople eliminated by human indifference, disease, or deliberate destruction. Rounded up in the bush, some of the people were sent to camps that mushroomed on the screen of the computer, camps so far away that no man or his soul would ever return; others were detained at the nuclear sites to help with the research.

Anawari felt hopeless in manipulating the computer to reveal their fate. Suddenly it mattered whether a man had died confined in a desert camp or was wiped out by a nuclear blast. Anawari tried to squeeze out from the machine more than just the figures. On the screen in front of him appeared data on the animal population in the nuclear zone listing numbers of feral camels, donkeys, and horses and, for some reason or another, referring to dingoes as well. "There are no inhabitants in the area," concluded the statistical report. They must mean "white inhabitants," thought Anawari and patted the machine: "You can do better than that, surely—come on, pal." The computer suddenly brought forward data on children taken away from each particular tribe as they were rounded up; Anawari was especially attentive to this revelation, fearful that even one detail might escape him. He stared fixedly into the machine as it traced these children through the white man's institutions and into maturity, and he recognized the names of many of his schoolmates among them. Anawari snatched up a pencil to note down all these details. He must write to his friends and tell them of their true tribal origins; how wonderful that they would know the truth at last. At school all the black boys—Jumbuck, Aroitj, Namir, Ily, Zambo, Ruwe, Yarto, and he, Anawari, had ganged up, and had dreamed of forming their own tribe. They had even performed a ceremony—they called it *mullina,* but Anawari found out much later it should have been *mallinya,* a second initiation rite; but then none of them knew

38

much about tribal things in those days. They would probably never have generated much enthusiasm for the tribe if it had not been for a camping excursion in the mountains with the boy scout troop from school. Maybe it was the smell of virgin bush, not yet trampled by the white man, that gave them the spur to draw apart from the white boys and seek their own world; or it could have been . . . they had stumbled across the remains of an old Aboriginal camping ground and . . . yes, that had finally made them strong and resolute. Anawari was angry with himself that he had allowed such an important event in his youth to grow dim in his memory. At that old camping site, they had found bones, a rock on which the Aborigines had sharpened their implements, and . . . yes, a stone ax; none of the boys had ever held one in his hand before.

Anawari remembered how they had called each other "Brave" and had sworn not to go back to school but to stay in the bush and form a tribe. They never did get around to finding a proper name for their tribe, but boylike, enjoyed the excitement of choosing a leader—the one to be called "Big Chief." How little they had known about real tribal life—but that should not really surprise him—the white school did not teach such things. How could these dispossessed boys know that their tribal brothers needed no clan rulers, that they were governed by their customs and a group of tribal elders interpreting it? In spite of knowing so little, the boys had nonetheless felt compelled to break away from the white man's world, and to search for a life they hardly knew existed, but which became more and more an undeniable part of their existence. Anawari had the honor of being the first and only one of the boys to undergo the initiation ritual. He had been stretched on the ground close to two boys, one clapping two sticks together and the other holding a long stick pressed against his lips to symbolize the *didjeridu,* while imitating the rumbling note of the instrument. That must have been Namir, as he had been elected Big Chief and had the sole right to lead ceremonies (years later he discovered that *maijada* was the proper word for rites master). The other boys, stripped naked and daubed with mud from a nearby creek, had danced around chanting, but no one really knew how the *mullina* should be performed, or when and how to end it. The young tribesmen's sweat flowed freely and mixed with the trickles of blood from leech bites on their bare legs; one of the boys dipped his finger into the scarlet runnel sliding down his mud-plastered skin and, borne along by the excitement of the ritual, marked Anawari's chest with a bloody zigzag pattern. Inspired, the others followed suit until even Anawari's face was marked with lines of blood.

Years later Anawari still wondered just how close he had come to real initiation. Their makeshift *mullina* had come to an abrupt and undignified end when a search party—the forest ranger followed by a panting group of the "holy brothers"—had rushed unexpectedly on the scene and spoiled the ceremony. Anawari had hoped for another occasion when the boys could come together in the bush and recreate their *mullina,* but the chance never came. The Aboriginal boys were taken immediately back to town, confined to the school building, and required to spend a good part of each day kneeling on beans and praying to be forgiven for their heathen behavior. A small hope had remained, however, that they might stage a *mullina* secretly at night in their dormitory, and they might have done so but for the absence of their ritual leader. The Big Chief was no longer with them, and when questioned, the brothers explained that Namir had retired in solitude and dedication to pray, to prepare himself to take his holy orders and join the brotherhood. Without Namir the ceremony lost its authority, and besides, Anawari felt that it surely must be improper for him to conduct the ceremony for his own initiation.

Now, staring at the computer, Anawari saw nothing referring either to himself or to his old schoolmate Namir, but there was still a chance that the screen might offer up a clue to the beginning of that long and lonely road by which Anawari had been led into the white man's world, and Namir . . . he was . . . who knew where? Like a spiteful human, however, the machine opposed Anawari's desires and unexpectedly switched programs. Details of distributing food rations in displaced tribal camps appeared on the screen. Anawari turned his back to the computer and looked out the window.

An old man was walking slowly toward the entrance of the Welfare Centre, and as Anawari watched, the bent figure reeled to the left and right as though he would never reach the doorway before collapsing. The old man seemed familiar—it was Nupuru! Anawari reminded himself to ask him in which of the tribal dialects the word *karan* is used. The elder, supporting himself with a rough walking stick that stood a good meter above his head, reminded Anawari of something from his childhood—something from his schooldays with the brothers . . . yes! . . . a picture of Moses on the way to Egypt.

Nupuru stumbled over the doorstep, and Anawari ran to support him until he reached the counter. White patches of dry scurf covered much of the old man's skin, gnarled scar tissue puckered his scalp, and one of his eyes was missing, leaving only a weeping hole, the tears from which had smeared muddy tracks in the thick layer of dust on the wrinkled cheeks.

Anawari forced a smile. "What can I do for you, my friend?" Nupuru said nothing, but formed a cross with his two index fingers. Anawari hurriedly gave him a handful of the biscuits marked with the shape of a cross.

The computer still galloped dementedly on, thrashing out its pile of data, instructions, and advice; it even printed daily ration lists for inmates in tribal displacement camps. Anawari glanced warily into the old man's face but saw there only the serenity of a man wrapped in his own dreamlike world; even the elder's one eye had adapted to his state of calm, for it seldom blinked. His whole demeanor exuded a secretiveness, for which Anawari was grateful, for he and the old man shared a secret that had to remain just that. Not long before, during Anawari's last holiday, he and Nupuru had spent almost a month together in the bush, on a trip into the wilderness that not only had increased Anawari's tribal feeling but had taught him more about traditional Aboriginal lore than any written or even spoken words could ever have done.

They had drifted south through the bush and after many waterholes reached *pulkarin,* a rock somewhere in the vastness of the desert. The rock looked no different from any other boulder except that one side of it appeared smooth. "Home of *karan,*" Anawari was told. The old man rubbed with his palm the smoother surface of the boulder and uttered some words of a tribal chant. It was explained to Anawari later that by rubbing the rock, little karan, souls of unborn children, would swarm out. They are no bigger than a midge and can only be seen by the eyes of *nangari,* a medicine man, as they hover over tribal country searching for a woman to mother them. "The little fellows prefer someone kind and young who is able to look after them well," explained Nupuru.

No white person in the settlement had known about the journey, not even Ann, for Anawari had told her that he was going on a prospecting expedition. He had equipped himself with a small hammer and a mineral hunter's manual, and had returned with a bag full of rock samples, convincing everyone that it was a business trip, such as every white man in the settlement made now and then. "And how are they treating you, down at Camp Menzies?" he asked. Now the old man kept quiet. Anawari had not intended to put his friend through the computerized system of data gathering, but leading questions seemed to ask themselves almost against his will: "You're a Para elder, aren't you, and you have two younger brothers?"

Nupuru raised three fingers. "Mundjon, Warri, and Kaltu." The last was most likely a half-tribal brother, for he lived in a different camp.

An office memo written in red by Superintendent Hunt's own hand was taped to the office side of the counter. For more than a month it had enjoined Anawari to seek information on these three tribesmen, and urged him to acquire details about their life and activities in the ranges. The men had lived in the bush round the Kunamata Mountains and had only been brought to the settlement a year before. Anawari vividly remembered the arrival of the brothers, their appearance, and even their names, but he was never sure which was which. They called in at the office now and then for a handful of food, or some worn-out clothes, and whenever they were about, the computer had a field day recording information, but there still had to be something that had not been revealed and that Superintendent Hunt desperately wished to know. No matter how important it might be to the Big Boss, Anawari tried now to think of a way not to cross-question his old friend.

Nupuru leaned forward. "Mundjon and Warri are gone."

"Oh? Well, they'll soon be back, I'm sure."

"No one comes back from the hospital."

An uneasy thought struck Anawari. "Come on, have some biscuits."

He took the old man by the shoulder and led him behind the counter into a back room at the end of the hall and safely out of range of the prying computer. The machine was now issuing a press release about a certain surveyor appointed recently to re-establish the northern boundary of the Nuclear Development Area— but through the closed door its ranting was reduced to nothing more than a whisper. "How long since they went to hospital? One? Two? How many days?" Anawari showed three of his fingers; the Para tribal language had no words for any number higher than two, so the numbers had to be demonstrated.

Nupuru held up five fingers.

"Were any of the fellows terribly ill?"

"Only like me, rolling mist sickness. Nothing more."

"Hell! Is there a single Aborigine hereabouts who's free of it?"

It was scarcely a week since Anawari had chatted with Dr. Tinto during a farewell party for Ann—where he had been the only black in a mob of whites—and when he mentioned rumors about the rolling mist sickness, Dr. Tinto had replied: "Suspicion, Rev.; the Abos are the most suspicious people on earth. They had about forty thousand years at hand to develop that. Aren't you lucky we emancipated you?"

"Who took your brothers away?" asked Anawari now.

"The sergeant and a nurse. They came to the camp and dragged my brothers into a police van."

"Which nurse? Do you remember?"

43

"Redheaded."

"Huh! One of the bloody twins." In Dr. Tinto's medical team were two sisters, both aged around thirty, and almost identical in face and dress. One was Pat and the other Pam, and Anawari had become thoroughly confused trying not only to tell them apart but to call each by her right name. To avoid embarrassment he jokingly called them the "Twins."

As Anawari led Nupuru toward the entrance again, the old man stopped for a moment with his one eye on the basket of oranges. Two days ago that same basket had contained only a handful of fruit but now it had been filled, though when and by whom, Anawari did not know. For years he had distributed the oranges to Aborigines whenever they called at the office, but only now he noticed that the number 25 was stamped on each piece of fruit. If I let the poor old fellow go without any of those, he'll live a bit longer for sure, thought Anawari as he escorted his visitor to the door.

CHAPTER 5

The night drifted to its end; like a pigeon caught in a net, the dawn struggled through the branches of the mulga trees before creeping into the leaden sky and spreading the morning light.

Lying on the floor of the back veranda, Anawari pulled the blanket over his shoulder to protect himself from the breeze. Another day on the way—two kinds of days, he corrected himself—one for us Abos, the other for the whites. Stunned, he held his breath, fearing that his thoughts would float away in the air like a speck of dust. From the adjoining room came the noise of a foot stamping, and the veranda floor shook slightly. "Wake up, Reverend, Sir—Christendom is calling you!" Laura was speaking through the open door, but when she spoke again a moment later, it sounded muffled. She must have been in the kitchen. "Keep following the boss blindly—they'll soon make you a bishop." Last night she had teased him even more: "The whites have never had it so good. They have pinned all those phony badges on you— loaded you like a Christmas tree. Just help them to get a few more Abos and they'll make you into a saint, Reverend, Sir."

Had she come to tidy the place or anger me? wondered Anawari. Most likely Laura was honoring the place where she had lived for years and was agitated at seeing him instead of Namir. What *had* happened to him? He must remember to ask her again.

"Sorry I robbed you of your bed last night." She had brought out two mugs of coffee and hurriedly put them on the floor. "Did you feel cold out here?"

"I like sleeping outside." Anawari grabbed the edges of his unbuttoned pajama jacket and held them against his chest. Had she seen the tribal marks on his skin? He hoped not. He was angry with himself for not taking precautions and turned away to button the garment.

She sat on the floor. "Namir liked to sleep out here too. He used to watch the campfires glittering in the dark and chanted in a whisper:

> Enfolded by desert lies Tjuta,
> beyond the far horizon lies *Tjamu ngura*,
> Enfolded by plains lies Tjuta
> dimmed by the enveloping dust lies my lost home."

Laura moved her hand restlessly, reached for the mug, but finding it was still hot, left it quickly. "Tjuta . . . that must have been his tribal country."

Anawari doubted now that there had been any telephone call from Ann. No, he did not mind if he had been deceived—in fact he felt somewhat apologetic for not being able to comfort Laura. The house looked an empty shell now, the bed where she and Namir had slept . . . yes, there was still a large metal trunk under the bed with a thick layer of dust on it. It must be some of his belongings—Laura had better have the stuff; she might have the key to open the padlock.

Laura said absently, "I often felt he might walk from here across to the tribal camp."

"Where is Tjuta, actually?" Only now he remembered hearing it earlier from the tribal woman in the desert.

"I checked every map—there is nothing about it in any index. He might not have known the location either; it looks as if it was a place the tribal elders kept to themselves, exclusively."

"Do you have his photo?"

"No. I had one at work, but the sergeant took it." Her mouth stayed open for a while. "There should be a photo of him with an old, blind man; it's a bit blurred, though. I took it in a tunnel at Bidi when we were there looking for gemstones. Ann was there too; she might have a print."

Anawari reached for his mug with one hand, the other holding his pajamas in case the button should give up. Ann had never told him about any gem-prospecting trips. In all the years they had been together, she had only mentioned Namir a few times and hardly ever by name. "Dr. Tinto often worded us up: That man was going to snap—no clerical garb can conceal a savage mind forever."

Would Ann say the same thing if anything like that happened to him too? She would not like to hear him mumbling that tribal chant. Those marks on his chest, now; yes, she would ask all about them. Anawari held the mug against his mouth, but his hand trembled, spilling coffee down his pajamas. "That stuff . . . you should have all his belongings." He spoke suddenly, fearing the silence.

"What stuff?"

"The trunk under the bed; that must be his."

Her mouth opened, but it took a while for the words to come: "Ah, the gelignite—it'll have to be disposed of, I suppose."

He had slept over that trunk for years now, Anawari remembered, biting his lower lip.

"We needed gelignite for prospecting. You can keep it in case you ever get to Bibi. We struck some good pieces of opal on holiday."

The sound of a motor springing into life came from the direction of the hospital, and a moment later a helicopter swung into view, sweeping low over the mulga trees and the house. "Off they go to that dead camp," thought Anawari. The machine was so close that the police badge on the sergeant's chest showed clearly, and Dr. Tinto could be seen at the window with a pair of binoculars up to his eyes.

47

Laura tracked the machine through the air. "The bosses are going to manage without you today."

"It'll be Doc's field day—the sergeant has discovered a jackpot for him. Did Namir often accompany them into the bush?"

"Not willingly. 'I've had a gutful of that,' he used to complain after every trip."

Should he tell her that they were together at the holy brothers? Perhaps he might have mentioned him to her and talked about that ill-fated initiation ceremony in the bush? No, better wait to see that photo. Even then, one couldn't be so sure. He, Namir, and Ily—another schoolmate from the group—were so much alike, often indistinguishable. The other boys called them the "Siblings," and it was a popular game at school to try and tell one of them from the other. Once Namir coughed during Mass, and the brothers placed Ily in solitary confinement for three days. Leading a small deputation, Anawari went to the school principal to explain the mistake and was told, "It is often impossible to recognize one dark face from another." The principal then went on: "Perhaps you should have stayed in that tribal wilderness and perished in the nuclear blast. Pray to Him who brought you to us."

Coming closer to Anawari, Laura whispered: "You know he had some marks on his chest—real tribal stuff? They appeared on his skin overnight."

Anawari held his breath. The sound of the helicopter still floated in the air, now muffled by the distance.

Laura emptied her mug. "An elder from one of the camps told Namir that he was initiated as *wankar,* half man. The tribes do that to their youth; I doubt if anyone talks about it."

Anawari stood up. "I have to get ready for work." He could not remember if he had ever acted so rudely to a visitor before, but now he wanted to be alone. Though he had lived with the whites for as long as he could remember, in times of stress he always felt easier without the company of others.

"Thanks for letting me stay." Laura was leaving.

How sure could you be in here? Laura's eyes were a transparent blue and seldom blinked. Beyond them he envisaged a world he knew little about.

"Shall I call in again tonight?" asked Laura at the door.

"Do! Please . . ." the words were out before Anawari stopped to think.

"Oh dear, I've just remembered—I have an assignment at the hospital later today—it might keep me there until midnight."

"I suppose there's always a mob of tribal patients for you to look after."

"Not so many, really. We never keep anyone in hospital unless they are brought in for observation; and they're always 'terminals' anyway."

"What about someone who becomes really ill?" Anawari tried to sound casual.

"He is disposed of as usual. Hasn't Ann told you?"

"Ah, yes! The customary treatment." Anawari forced himself to smile. "Well, call here—any time. It doesn't matter to me if you're late."

"Oh, I do like your door knocker," remarked Laura.

Hanging from the door handle was a wooden stick colored red with ocher and with a design of white lines winding outward from an unpainted center. Is this how a local message stick looks? Anawari wondered. He had seen many similar objects before; in the museum there was quite a collection of them, but slightly different in design, and he had been told that the sticks belong to the Pangeran tribe, so long extinct that no one alive could read the message. After his visit to the museum Anawari had dreamed of a huge tribal warrior—a mountain of a man—on whose shoulders rested the entire Aboriginal spirit world, and message sticks, identical to those in the showcase, were sent throughout the country calling all tribes to send food and water for the man supporting the sky. Anawari thought that, through his dream, he had unearthed a secret of history that would otherwise never have come to light, so as soon as he could gain admittance, he rushed to the museum and told his story to the curator. The white man was terribly polite, but disapproving. "It would be proper for a man who holds the sky to call for nourishment only from the Lord."

After Laura had gone, was safely through the front gate and out of sight down the street, Anawari took the message stick down from the door, peered closely to see the fine detail of every line and curve, and moved his fingers gently over it as though any harsher touch might distort the content of the message.

What important news was being so directed to him, and why? Anawari knew so little about communication between one Aborigine and another; was this a commonplace passing of a message, or an urgent call for help? There were several books, he knew, that might tell something of the mystery, but all were written by white men, and Anawari felt an inherent discomfort at using such a reference to discover his ancestor's customs. Besides, even if he had wanted to read what the white men had to say about the message sticks, the books were inaccessible in the library at the hospital. From time to time Ann had brought home a volume or two, and had often read him a passage here and there when she came upon something particularly fascinating, but it had never been suggested that Anawari should use the library himself. All that knowledge lay buried somewhere deep inside the hospital building and was, it seemed, destined for the eyes of whites.

In the afternoon, after he had rested, Anawari walked into the Menzies Camp with a small bag dangling from his shoulder. He had only rarely come that way before and, looking about, realized that some years must have gone by since his last visit. The camp had no defined boundary, but occupied probably a square kilometer of bush. At some earlier stage the spinifex, small bushes, and clumps of tough grass had partly covered the red earth, but the occupants' constant activity had discouraged the stunted and scattered greenery until it finally gave way and became a patch of desert. The road, a neglected track of mixed sand and red dust connecting the camp and the settlement, was scarcely used except by the "rations" truck, which called once a week to dump lumps of clumsily slaughtered cow in the dust for the locals to distribute among themselves.

Outside the entrance to the camp, near the Sir Robert Menzies commemoration plaque, Anawari caught up with two naked children carrying, between them, a heavy oil can that slopped water in the dust as they staggered under its weight. They moved very slowly, and stopped often to catch their breath and ease their cramped fingers. Anawari felt sorry for the kids, and he picked up the container as he passed, saying a few friendly words as he did so. Both children looked horrified, however, and they stared at him for a moment before running quickly out of sight toward the center of the camp. Anawari walked on carrying the tin and stopped at one of the huts. Under a roof made from only a couple of branches sat a woman, and as Anawari approached her from behind he coughed; but there was no sign that his voice had been heard. Anawari wished to be rid of the heavy container. She could be blind and deaf, he thought, and touched the woman's shoulder; the stiff body slid sideways to the ground and with it the small cold body of a child with its head leaning on its mother's breast and its mouth still at the nipple. The bodies had shrunk from living, human size to skin-covered skeletons, and lay in silence and despair, as they had during their last long days and nights, dreaming empty dreams of food. Their poor faces were dominated by startling prominent teeth and magnified eyes telling the story of their agony. It was uncertain how long these two had been dead; the wind had blown the fine ash away from around their fire, but no flies had gathered, as though the withered flesh had nothing to offer. A biscuit marked with a cross, such as those handed from the basket at the Welfare Centre, stayed jammed between the woman's fingers. Someone must have put it there not long ago, Anawari thought, or the dogs or insects would have polished it off.

Anawari went on through the camp, between rows of dead fires. Here and there a tree remained, darkened by a coating of smoke and dust, and providing a few families with the comfort of a support on which to lean the branches that formed their *wiltja,* scant shelter. The rare sheet of corrugated iron roofing often had no support, so only served its purpose by being partly buried in the sand sideways and gave little protection from the cold desert winds. Blankets were seldom seen, and most shelters contained nothing but a hole in the sand, dug between the corrugated sheet and the campfire, and made just large enough to accommodate a man and his family.

At last Anawari found Nupuru. The old man had a blanket stretched between two sticks to shelter him from the sun, and was constantly evicting a whole pack of dogs that had gathered to share the small patch of shade in which their master squatted. Anawari noticed that Nupuru did not hit the animals, and that his grumbling and pushing scarcely discouraged the beasts. Once outside in the hot sun, each animal immediately turned and walked straight back into the shade.

Anawari still carried the container full of water and now he set it on the ground. "Do you know who wants this?" He would have said "owns," but the Para language had no word appropriate for private possession. Since he had been in the settlement, Anawari learned that the people from the camps had become dependent on tap water just as much as on the air they breathed. There had been no rain for years, and the people spoke of it as though they had long forgotten when they had last seen it.

Nupuru eyed the container as his dry mouth moved stiffly: "It'll be of much use to many here." Anawari remembered that, when arriving at the settlement, the bush behind his house had been partly covered with scrub. At dusk he had often seen from his back veranda the people there silhouetted against the glowing sunset. It looked at first as if they were hunting possums or other animals that crept out at the end of day, but later he found out the scrub had been stripped of bark and leaves for the few drops of water it contained; that is, if there was any of it to be crushed out, for the plants, like the rest of the country, were dying of thirst. "I tried almost every *wiltja* but no one would take it." He felt embarrassed that no one wanted to drink.

"Leave the can there, behind the blanket. Someone will come and fetch it," suggested the old man. Anawari did as he was advised, followed by the dogs, which seemed not to have had water for days; as soon as he left the container, they jostled around it and tried to squeeze their tongues through the narrow opening to reach the water within. "Why would no one take it from me?"

"The people fear that you have come to punish them. We're allowed only to drink water at the tap in the settlement—not carry it to camps."

Anawari asked how long it was since it had last rained, but the old man could not tell precisely, for no tribesman had ever counted years in the desert. The drought had been about ever since the whites set up the settlement, even before that, when farther south the whites blasted *tjuta,* the country of Blood Gum Tree people. "It might never rain again," Nupuru suggested, for the rain could be frightened away just as could humans, and it had been chased by rolling mist that had run back to the sea. The sea, farther north on the other side of the desert, was about half a continent away, thought Anawari. The two children he had met on the road scuttled from behind one of the huts and dragged the container away with them; Anawari turned his head deliberately away and did not look in their direction. "What about your dogs? Where do they drink?" Should I say "dingoes" instead of "dogs"? he thought.

"They sneak into the settlement during the night. There's always a dripping tap to be found, it seems."

"Superintendent Hunt shoots dingoes, whenever he sees them."

"The shot ones do not come back." Nupuru tried to move enough dingoes from the shade to make room for his visitor to shelter from the sun.

"I'll be all right," insisted Anawari and sat down on the hot ground. The dingoes hardly had any hair; some of them were even without whiskers. Would they be suffering from mange or something else? wondered Anawari, and shuddered as he thought of these red raw bodies, like skinned carcasses, sleeping with Nupuru, but he knew that without the warmth of the dogs the old man would never survive a freezing desert night.

Anawari brought the message stick, wrapped carefully in a T-shirt, and was about to ask Nupuru to decode the message, but he was hesitant. Seldom had he addressed an Aboriginal elder on a personal matter. Maybe he should first chat a little—build the old man's trust. "I have no news, as yet, about any of your brothers, but . . . you may be sure that as soon as I learn something you will hear from me."

"No one ever comes out of that hospital building."

"One of them had a family, is that right?"

"The woman with a baby at the first *wiltja*."

The air in Anawari's chest hardened, and though he waited a moment for his breath to return, and opened his lips to speak, he found himself unable to form a single word.

The blanket behind Nupuru was full of holes, and through one of these the sun cast a beam on the old man's face to which his hand rose rhythmically as though to brush away an irritating insect. Around his brow was a roughly woven band, not only to confine his hair but to denote his status of "wise man," and when Anawari realized that it was made of spinifex, he was for a moment reminded of the picture of Jesus, crowned with thorns, that had hung in his bedroom at the college.

The last time Anawari was at the Menzies Camp, a special headband of pure silk embroidered with the Union Jack had been provided for Nupuru to wear, but everything in the camp had looked very different that day. Huge trucks had moved in blocks of prefabricated huts with air conditioning and screen doors, and two portable toilets had been installed. Each woman was given a dress for the occasion, and a small flag, and the men were each provided with a pair of shorts and a Royal portrait to be hung around the neck covering the chest.

The Queen flew in to open the hospital, and was escorted on an inspection of the Menzies Camp, followed by a whole swarm of cameramen and reporters. Accompanied by Superintendent Hunt and Dr. Tinto and a man from the N.D.A. in an open limousine, the Royal Personage was driven slowly through the camp without stopping, because of the flies and the dust, and poor

Nupuru had run alongside, bowing and repeating his well-rehearsed welcome speech. He never finished that speech though, for while bowing he had cracked his head against the stone-proof window of the car and fallen, unnoticed, in the dust. Every man and woman, well-schooled, was lined up along the route to sing "God Save the Queen," but was found to have some difficulty in remembering the words. The loyal chorus got only as far as intoning "God . . ." and stuck to repeating that one syllable till the entourage passed out of sight. Recalling the improvements provided that day, Anawari looked about for any remnants before he remembered seeing the prefabricated huts and portable toilets being loaded back on the trucks as soon as the visitors had left. The shorts and dresses were made of the same paper as the flags and posters, and had all lasted only until the first willy-willy swept through the camp and cleared away any evidence of a Royal visit.

"They want you to go," said Nupuru.

Anawari saw then that the old man held the message stick a few inches from his right eye. "Who's calling for me?" he asked.

"Your people."

"Where am I to go?"

"To your country, where your *karan* comes from."

A cloud of misery rolled over Anawari—he did not know where he came from, and he doubted that the whites had ever bothered to keep a record of the tribe from which he had been snatched, let alone when. So many times Anawari had stood in front of a map and willed himself to point to one part of Australia that he could call his place of origin—but there was nothing, not one subconscious flicker to give him a hint of from which part of the continent he had come. It is uncomfortable to have to admit that you do not know from where you sprang to life, and Anawari whispered to Nupuru: "Please! No one else must know about this."

The old man shoved and grumbled at his dingoes and drove them off, and Anawari was pleased that the souls of Nupuru's relatives, which were embodied in the dogs, would not overhear his secrets and tell them to the spirit world.

"I'm not sure where to find my mob."

"Far south—your people many many waterholes away."

Anawari glanced around to make sure that no one had come close enough to hear the words, and was disgusted to see, some distance away, an elderly man squatting to relieve himself, with a pack of dogs jostling about him. That man's lack of shame angered Anawari until he realized that for kilometers around there was no shelter, natural or man-made, where a human might retire in privacy. "Which tribe am I to look for?"

"You'll be told."

Drops of perspiration rolled down Nupuru's face and into his bushy white beard, and his one eye looked inflamed and sore. As the husky old voice weakened to a whisper, Anawari wondered if he had gone too far—pressed too hard in his demands of a sick old man. It seemed that Anawari had learned all he could for now; Nupuru was exhausted, so the many questions Anawari still needed to ask must wait. He must make another visit, perhaps tomorrow, to hear more of his ancestry—perhaps early in the morning or at dusk, without the blazing sun to dazzle the old man's eye. Anawari had avoided mentioning Tjuta, the tribe spoken of by the woman in the desert a few days ago; he had hoped to hear it again, but without suggesting it himself first.

On his way back to the settlement, Anawari moved off the track; desert flowers grew scattered here and there across the sandy soil, and though it took him some time, he wanted to pick an impressive bunch of every color to be found there in the bush.

CHAPTER 6

The broken glass in the window of Aboriginal Welfare had not yet been replaced, so Anawari squeezed through it once again, dragging with him the bunch of flowers. It seemed as though luck had come his way at last—the door leading from his office to the main hall had been left unlocked, and Anawari tiptoed through into semidarkness, for the only light in the hall came from the main entrance quite some distance away.

In addition to the reception area, the ground floor contained a number of rooms; passing on his way to and from this office Anawari had often seen Dr. Tinto, or one of his staff, coming in and out of these rooms, but good care had been taken that no confused outsider should wander from the hallway. A line of footprints was painted in fluorescent red on the floor, and on every door was inscribed WHITES ONLY or NO ADMITTANCE and an impressive drawing of a large snake with head raised to strike just to make sure that the message reached even the illiterate Aboriginal.

Anawari had no present interest in any of the rooms on the ground floor—not that they were not worthy of inspection but he suspected that in the hall, somewhere between the main entrance and the lift, was a monitoring device set to register the passage of every visitor, and he had no wish to have his presence recorded.

The lift served both upper floors, but Anawari chose to use the stairs instead—not only because he hated being enclosed in the windowless cubicle, but in case of mechanical failure; it would be just his luck to be rescued from a jammed lift by Dr. Tinto or Superintendent Hunt.

Anawari considered himself safe as long as he moved on tiptoe, for now he had the upper floors of the entire Y-shaped building to himself. Several rooms he investigated all seemed to serve a similar purpose, for each had sets of test tubes and other glass equipment of peculiar shape for laboratory research. He gave little attention to these rooms; there seemed little point in being distracted by something about which he knew so little.

At the end of one corridor Anawari came to a room that was as capacious as a theater, and in the middle of which stood a large table entirely comprised of panels of buttons, switches, and monitoring lights. On the floor in front of this, and next to a velvet-covered chair, lay a briefcase of crocodile skin lettered in gold: N.D.A. Anawari felt disappointed not to read Superintendent Hunt's name on it. In the Nuclear Age the names are unimportant; only the atoms matter, the trash they create, country they wipe out, and most of all, the lethal scars they leave on the human body, and on the soul. He sat at the table and, for a moment, felt like a man who has been given a mandate to rule the world. The buttons were numbered, and when Anawari found the board listing code references, he immediately realized that each Aboriginal camp, house, even each individual in the settlement, was in some mysterious way connected to the controller's table. When Anawari pressed the button coded for Menzies Camp, the image of a tribal face appeared on a large screen on the opposite wall—Nupuru! The old man sat on the dusty ground, holding a boomerang clasped against the shaft of his spear, and chanting to the horizon. A human silhouette appeared in the hazy air above the camp, and as the picture enlarged and brightened, it revealed the skeletal face of the woman Anawari had seen days before at the dead camp in the desert. The two remaining teeth in the skull hung from the decaying jawbone. "*Idi,*" she said, and the bones clattered, repeating the word. Anawari, tortured by the scene, hurriedly pressed another button but the picture did not move. Nupuru reappeared on the screen still chanting his words, which could not be heard because of the clatter of boomerang against spear. Anawari, assuming that the old man's chant was some funeral song of farewell to the tribal soul, silently bowed his head. Now he realized that his own visit to that same camp must have been monitored in just this way, on that giant screen.

Undeterred, however, Anawari felt compelled to press other buttons and was intrigued to view not only black people but whites as well, in whatever place or circumstance they happened to be. He even tried pressing the button assigned to himself, and though he at first felt cheated that the screen remained blank, he quickly realized that, as controller of the monitoring system, he could not spy on himself. A red light flickered indicating a replay switch, and when Anawari pressed this he instantly saw himself hanging down a wall with his foot stuck in a window frame, just as he had hung a minute or two before the sergeant had rescued him.

One of the buttons had had its number scraped off, and Anawari, poring over the reference register for any irregularity that would help identify the mystery number, found a dark blot superimposed on, and concealing, the number beneath.

Anawari very seldom came in contact with Superintendent Hunt; they had little in common, and on the rare occasions they did meet, they quickly ran out of appropriate conversation. Anawari reasoned that this was because each subconsciously knew the attitude of the other, so that there was no need to communicate in words. Now, as Anawari pressed the disguised button, that same man appeared on the screen just a few yards away, sitting at the edge of a rock pool in what at first appeared to be some mystical meditation. The scene faded before Anawari could study it in detail, and he was regretting the lack of opportunity to satisfy his curiosity when the screen lit up and Hunt was seen again. His pose was the same as before, except that one of the Twins was now in the picture, tossing something into a pool of water. Anawari understood that his boss was out somewhere in the company of a young female and whispered, "Dirty old bugger!"

The sound of a typist at work came from an inner room; long periods of rapid pounding were interspersed with only very short intervals of silence, but when Anawari followed the sound, he found only a madly galloping teleprinter. He leaned down to read the words being printed out at full speed: DR. TINTO RE YOUR NOMINATION NOBEL PRIZE FOR SCIENCE INFORM US LATEST DATA YOUR WORK ON GENETIC ENGINEERING.

The machine busily spewed on, adding to the pile of paper already heaped before it, but Anawari had no further wish to look, even though he knew that everything written there would, in one way or another, be concerned with Aborigines. How he hated machines such as this one, which with such efficiency, such ferocity, blindly served their white masters in a relentless conspiracy to hunt down the Aborigines to the last man.

Acquaintance with the teleprinter had shaken Anawari, not because of the news it transmitted, but because of its ceaseless hammering; the noise distorted his thoughts. It distracted him from his purpose, and now that he was aware of being watched, at any time, on the monitoring screen, he knew he must continually keep his wits about him. By the time he reached Laura, however, Anawari had composed himself, and even if something of his mood still lingered on his face, the bunch of flowers in his hand would surely nullify it.

"Thank you! Aren't they pretty! One of Namir's friends—Ruwe—often used to bring me flowers. Did Ann ever mention him? We were all at the Seminar for Aboriginal Assimilation. Very bright young man, he was—everyone expected that Ruwe would become . . ." She paused, searching for the right word.

"You seem to be the only one slaving," interrupted Anawari.

"Ann's work has piled up—they insisted that I finish it."

She was busy injecting oranges, though the job was done mainly by a machine. Every three seconds, a piece of fruit rolled through a duct from a large feeder vat and was grasped for a moment by a pair of mobile jaws. A descending needle punctured the orange and injected the prescribed amount of a medical substance, and a second later, the jaws parted to drop the fruit into a bucket below. It was scarcely an impressive spectacle, but Anawari pretended to be very interested. Laura showed him the screen, above the machine, where a computerized number advised the weight of each orange before and after the injection, indicating the quantity of introduced substance. "Ann hardly told me anything about the seminar."

She looked at him over an orange. "It was conducted by Professor Blair from the N.D.A.—he spent some time in the settlement before the hospital was built."

That was before Anawari had arrived.

"They say he wanted to name the hospital 'The 1833,' in memory of the year they abolished slavery. The N.D.A. did not fancy the idea. That year marked the beginning of the campaign to wipe out all those tribes in Tasmania. They advised using the name William Wilberforce instead. Have you read his book?"

"*Abolition of Slavery Act—1833*, you mean?"

"I'm talking about Blair, not Wilberforce."

"No, but I've heard some of his speeches."

"You'd better read it." Laura leaned forward. "He dedicated his book *The Custodians of Fire* to his old-timer superintendent, Hunt."

Anawari sat by the workbench. In front of him the stream of oranges ran through the machine. Had he ever read about the Tasmanian campaign? How many tribes were there—ten? twenty? What were they called? Instead of the tribal names, Anawari knew only that of Truganini—yes, that was the name of the woman—the last surviving Aborigine. She saw both the beginning and the end of the campaign, led by the white man Arthur: Colonel, Governor, or Sir—however his master had honored his name. Yet that had happened almost a century ago. In the bush, man is no longer hunted with punitive expeditions; in the Nuclear Age you press a button and it wipes out a whole tribe.

Anawari watched an injected orange roll into the bucket; a new chapter is about to be revealed, perhaps several of them, a whole epoch. He had no way of predicting what the unearthing of the story would bring about, but judging by earlier experiences, the longer events are shrouded in secrets, the more horrible they look. Most of them are larger than life, each charged with the search for human loot—the savagery that scholars like that man Blair call "our black experience."

Laura suggested that he should read *The Custodians of Fire*. "I must get you a copy." The book, Anawari was told, claims that the Aborigines discovered fire and utilized it by burning the bush systematically to enhance new growth of grass and scrub from the soothed land. According to Professor Blair, this meant the beginning of Progress, which later spread to other continents and led to the first agricultural settlements. The Aborigines had no knowledge of this, but nevertheless, the Industrial Revolution was achieved through the proper use of fire and the credit for it should go to the Aborigines who discovered it. Fire, which gave the world wisdom and comfort, came finally back to tribal Australia to benefit the men who lit it first. "He thinks of a nuclear blast as the greatest fire of the lot," explained Laura.

Anawari's lips swelled with words that he felt unable to hold back: "Did Namir swallow all that?"

"His friend Ruwe was the only one who argued the most—challenging every word. He shouted at Professor Blair once. . . ." The stream of oranges through the duct distracted her and she switched the machine off, then on again. "He said, '. . . because of people like you we're now five hundred tribes less!' "

Ruwe apparently got his hand on a copy of an old manuscript by a certain missionary, Father Rotar, on which he built his argument that Progress, whether it comes with a steel hatchet or a nuclear blast, is equally alien to tribal man. The old missionary claimed that no Aborigine would deliberately set the bush on fire for it would mean burning his own home. Among the desert tribes where plants mean life, the trees are reincarnated tribal relatives who have come back to provide shade; the trees also offer bark and leaves to a man suffering from thirst, allowing him to crush them into juicy drops and have a drink. " 'Aborigines had no part in that madness,' " Ruwe often said, quoting Father Rotar.

Anawari assumed that the polemic actually was about the nuclear testing and wondered what the Church had to do with it; he was told that Father Rotar spoke as an individual for he had lived among desert tribes before their land was taken by the N.D.A. "Remarkable man." Laura spoke with such admiration as though she knew him intimately, and that prompted Anawari to ask about Father Rotar's color. "His skin's white—under it he's all black." This was perhaps the first time he had heard about Father Rotar, but he hardly gave any thought to what the man might have achieved for the desert tribes. However wholeheartedly the whites struggle to help, they always have their own world to fall back on and Anawari felt far more interested in what had happened to Ruwe. His old mate might be on to forming a new tribe—the idea they thought of when in school.

Laura suddenly remembered something seemingly important, for her voice rose: "There was another fellow at that seminar—Ily—old mate of Namir and Ruwe apparently. They all shared the same room as they did years ago." And she heard often Ily repeating, "At least here they let us say what it is like being black."

Ily would have been just the right man for that seminar, thought Anawari. He had read in the paper that his old schoolmate, who had made quite a name as a surveyor, was to marry the daughter of a politician. Does Laura know that Ily has joined the N.D.A. too, if one is to believe the computer? Above the workbench, Anawari's photo was pinned on the wall. It had been taken soon after their college days by his schoolmate Ruwe. Yes, they had been friends for a while. None of them ever spoke about those five hundred or so extinct tribes, and it seemed then that there was something more urgent to worry about. Ruwe had made dozens of photos of Anawari, manipulating the light skillfully so that it was hard to detect the real color of his skin. Whenever he applied for a job, Anawari enclosed one of those photos and often wondered how anyone could have detected the Aboriginal features when they were so well concealed in the print. The photos did no good—after he had collected a pile of job rejections, Anawari burned all but one print, which Ann had unearthed recently among his old papers. However, when applying for his present job with the T.R.A.C., Anawari enclosed no photograph but instead had placed Ily's name as a reference for good character. The trick worked. "That fellow Ruwe . . . is he still about?" Anawari thought it best not to reveal that he knew the man.

"Surprisingly, the old professor befriended him. Ruwe was given a grant to write a book."

"About those tribes?"

Laura's lip twitched ironically. "No—the book was to be about the disappearance of the Snow Man. He was off to the Himalayas soon afterwards—that is where he was last heard of."

One of the oranges must have jammed, for the machine was whining. Laura hurriedly switched the power off and began to empty the vat. Glancing at the photo again, Anawari guessed that what looked like scratches on his face must be marks made on the back of the print, and lifting it up found "505/11" written in Ann's handwriting. "It must be a boring job jabbing all those oranges. Are we really in need of so many?"

"They'll all be used," said the girl. "You must have seen the plane carting boxes of them."

"Healthy looking fruit." Anawari evaded a direct answer.

"Ann must have processed so many of those—enough to tranquilize every black man."

Do any of them know how the oranges are used, he wondered? Laura rattled the injecting device and then, setting the machine going again, looked at him. In the depths of her pale eyes, Anawari caught an image he had seen in the desert, days earlier—an Aboriginal woman mourning her dead child. The blue eyes blinked. "It'll make an impressive photo, seeing this stuff consumed."

Anawari looked aside. A complete list of the hospital staff and the white population of the settlement chalked on a blackboard hanging on the wall above the fruit-injection machine showed the score of each participant in the "Hunt." The sergeant led with 99 points; Anawari had expected Dr. Tinto to be running second, but Superintendent Hunt, with 73, stood one point ahead of the doctor; the other contestants had far lower scores and stood no chances of qualifying for the prize, whatever that might be. "Look at Hunt's score—the old rooster's doing pretty well," remarked Anawari.

"Yes. It's the first time that he's been ahead of Dr. Tinto. He was behind last week, but I suppose the two natives he brought in some days ago pushed him ahead."

The men might be Nupuru's relatives? Anawari looked at the girl. "Where did he get them?"

"Don't ask me. . . . He says he baits a fishing line and leaves it in the desert."

"He must be joking. . . . It sounds a bit peculiar."

"Peculiar, all right! Most of the Aborigines he's caught have died soon afterwards; they're hardly any use in our research program at all. Still, no one complains; we're all mainly concerned with solidarity, I suppose."

Anawari examined the list more carefully and saw that the women's scores were far below those of the men.

"I'm excluded, see?" Laura laughed, then her face hardened again. "The women have their own contest—the one with the best score will accompany Dr. Tinto when he goes."

"Where does that odd name come from, anyway?"

Laura looked at him: "A device to measure shades of color is called something like that. Haven't you heard of it?"

No, but Anawari had suspected there must be something of the sort. How else could the blacks have been classified? "Is Doc leaving?"

"The research project has to end someday; even if you use trees or rocks, instead of Aborigines, those will run out too."

Anawari felt uncertain if they were talking about Dr. Tinto or his research. "Suppose there is nothing there?" He wanted to be vague. For some time now he had suspected that Dr. Tinto was engaged in dual work for T.R.A.C. and the Atomic Authority; perhaps there was a third part as well—toying with the old ambition to create a new form of life. According to that mysterious helicopter pilot, Roger, "The whole country had died—the humans are rotting now"—that would be quite a promising field for any scientist to poke under his microscope.

A note of discontent colored Laura's voice: "He succeeded in splitting the human cell of the Aborigines affected by the nuclear tests around here. He tries now to preserve their life properties in a special environment totally isolated by plutonium waste. That alone could fetch him the Nobel Prize, so the rumor goes."

The meaning of this science stretched beyond Anawari's grasp.

"It's unclear to most of us as well." Part of her cheek twitched nervously. "It's like preserving a gecko in a spirit jar, except that they hope to bring it to life if the Boss ever feels like it."

Professor Blair—yes, he talked of it, remembered Anawari. He had heard him once, on radio, with Dr. Tinto, the possibility of preserving tribal man and revitalizing him from time to time, giving him a new lease on life—for another forty thousand years, perhaps. How could he have forgotten that? The two men sounded like white gods, with a mandate to decide who will live and when. "All that scientific fiddling is done here at William Wilberforce?"

The vat ran out of oranges and Laura switched off the machine. "Only the samples are gathered and processed here. There are a number of similar centers to ours, collecting data on Aboriginal biology and culture. The core of the scientific work is at our main center in Canberra." Anawari felt uncertain whether it was the doctor's real assignment or a pretext to shield more sinister work. For a moment it surprised him that Laura and others who let themselves work on a mysterious project that was wiping out the desert tribes would believe in a slimy pretext but . . . yes, he, too, was working on that project and until almost yesterday had followed his white masters like a blind pup, in spite of his color. Had the people working in Auschwitz felt like this? There was a chimney there too, bigger than the one here. Could anything be bigger than five hundred tribes? Frightened by what would be the answer, he muttered quickly, "Of course, you went to that seminar in Canberra."

She nodded. "I doubt if it'll work. Namir, you know, argued

that if tribal man were brought to life decades later he would die instantly when he saw what his country looked like."

Namir does not seem to be among us to argue any longer, thought Anawari, though he said nothing.

"Would you like a cup of coffee?"

"No, thank you."

"I'm having one."

Anawari was too suspicious to eat, drink, or even touch anything in this terrible room in which he found himself. While Laura was busy with the coffee machine, Anawari turned again to the blackboard; none of the participants among the women had a clear lead, but the Twins and Ann were tied in front, each with the same number of points.

The clatter of the helicopter reverberated outside, hovering above the courtyard, then slowly subsiding onto the concrete slab enclosed by the two wings of the building and the back wall. They're back, Anawari mentally alerted himself. Dr. Tinto stepped from the machine leading an Aborigine on a chain. The captive made no attempt to resist or break away as so many others had done, but limped slowly behind the doctor, dragging his leg, which appeared to be injured. To hasten their progress, the sergeant walked behind, prodding the black man with a bundle of spinifex. Though it surprised Anawari at first that the Aborigine put up no resistance, he concluded that the man was too light-skinned to be a full-blooded tribesman, and prior contact with the white man had taught him the futility of resistance.

"Hey! This is getting interesting," said Laura.

Anawari looked at the girl in surprise.

"Dr. Tinto has scored this time; that makes him even with Mr. Hunt. They both have exactly the same number of points. Unless, of course, one of them gets *nangari*."

Anawari looked at her out of the corner of his eye.

"The medicine man will get top score. He has a personal count that is more than the whole tribe." Her voice had hardly altered.

She might be setting me up, he warned himself, and tried to

sound casual: "I thought those *nangari* were an extinct species."

"Namir used to know one of them. He gave him back his *karan*." According to Laura, and what she must have been told by Namir, when the whites abducted him as a child, his *karan*, that cornerstone of life, deserted the body and ran back to the bush. It went to live on its own, hiding among the scrub and searching for nectar to feed on, though in the prolonged drought there would scarcely be any for it to live on. The *karan* was still there some years ago when Namir came to work in the settlement, but so weak that a local medicine man easily caught it and placed it back where it belonged, extracting from his body the soul put there by the whites.

Anawari felt ashamed; there were four camps of his people still about, yet it was from a white that he had to hear of something so important about his ancestral life. Laura went on explaining that they had initiated Namir as a tribesman. "He could have been *wati*, a full man by now, if things had gone well." Anawari wanted to glean more information from Laura's chatter but he realized that Dr. Tinto should not find him in this part of the building, so he excused himself and hurried toward his own office.

CHAPTER 7

Anawari was summoned to his office early next morning, without any prior explanation as to why he must hurry to report in, several hours before his normal starting time. During most of his life, however, Anawari had been accustomed to seldom knowing what the white bosses expected from him, and never being told the purpose of the finished task, so that he could not be surprised at this unexplained command.

As he arrived in his office, he was joined by the sergeant, who came in from the courtyard leading his captive. "There you are! I told you the bastard would never get away, didn't I?" There was a victorious smile on his face.

"So! You have your hundredth point at last."

"Well, that would have been fine but . . . Dr. Tinto claims this catch."

They spoke in English. It was seldom that any Aborigine brought in from the bush knew the language except, occasionally, one who had lived for a time among white men before returning to his tribal country.

"The bugger is not as wild as I thought—he does not scratch or bite, but even so, you see to it that he's safely back in his box after you finish with him."

Along the courtyard wall stood a line of cagelike boxes mounted on wheels, and of a size that would pass through standard doorways, fit into the lift, and even squeeze into the sergeant's "paddy wagon." Each newly arrived captive was placed in one such cage, moved about from one section of the building to another, and seldom let out at all. Each box had a self-cleaning device that, with understanding and cooperation from the inmate, worked semiautomatically and consisted of a built-in bucket with a self-closing lid, and a bottom outlet that opened into a flexible hose. In the courtyard and throughout the building were several points designed as terminals at which to park a cage and plug the bucket hose into the wall outlet provided. When this was done, a vacuum system immediately began to draw off the human excreta, but problems arose in persuading the captives to cooperate. Most of the Aborigines had spent their entire lives in the bush, and followed the practice of never relieving themselves twice in the same spot, so having used the bucket once, they stubbornly refused to lift its lid again.

The hygiene problem had become less worrying lately though, for, with Ann's help, Anawari had won a long campaign to take personal responsibility for the captive bush Aborigines. Under his management, methods were changed, and only those who showed uncontrollable savagery and viciousness were condemned to a cage, while the others were expected to learn, from Anawari, that they must be grateful to the white man for the privilege of staying alive. Perhaps it was the importance of this job, and the success with which he had communicated with the tribal people, that had prompted the authorities to confer on Anawari the title of Reverend; he had also been issued a Salvation Army cap, a Red Cross badge, and a shirt embroidered with the white flag emblem of U.N. and the U.N.E.S.C.O. insignia.

"Here! First let me help you with that wound," said Anawari after the sergeant had left. "Sit over here; not there—turn this way; a bit more—that's it! That's the way."

The captive was placed in just the right position for observation by the electronic eyes and ears of the computer, and Anawari kept him still for much of the time by pretending to be preoccupied with the wound on the man's upper thigh. This at first appeared to have been caused by a spear, or perhaps by falling on a jagged tree stump, but as Anawari washed away the dust and blood, he realized that a bullet had neatly punctured the skin and thigh muscles on the outer leg and then torn tissue and flesh wide open where it had come out. The captive's skin on both wrists was bruised, torn, and bleeding; he must have had a tough time breaking loose from his chains, and his final success was probably due to his wife's help—for the man could hardly be any other than the one called Gara—and . . . Anawari's skin crept with guilt as he thought of the child dead among the bushes near the camp, for he . . . yes, he . . . had set the bait for that small victim.

The man was indeed Gara, and though he spoke the Para tribal dialect, it was without fluency; his words came stiffly and the stress often fell on the inappropriate syllable. His skin and, in fact, much about his appearance puzzled Anawari, for it showed him to be more likely a half-caste man than a full-blood Aborigine; his forehead was not as broad, and the hollows about his eyes looked shallower than those of a Para tribesman.

This man was not circumcised! This unexpected discovery stunned Anawari, and it took him a moment to react; then with a rush he snatched the vinyl canopy of the computer and threw it to Gara. "I'm a man of God. Nudity, for me, is a sin," he said in English, raising his voice to make sure that the machine would register the statement. The captive must have understood his words, for he pressed the canopy against his abdomen, concealing the greater part of his torso. The telephone rang unexpectedly and though, at first, Anawari ignored it, the caller persisted; it was Dr. Tinto wanting to know if the data on his latest catch was ready. That whole mob of white vultures is after his soul, thought Anawari, and answered, "I'm encountering some irregularities—I'll be a little longer than usual."

"You have a comparable salary to any white, and the assistance of the best computer network. Get up off that black ass and do some work, eh?"

The blood rushed to Anawari's face but he forced himself to answer amiably: "It'll all be processed by tomorrow, Doc, so

71

you'll just have to sit patiently on your white hole and wait till then. OK?"

This conversation done with, Anawari caught Gara's expectant gaze, but there was nothing to be said. He now knew that every movement and word in the Welfare Centre was monitored, and fearful of revealing his sympathy toward the captive, he spoke in a loud stiff voice: "Let me get you some clothes, Brother. Stand here . . . that's it . . . while I take the measurement of your shoulders." Everything said was part of a standard set of words, and this ploy was to get the man's chest against the computer screen for identification of the tribal sign on his skin. Anawari wished to do this part of his task efficiently, for he was, himself, eager to read the result. The marks on this man were nearly identical to his own, except for a difference in the size and number of winding spirals. He longed to pull off his clergyman's garb and compare the two sets of marks, but to expose himself so in front of the computer would reveal to the bosses that he had been recently initiated and this would surely be seen as backsliding into tribal ways. Anawari pushed his hand into his shirt, and while staring at the marks on Gara's chest, went carefully with his fingers over his own.

The moment finally came to press the button and reveal the computer findings on the tribal identity of the interviewed Aborigine, but as Anawari impatiently watched the screen the formula "T.468" appeared instead of a tribal name. Anawari had no need to refer to the card register—he knew from memory that the code denoted an extinct tribe; he also knew that the computer had classified the ethnic name and locality of the tribe before registering the "extinct" code, but to reach the information would require hours of pressing buttons and wheedling the machine into revelation of the data.

Anawari had already spent so much time fiddling with the computer that he feared any more might arouse the suspicion of his boss, or of someone checking on his work. There was a tiny hope, however, that incessant chatter might jam the machine and prevent efficient recording of the program. "Here, put this shirt on . . . pardon me, it's a jacket last worn by a corporal of the Desert Regiment of Her Majesty's Army. It's worn only once during a short exercise. It looks a bit dusty, yes—but that will do no harm. All this help comes to you through the love of Jesus, who, by the way, is watching us and . . . "

"Spare me the agony, please," said Gara in English.

The words hit Anawari like a hammer, and would have left him speechless had he not been so aware of being constantly watched. "Ah! I see, you don't like corporal's jacket. What about a sergeant's; a lieutenant's?—There's a whole regiment of discarded uniforms in that room over there, all for your fellows. Here, please, just step this way. There's plenty more to choose from. Come over here, my friend." As he spoke, Anawari led the man into the dim storeroom at the back of the office and whispered into his ear: "We're being watched. Keep your mouth shut; I'll try to help you out of this mess."

When the two returned a few minutes later, Gara was wearing a discarded greatcoat and Anawari buttoned it up as they walked. They moved through the office, past much of the monitoring equipment, and paused long enough for the computer to record every detail.

A dust storm was raging when Anawari and the tribesman walked out into the courtyard. The space between the building's wings and the concrete wall was filled with whirling dust, being shipped ever faster by the whining wind, and though he was uncertain whether his words could be heard, Anawari nevertheless used the opportune moment to repeatedly reassure Gara that a way out of the situation would be found. They walked straight toward the back wall where Anawari expected to find a row of cages, but only after reeling and fumbling about in the flying dust did he, at last, bump into one of these, and wrenching at the lever of its lid he closed Gara inside with a few whispered words of hope as his only comfort.

When Anawari returned to the office, the computer telephone was ringing impatiently—"Control" was demanding full details of the last program; Anawari explained the difficulty he had encountered in ascertaining Gara's tribal identity, and offered assurances that the interview would continue the next day to the best of his, and the machine's, ability, but voiced his uncertainty of a positive result in such difficult circumstances.

"Apply conventional methods, Reverend, Sir," advised the computer.

"I'll do that most certainly; thank you, madam." Anawari knew that he was addressing the same recorded voice that called so regularly, but it had never before addressed him as "Reverend, Sir." The recording at Computer Control must have been modified lately, but even though the wording was slightly altered, the voice remained the same. The happenings in the dark labyrinths of the machine did not occupy Anawari's thoughts for long, however, for at that moment he was rejoicing in a minor victory over the machine. The computer's advice to "apply conventional methods" meant permission to build the captive's confidence, in the hope that he might voluntarily reveal the details of his tribe and life. Any data thus gathered could then be fed into the machine independently of any previous program, and Anawari might yet discover his tribal origins without attracting adverse attention. He was jubilant—not only with hope but with his victory, albeit small, in the contest with his masters.

The day drew on, but the storm still raged. Now and then the wind was momentarily still and the air cleared a little before a new gust swept in, and during one of these lulls, Anawari peered out to see how Gara fared in the storm. The man lay huddled on the bottom of the cage while the wind flopped the loose ends of the greatcoat, and Anawari wondered if he should take Gara a blanket. A gust of wind flung sand against the window and the dust rose again outside, and yet the air was not so murky that it would conceal his presence on such a suspicious mission if the sergeant glanced out his window on the opposite side of the court; or maybe Dr. Tinto might be peeping from one of the floors above. At that thought Anawari looked up to where the upper rows of windows could be dimly seen through the swirling dust, and as he watched, an empty cage came swaying down through the mist and bumped onto the concrete slab near the back wall. The steel rope hooked to the cage roof became slack, dropped loose, and snaked smoothly upward again. The dust eddied and Anawari saw a steel arm and pulley reel in the cable, swivel swiftly and disappear from sight on the roof far above the courtyard. Anawari had never seen the crane before, and could think of no reason for hoisting the cages onto the hospital roof, but any further consideration of the mystery was interrupted by a voice from the doorway: "Ann rang." Laura stood with her head poked around the half-open door. "She'll call you back in about an hour. Wait here and I'll have it put through to this telephone."

"Why not at home?"

Laura smiled. "Oh, I just thought it would be nicer if we weren't disturbed there."

With an hour to wait, and a satisfactory excuse to give any curious passerby, Anawari had the perfect opportunity to interrogate the computer for an answer to the T.468 code, knowing that he must be prepared for a battle of wits. He knew that he was dealing with a tough electronic beast, programmed not only to provide data but to deceive the unwary—and his first results confirmed this opinion, for the screen immediately flashed the red-letter warning: "The material you seek is 'Classified.'" "Don't sell me that one," whispered Anawari, and persevered with several program combinations until the machine was finally persuaded to begin issuing information. A chart of tribal territorial divisions in the Nuclear Development Area appeared on the screen, dated before that entire part of the continent had been assigned for military use, and had therefore assumed the status of "Prohibited Area." Anawari, triumphant at outwitting the machine, watched as the computer galloped through details of the campaign to hunt down the natives of the Tjuta, Para, and other desert tree tribes in the vastness of their bush territory; of transferring them to government settlements hundreds of miles away. Statistics on displaced natives flooded the screen, with each Aborigine referred to only by a number, and so often described as "missing, presumed dead" that a picture of chaos and misery was painted even by these bare and unembellished figures. Anawari had an eerie feeling that the word "missing" referred to the Aboriginals detained by the Nuclear Development Authority. There was no way to con the computer to reveal their fate or why they were held, but Anawari persisted, feeling determined to press on till the machine broke down.

The word "Walpa" came up on the screen several times as the cause of breakdown of tribal order and the catalyst of ethnic extinction; at first Anawari thought the word must be the name of a tribal leader responsible for his people's misfortune, but when he tried to consult the computer on a separate channel, the only answer was the repetitious INFORMATION CLASSIFIED.

Anawari was not so easily persuaded to give up; he tried another program, this time seeking only information on the tribal word *walpa* without reference to a tribe or territory, and was at last given an answer—"Storm." How could a single storm render a complete tribe extinct? Anawari found himself walking out of one mystery into another.

The telephone rang at last, and brought Ann's voice, vague and distant. Anawari felt exhausted and disoriented, as though he had been awakened in the middle of a nightmare.

"Listen to this! You're going to be knighted. I've just heard it on the 'grapevine.' "

"But why?"

"For service to humanity."

"Whose service?"

"Yours, darling! Remember that campaign we had for the banning of box cages being used to restrain Aborigines?"

"Yes; but look here, the boxes are still out there in the yard."

"Ssh! Now listen to me! They're paying tribute to you for that campaign. Look it up in the Queen's honors list if you don't believe me; your name will be there, I promise you."

As Anawari began to protest, a click severed the telephone connection, and Ann was gone.

CHAPTER 8

t seemed to Anawari that his battle with the computer would never end. The following morning he found his thoughts continually returning to the figures Ann had written on the back of the old photograph, and he became more and more convinced that this must be the code giving access to some secret file and the answers to all his questions about himself. Anawari first set the computer onto the inquiry program, and then punched 505/ . . . Here his memory failed, beyond a conviction that the remaining number consisted of no more than two figures; his optimistic calculation that a total of twenty separate combinations would cover all possibilities was quickly disproved as realization dawned that there were dozens of combinations of two figures. The laws of arithmetic were more complex than he had imagined, and attention would surely be drawn to the computer experimenting thus, for hours. Not only Superintendent Hunt, but almost everyone in the building, would learn that Anawari was attempting to break into the classified data of the computer.

There was no choice but to write down all possible combinations of two numbers, study the result, and hope that one pair would strike a chord in his memory.

Anawari was almost halfway through his mammoth task when he was distracted by the opening of the door in the main hall, and Laura appeared, pushing a trolley. "Tea or coffee, Reverend, Sir?" she asked.

"I didn't ask for any tea." Anawari had never before been offered such service.

"It'll do you good."

"Have you run out of people to serve?"

"Well, yes, I have, actually—the sergeant and Pam have flown off to the desert again. . . . "

They must have left pretty early, thought Anawari. I didn't hear the helicopter taking off.

" . . . Pat is somewhere in the bush with Superintendent Hunt."

"What are they doing out there?" asked Anawari, hoping that he didn't sound unusually curious.

"They're setting traps and fishing lines—at least that's what they always say—you know how crazy old Hunt is about catching natives. He's just itching to score that extra point."

Anawari cast a sharp look at Laura, wondering if she had been sent here, or if she had come on her own initiative. She wore a pendant—the remains of an old seashell; its edges long ago worn away, leaving only the shape of a large coin. It hung from her neck on a string made most likely from animal fur or something else—Anawari could not tell. He had last seen that pendant hanging on the wall above Ann's working desk and had wondered then whether the string were spun from animal fur or human hair.

"So there's only me and good old Doc left in the building. Which reminds me—the Doc sends you this, and wishes you the best of luck with your job."

It was a box of sweets. Presents had been so scarce in Anawari's life that he had never refused any when offered, but this time he felt that the gift was more sinister than cordial.

"No—please keep them yourself," he insisted. "Anyway, my life is sweet enough without those." He looked at the pendant again. Ann told him it had been given to her by her boss. They must have found it in the bush—the string still looked rough though probably used by generations. Spun coarse by tribal hands it stays that way. In the bush the people do not know of wool or silk.

Anawari panicked. "Our friend here is watching. . . . " He rolled his eyes toward the computer.

From the top of the filing cabinet Laura grabbed a copy of the book *The Custodians of Fire*, which she had brought in earlier, and flung it into the machine's feeder tray. "Digesting that should keep the monster quiet for a while."

Anawari still had no idea whether the girl had been sent as an informer or whether she carried on this way through her own foolishness, but he suspected that she might be titillated both by her desire to fight for the Aboriginal cause and by the opportunity to compete against Ann. Whatever her real motive might be, Laura leaned toward him and whispered, "They're closing in on *nangari*."

He stepped on her foot and, setting his face grimly, said hastily, "I'm busy, can't you see?"

She took no notice of him. "We ought to warn the man."

Why is she panicking? The medicine man is like a nocturnal lizard—that small reptile that buries himself in sand to escape the harshness of the heat and comes up at night to search for food in the desert.

"They're after him. Could I speak to that captive? Please—he's a friend of Namir's."

Who? Gara or *nangari*? Safer not to ask, thought Anawari, and said, "I have to do an urgent job for the Doc, can't you see?"

She stood at the doorway for a while, not knowing what to say or do, then suddenly cried: "Oh, help! I forgot to check the final reading. . . . " Laura must have remembered something vitally important, for she rushed out into the hall without pausing long enough for her words to be properly heard. Anawari was furious with himself at not knowing how to handle the situation. He looked out of the window—and saw old Nupuru walking slowly toward the building; he realized that Nupuru was not coming inside when the old man stopped at a water tap near the side entrance, knelt, and let the water run over his head. He drank only a little and though it seemed strange that someone should walk all that way from the camp not to quench his thirst but merely to cool his head, Anawari was becoming accustomed to being a spectator of things inexplicable. With the water dripping from his long hair and making runnels through the dust on his chest and shoulders, Nupuru walked, not toward the road but into the scrub, where a pack of dingoes sprang out to greet him. The animals must have been thirsty for quite some time, for with lolling tongues they jostled to reach the drops of water falling from the man's hair; Nupuru knelt to let them drink more easily.

The scene somehow reminded Anawari of the captive, and he crossed his office to the opposite window to see Gara lying in the cage, unable to shelter himself from the full glare of the sun. Anawari, feeling guilty, was sure that the captive was without food or drink, and his first thought was to rush out there with a handful of biscuits and a bowl of water—but as he expected the girl to return any moment, he restrained himself; he did not wish to give her a reason to come prying after him into the courtyard. One problem at a time, old boy, he counseled himself. The computer galloped madly on, digesting page after page of the thick book. Inhuman great beast, he thought.

Laura walked slowly to the doorway with gloom clouding her face. "I've got bad news for you, I'm afraid." She paused for a moment, obviously searching for an appropriate, elusive word, then blurted out, "You're positive."

"Come on! Cheer up, my girl," said Anawari, putting his arm around her shoulders, for he was under the impression that Laura was the one struck by trouble.

"No! Don't touch me! You're contaminated . . . by radioactivity. That happened to Namir, too."

It was difficult to comprehend; Anawari found himself smiling foolishly in disbelief.

Laura whispered: "There's a device at the main entrance which monitors any radioactivity present as each person enters. I've just checked the detection data now—it must have happened pretty recently."

"Does anyone else know this?" Anawari's voice was dry.

Laura said nothing but scribbled on a piece of paper. "I blanked out the record," and then murmured, "Let's hope it hasn't gone into the system." She glanced at the computer.

Alone again, Anawari tried to fathom the puzzle of how he had become contaminated, and . . . the raid on the dead camp, with the sergeant, came to mind. He saw again the old blind woman, her rags whipped about her in the dusty wind; the setting sun cast a momentary glow on the dead campfire but faded again, leaving cold, gray ash, and as darkness fell on the imaginary scene, Anawari fancied he heard the faint sound of a *didjeridu*.

If anyone was to be contaminated by human contact with radioactivity, Anawari reasoned, it should be the sergeant, or the others dragging tribesmen from the desert; so it seemed most likely that someone in the settlement had arranged for him to be contaminated. Furthermore, he could not recall whether he had used the main entrance or the side door for the last two days.

It was midafternoon when Anawari finally attended to Gara; in one hand he carried a billy can of water, and in the other a paper twist of biscuits; on reaching the captive he had to put both on the ground to lift the lid of the cage.

Gara must have been suffering during the long thirsty day, for he snatched the billy can and gulped its contents without a pause for breath; and when some of the water spilled from the corners of his mouth onto his beard, he wiped the long bushy hair around his chin and sucked at the drops thus gathered on his fingers. Anawari wondered where it would be safer to talk—there, or inside the building—and though he knew by now that they would be overheard wherever they went, outside, in full view of every eye, seemed somehow less secure. "Come inside. I'll get you some extra clothes. It can be terribly cold here at night."

The storeroom was piled with bags containing army uniforms which, though discarded, were hardly worn. The uniforms, it was rumored, had been previously used on dummy soldiers set up near nuclear blasting sites to test the impact of new weapons. They came through undamaged, but contained much dust and sand pounded into the fabric and weighed more than usual. The uniforms smelled of . . . Anawari was unable to tell if the smell came from burnt wool fiber, melting sand, or something else. Sacks of uniforms were stacked everywhere, even across the only window, so that the room was dim and offered privacy. Anawari felt that he was about to face a particularly delicate task—he had never interviewed a man from an extinct tribe, and knew of no other such occurrence. He considered it to be of such importance, in fact, that he felt he should apologize for not choosing a more imposing place for the interview than a half-dark room stuffed with dusty bags. Perhaps, however, there was a symbolic fitness in the dreary surroundings, for everything Anawari expected to hear would be full of sadness—even tragedy. "That's a good patch of desert, the area around the Kunamata hills; a nice piece of tribal country you have there." Anawari wondered whether the man belonged to the Para or the Pipalia tribe.

"It's my wife's father's country, not mine."

Anawari had never heard of a local Aboriginal custom permitting a tribal man and his son-in-law to live together: it would not be traditionally so. However, since the southern tribes of the desert Aborigines had lost their land and many had fled north to their neighbors' territories, the customs were bent to allow man to survive. "How nice that the two of you can get along so well," he remarked. Did his wife say they came from farther south?

"Most of the people have gone. Some were wiped out by the nuclear blast, the others choked by the rolling mist that followed."

Anawari hoped to learn something about the detainees held in the Nuclear Authority, for he could not hope to be told about them by the computer, even if he had all the time in the world to persist. "You're from some mob down south by the look of you. Am I right?" The man from a European father and a tribal mother was born sometime in the 1930s, at a time when tribal children were taken from their parents and put in white men's institutions, so that they would not grow up by the campfire and inhale the evil of the bush. When abducting the children at that time the whites claimed that tribal infants had to be placed in state institutions where they could learn to eat with spoons; when they grew up, they could return to the bush to teach their relatives how to boil a billy can. Anawari had learned earlier from Laura that, some decades ago, Father Rotar had campaigned against child abduction, claiming that the whites were converting tribal youngsters into *janizary,* indoctrinated fanatics who would return to the bush with a sword, bringing tyranny and not a billy can. Gara's father must have thought that too and left Australia, taking his son to Europe. Decades later Gara returned to his tribal relatives. "In time to see the country blasted by nuclear fury."

Anawari had a feeling he was meeting a close relative. "At least you found out where you came from. I still don't know anything about my tribal mob."

In the dim light coming from the doorway, Anawari glimpsed a spasm that flashed across Gara's face, as if he had been about to say something, but for some reason changed his mind and swallowed the words unspoken. After a pause he said: "The whites should have told you, after all the good service you have given. . . . All the faith you have shown."

There's no need to muck about with this fellow, Anawari warned himself. He knows far more than most of us do. "You're familiar with tribal skin marks then . . . on a man's chest, for example?"

"No. Not really. I'm only *wankar.* . . . I haven't been fully initiated yet—but you noticed that."

Anawari wanted every detail he could gather. "How did you find your mob, then?"

"An old fellow at Bidi told me. They call him Patupiri—the bat. He has more information in his head than all the books put together. . . . He can tell you all about any sign or tribal mark."

Anawari thought to ask who put him onto that man, but avoided sounding inquisitive. "I hope he's still around."

"He should be; he lives underground in an old mine and . . . well . . . if you keep out of the white man's way long

83

enough, he doesn't trouble you much." Gara stood up, walked a few steps, and then poked his head through the doorway to reassure himself that no one was eavesdropping before he whispered: "Why don't you try the local medicine man? He's a *wati*, a very wise old fellow."

"How would one go about it?"

"Your predecessor here must have known him."

"Yes . . . well . . . I should really try that." Anawari was eager to change the subject. "When you were down at Bidi, did you go to see your country? It should not be farther than a few waterholes—if the old man, Patupiri, is faithful to his territory."

"Ha! You need to have white skin to go there. They would not let in even Father Rotar; Takapiri has been his home, you know."

Anawari did not ask much about Rotar, for he worried mainly about black souls driven out from their country. He gathered from the chat, however, that the white missionary had been accepted as *wati,* tribal elder, by the Tjuta and the Para, entering into skin relation with both Blood Gum and Ghost Gum people, who gave the man full ritual responsibility as leader of a large family, and later, as the Nuclear Authority intruded into the area and death followed, Father Rotar inherited a number of other families from his deceased tribal brothers. Thinking of that, Anawari suddenly remembered that when raiding the death camp with the sergeant, he had seen a strange object on the ground near the skeleton woman—a knife, hastily made from a piece of discarded metal. Some nights ago, dreaming about that woman, he saw that knife in her hand while she dug *marku* grubs from the root of a mulga tree, and it became clear to him that the tool was made from an old cross, the longer bar of which had been filed to form a blade while the whole cross-section served, partly severed, as a handle. Anawari now wanted to ask if Rotar had been married but remembered that among the desert tribes no celibate could achieve status of *wati*. He wondered if Gara was related to that man and asked, "Where will you go when you leave then?

Will you head down south and sneak into Takapiri Lake country? Or go back to the desert to your wife?"

Gara stared at him with wide-open eyes. "There's no way out of here, mate. The cages all come back to earth empty and pile up waiting for more occupants but . . . the bush around here is fast running out of black fellows to fill them again."

Outside, the red evening glow had melted into the storm clouds banked along the horizon, and darkness had fallen swiftly, as it does in the flat inland; the time to leave the office had long passed, but Anawari found himself quite unable to face shutting Gara in the cage once more. It seemed inevitable that they should both stay in the building. So Anawari set about arranging Army bags so that they might spend as comfortable a night as possible. Tomorrow, Anawari hoped to find the courage to escort the captive through the courtyard, and to squeeze him back into the cage, but . . . bravery is chiefly a daytime business, he told himself.

CHAPTER 9

Anawari dared not absent himself until the weekend, but when Saturday came he was up at the crack of dawn and walking down the road while the entire white community still slept; and about half an hour later, as the sky grew light, he reached Camp Fraser.

Anawari had seldom come that way before; his last visit must have been more than a year before in the company of Ann and the Twins . . . yes, it was just before his engagement, because . . . he remembered being burdened with the thought that he really should marry a woman of his own color, and stick to his Aboriginal heritage; but in his life, circumstances had seldom turned out the way he would wish. There were dozens of youthful girls in the camp from whom to choose *kuri*, a wife, and although all were spindle-legged and skinny, they nevertheless had the pointed firm bosoms of which he had often dreamt, but had never found among white women. The tribal girls had rough skin, weathered by sand and wind, and they washed their hair only when rain came, if it came at all in a year. They wore little more than a *mawulyari,* a scrap of cloth made from spun human hair and animal fur, and covering nothing but their genitals, but even if any tribal girl had appeared attractive and acceptable as a match, Anawari would have felt powerless—he seemed utterly without will and it was Ann, not he, who had planned and organized their forthcoming marriage. Although a year had passed, time had made no mark on the camp—the Aborigines still slept in scattered pits tunneled into the sandy ground, reminding Anawari of abandoned diggings from the gold rush era. Here and there a lucky resident had a sheet of corrugated iron stuck in the ground as a shield from the wind, but nothing else broke the monotonous flatness of the terrain. The sparse native trees had been, long ago, burned in camp fires, down to the last scrap of charcoal, and now wood, which had to be carried from far away, was hard to come by.

There were only old people about, Anawari saw, and there, in front of him, was a pathetic group coiled and cramped in the bottom of a pit. They lay naked, calm under the spell of long despair, as if powerless to move or speak. The scene momentarily reminded Anawari of a film he had seen long ago, of mass slayings during some European war, and the cold bodies being dumped into one great hole; but he quickly drove the unpleasant image from his mind.

A woman rose from the hole hardly two feet away and, despite one arm and half her face being paralyzed, she attempted to make something known with grimaces and gestures. Part of Anawari's mind saw the figure as that of a ghost risen from the horrific film scene of so long ago, while his conscious mind wrestled with trying to understand her message. The old woman seemed to recognize Anawari; one side of her mouth jerked spasmodically, but instead of forming words, she only bared a row of yellow teeth caught in a pose much like that of a dying animal drawing its last breath. Anawari recognized this as an attempt to smile and thought that the woman was begging for food or clothes, but with the help of her gestures, he realized that she was trying to direct him toward one of the holes farther along the shameful row of camp sites. The hole the woman indicated had a sapling plunged into the sand at the bottom and protruding some feet above ground—perhaps to support a blanket—a piece of old canvas or a sheet of rusted corrugated iron as some form of shelter for the occupant.

Crouched in the hole was Kaltu, a tribal elder, who struggled to rise and to move the pack of dogs that lay with him for mutual warmth during the night; the man leaned against the sapling and, supported by it, climbed out onto the edge of the hole.

Anawari was about to say that the upright shaft looked like a flagpole, but realized the words translated into Para tribal dialect would make no sense at all. Kaltu, however, sensed that his visitor's attention was drawn to the pole and said: "It's in case of sandstorms. If a storm should come in the night, the pole will show the place where the sand buries me and my dogs."

Anawari doubted the glib story; it seemed that the sapling must have some other purpose, but no hole in the entire camp except Kaltu's had such a marker; however, one would have to belong to the Para mob to know all their secrets. "I thought you might have gone to the *intichiuma* with the rest of your fellows." The absence of men from the camp was so obvious that Anawari assumed they had all gone into the bush to hold a rainmaking ceremony.

"No right time for *intichiuma* yet."

"Where are all the men then?" asked Anawari.

"Taken to the hospital; young men, women, even children—here only the old people are left."

"Did every one of them have the rolling mist?"

"The sister says so."

Dead silence fell between the two men.

"I'm in trouble," Anawari admitted at last.

"What about your boss, can't he help?"

"No. He only helps white fellows. And haven't we our own boss?" When visiting Menzies Camp earlier, Anawari was left with the impression that Nupuru wanted him to see his brother Kaltu, who might lead him to a secret hideout in the bush; but now, seeing how cautious the tribal elder was, he thought not to mention Nupuru at all. "Would you take me to *nangari*, to our medicine man?"

"Him—he's not around."

Some time before, Anawari had found a sizable piece of crystal in the dirt of an abandoned camping place in the desert and, thinking that the medicine man should have it, had passed the crystal to Kaltu, knowing the precious piece would find its rightful place. "You know quite well that I am one of *nangari*'s men, too," Anawari pleaded.

"He could be somewhere in the bush; but far away."

"Well, suppose we go there; we might just have the luck to see him."

"It has to be a sunny day; no cloud—no dust storm."

Anawari thought it must be a tribal custom not to deal with the medicine man during bad weather and did not question the condition; besides, the day had every chance of turning out to be bright: nearly every day in the year was just that.

The two men set off into the bush the following morning, with Anawari carrying a canvas bag of water that he hoped would suffice for a day or two. On his office wall was pinned a copy of an early exploration map showing a number of waterholes in the area, and he knew that no experienced tribal man ever died of thirst in the bush, but in this harsh desert no tribal skill or determination could compete with the whites' indiscriminate drilling of bores to suck dry almost every waterhole hereabouts. It was never quite clear whether the bores were sunk to provide the settlement with a regular supply of water, or to make the tribal Aborigine entirely dependent on the white man for his drink.

Though they carried no food, Kaltu had a spear and a boomerang with him, and though the old man suffered from poor eyesight and walked slowly, Anawari was convinced that in his company one need never go hungry.

About noon the travelers came to a long-dry waterhole where the remaining trees offered welcome shade after the long hot march. It surprised Anawari to find some greenery after the prolonged drought. Kaltu explained that the tree had *karan,* just as humans do, and as the country around dries up, often it leaves the trunks for another place. Left without soul, the trees wither, shed their leaves and bark, and eventually turn into skeletons.

There are no differences between humans and plants, for when times are hard, man could turn into a tree, though no soul would be foolish enough to do that during a drought.

When the travelers stopped again, Anawari was shown *witjinti,* an old corkwood with twisted limbs and twigs, which looked as though someone had been there twisting every branch as it grew. Some torture like that happened during mythical times, and *witjinti* has not been able either to recover or die since then, for the twisted branches prevent *karan* from leaving. According to Kaltu, "That's what plunderers do to a woman." The tree originally had been a girl who, seized by intruding Ninyas, had been taken south, far away from her tribal country. Ninyas are malevolent spirits; they live underground in deep caves covered with ice, through which perpetually roams a cold wind. Their victims are taken to that subterranean world, and no woman, except Witjinti, has ever come back, for the tribal medicine man took the form of *wonambi,* serpent, and crawled down into the caves to search for her. He found the girl and showed her how to escape from the subterranean world through the crevices of the rocks, and so she came out in a range somewhere south of Lake Takapiri at a time when the country was in the grip of the worst drought known to man and the spirits. To enable her to cross the desert on her way home Witjinti was given *maban,* a magic seashell, with which to make rain whenever she needed water. As she traveled across the world of sand, she left behind a string of waterholes where she camped and where, after she left, the trees began to grow, comforting any traveler who came that way. Through the desert ventured a band of Pungal, light-skinned people who, the legend says, could drink human blood in absence of water and travel faster than anyone else. When they stumbled onto one of the waterholes, they followed Witjinti's tracks, hoping to steal the secrets of the rain. It took many camps to cross the desert country, especially traveling alone. Learning that she was followed, the corkwood girl hung *maban* on a string and carried it suspended from her neck. At night she would bury herself in the sand, and though the Pungal raided the camp, they found neither *maban* nor the girl;

not until one of them stumbled on her hand, which she had poked out of the sand during a dream. To make rain, one needs to know what to do with the seashell and needs to know the right words to chant. The Pungal twisted Witjinti's fingers, broke her limbs and neck, and crushed her bones to force her to reveal the secrets. The tortured body of the girl turned into *pulkarin,* a life-giving rock that is still there in the country near Lake Takapiri, while *karan*, her soul, traveled north and, on reaching her maiden tribal country, turned into corkwood. "Nowadays *nangari* keeps the secrets of the rain; none can steal it from him," explained Kaltu.

Some distance away from the corkwood tree, as if supporting the far end of a sheet of cloudless blue, stood a group of hills that, seen across the wide plain of red sand dotted here and there with clumps of dry grass, appeared to be an island adrift in a sea of molten air. Kaltu grew suddenly impatient and began to hurry— only deviating from a beeline toward the hills to dodge clumps of spinifex. Something not apparent to Anawari must have alerted the old man: a stirring breeze, a premonition of danger, a whisper in the air? Who knows? It was clear to Anawari, however, that some unnamable sense possessed only by such a man—a hunter for most of his life—was sending him scurrying for shelter before the shadow of his predator could fall across his own.

At the top of a stony rise the two men leaned against the concealing rocks and stared into the distance—a ribbon of dust could be seen billowing and subsiding in a line as straight as a spear's flight across the plain and heading toward the hills. Though it was too far for the sound of a car engine to be heard, Anawari felt more than sure that the dust flew from the wheels of a vehicle driven by whites from the settlement. He didn't think that they were looking for him, but if they met, he would feel uneasy at being discovered wandering about in the desert—particularly in the company of a tribal elder. Well . . . if he was caught, he would have to think up a plausible explanation—on the other hand, why bother? The best excuse would be only half-heard, for the whites would hear only what it suited them to believe.

Fear of being discovered turned Anawari's thoughts away from the wish to see *nangari,* and he searched for an excuse to cause Kaltu to lead him back to the settlement. He looked the old man in the eye and was about to say, "Let's get the hell out of this," when he suddenly found that the words had deserted him. His mouth opened and shut a few times, while his hands beat ineffectually against empty air, but no words would come.

Often during his life Anawari had cursed himself for cowardly behavior—he had avoided confrontation and never faced a real test of bravery—but this time he had come eye-to-eye with a tribal elder and felt the choice was no longer his. Mobs of Aborigines moved around the settlement every day, and there would hardly be a man among them whom Anawari had not faced across his counter at the Welfare Centre, yet he had never once looked into the depths of their eyes, or tried to see into the soul behind the calm, serious face and silent regard.

"They'll never get us." Anawari heard his own voice as if it were that of a stranger.

Kaltu pulled a small mirror from concealment under his *nanpa*—his belt made from spun human hair and animal fur—hooked it to the top of his *kulata,* a long hunting spear, and lifting the spear high above his head, reflected the brilliance of the sun toward the distant hills. Anawari wondered whether it was a message telling someone far away that the two travelers were approaching, or a warning about the whites on the move toward the Kunamata Mountains. Since it could be no one but *nangari* in the hills, Anawari now felt sure that the two men often used the same means of communication—the sapling in Kaltu's sleeping hole at the Fraser Camp was used, just as the upraised spear had been, to flash mirrored messages to *nangari* in the hills, but only on a clear and cloudless day. A feeling of deep content, almost of jubilation, filled Anawari's being with the understanding that he himself, the whites, and the whole computer system working day and night had been outwitted by one tribal elder with a mirror. Anawari watched the line of dust, which subsided for a time only to billow again some distance closer to the ranges. "Are they after *nangari?*"

"They never track him down," muttered Kaltu.

92

It was now more than a year since Superintendent Hunt had instructed Anawari to keep his eyes and ears open for information on the witch doctor; Anawari, however, used the milder term "medicine man" as he initiated procedures to track down the wanted man. All available personal details of *nangari* and his traditional activities were programmed and fed into the computer on a "classified" tape and behind the counter, well-concealed from visitors, was a list of discreet questions to be included in conversation with every Aboriginal caller, leading him to reveal what he might know about the medicine man. Yet the computer came out with nothing, and that had angered both Superintendent Hunt and the sergeant. Anawari, on the other hand, was not particularly surprised, for he had the idea that the wanted medicine man was not a physical being but a spirit, and therefore a subject Aborigines seldom discussed even between themselves.

On that holiday in the desert Nupuru had told Anawari an ancient story about *nangari*—a spirit or human medicine man who was the only black soul left in the bush. It happened during the time of that great mythical drought, after the Pungal stole *maban* but felt unable to make the rain. They spread throughout the country, drinking the blood of tribal people. The Pungal seldom ate anything but human flesh and never failed to sprinkle a pinch of salt over their victim, so the country they passed through soon became littered with skulls; these turned into gibbers strewn about the whole area, which became first a rocky plain and later, ground gradually into red sand by the wild winds, a desert. "Step on from one rock to another," advised Kaltu as they walked along the crest of the rise.

Anawari cursed himself for wearing heavy boots, which left a deep print whenever he trod on soft ground. He should have worn some lighter footwear or none . . . but no, the skin of his soles was too soft to walk barefooted as did his companion.

"Drag this behind you"—Kaltu handed to him a large scrubby branch—"it'll blur your tracks."

The medicine man often walked in *kadaitja* shoes like that first pair *nangari* of the old time had made. According to Nupuru he made them of emu feathers and animal fur mixed with blood; he made them oval-shaped so that the track left behind might never reveal which way the wearer had traveled. One shoe had a tiny hole in it through which a small toe might peep—for that toe had an eye—and guide the medicine man along the right path. So good were the *kadaitja* shoes that wearing them, *nangari* had sneaked unnoticed to the Pungal's camp. In his mouth *nangari* held *tjuringa*, a sacred oval stone, said to be the thumb of Witjinti, for it came from Pulkarin, the fertility rock near Lake Takapiri. The stone contained the life of every tribal man in the country. In his palm the medicine man carried a magic spear, hardly bigger than a straw, with which to pierce the tongues of the cannibals and let their blood run into the red sand. No Pungal had ever noticed *nangari*'s magic—the spear wounds healed quickly and the colored sand concealed the spilled blood—but though their bodies struggled awhile, they died soon after. Anawari was told that after the old medicine man rid the country of all the invaders, he "breathed" life back into the gibbers, which turned into trees. Then from these trees spread tribes of Ghost Gum, Blood Gum, River Gum, Box Gum, and other desert people.

It was late afternoon when they reached the Kunamata Mountains, climbing up steep rocks, over a ridge and on to a cliff top overlooking a waterhole in a rock pan far below. It was a place rare in the surrounding area; a place of water even after such a long spell of drought, to which must have flocked thirsty animals, birds, and humans from far away. "Ilgana," said Kaltu, pointing below as they squatted on the rocks.

Anawari felt deep content, as if some long-felt need had been filled at last. An old woman had told him once about Ilgana; he had heard the name later from children too, and about a month ago Superintendent Hunt had arrived at Anawari's home with a bundle of maps and aerial pictures of the area, over which he, Ann, and Anawari had pored all evening trying to pinpoint the exact location of the waterhole. Though they checked every millimeter of the charts and maps, and emptied a whole container of coffee, the dawn found them still at the worktable, with no more definite answer than that Ilgana lay somewhere in the ranges.

The sergeant would have flown over Ilgana now and then, but must never have sighted it—perhaps the water was so well hidden by overhanging rocks and shaded by the surrounding trees that no reflection was visible from above. At first glance the waterhole appeared to be inaccessible in a fortress of rock, but on closer inspection Anawari saw that a narrow gap between two huge boulders connected Ilgana with the tip of a long narrow valley, which, in its turn, joined the plain below. To reach Ilgana by that route would have spilled far less sweat than climbing the ridge had done, but as Anawari thought it possible that the valley may be *milmilpa*—a sacred place that the old man did not wish him to see—he restrained the impulse to question.

They rested on the cliff for some time, drinking from the water bags when their mouths were dry, and as the supply became depleted, Anawari rose to climb down the cliff and replenish it. Kaltu's hand touched Anawari's arm before he could rise, however. "Look down," and the old man glanced toward the narrow valley.

On the rim of the hill, in the shade of a gum tree, stood one of the Landrovers from the settlement, seemingly deserted. Kaltu whispered something, but so softly that Anawari did not catch the words, and stared toward the point where the path leading to the waterhole emerged below the cliff. The men waited silently for only a few minutes. Superintendent Hunt and one of the Twins appeared directly below, at the edge of the waterhole, carrying some jars with them. Anawari crouched lower and peered between two rocks to witness, in horrified excitement, such a scene as had cost the very existence of many tribes, but which the white man's delicacy had precluded him from recording. A terrible chapter of history would repeat itself hardly a spear's flight away and some unknown force, or . . . maybe sheer coincidence, was enabling him to witness the event. Of those who had seen this vileness in the past and were long since gone, there were few who had dared to speak, and those, too, vanished, leaving behind only a whisper.

As the two white people bent over the water, Anawari's determination to witness the poisoning of the waterhole increased, but the slab of rock sheltering Ilgana below hid the scene from view. The only way Anawari would see it was by lifting his head and peering over the rocks, but if this were done, even in a flash, the danger of being seen remained; so Anawari had no choice but to crawl around the outer side of the cliff to a new position—a small platform several meters higher up. As he crept around the rock, a dingo, running in the direction of the waterhole, stopped in front of him a short distance away. The animal had a large scar on one side of his head and held high up off the ground a leg that must have been wounded. As the dingo stood on the edge of a boulder, his ear above the scar flapped a few times, and Anawari realized that the animal was unable to hop backward to the other rock, so he moved out of the way to let the poor soul pass. By the time Anawari reached the upper platform, the visit of the raiding party seemed to be over and he saw only the back of the Twin carrying the jar and hurrying after Superintendent Hunt down the path toward the gap in the rocks.

Anawari knew the value, to Hunt, of live Aborigines, and taking this into account began to doubt that the Superintendent had actually poisoned the water. It seemed more likely that he had used some drug to perhaps paralyze the drinker until he could be collected, and added to the boss's score.

The whites reappeared on the other side of the gap, walking slowly down the path toward the car. The craggy terrain or the heat must have put a great strain on the aging Hunt, who leaned on the girl as he tottered forward. Anawari doubted that the old man would find strength enough to call back to collect his victims.

(Some days later the dingo appeared in Anawari's dream and, while flapping that ear again, tried to mutter some words. He thought that the animal, perhaps a totem, must have come straight from the mythical past and was about to pass on the secrets of life—an utterance that no human had heard before. "They stole my *maban,* magic shell—it might never rain again." The dingo tried to lick his wound, revealing a fine row of teeth.)

About half a day's walk from Ilgana, on the other side of the Kunamata Mountains, lay the Ulumbara Caves, of which Anawari had never heard. He doubted, in fact, that more than a few Aborigines were familiar with the site, for not only was it seldom mentioned, but it crouched, so well concealed in the hills that if Anawari had not followed Kaltu's footprints, he would never have found the way.

To reach Ulumbara one must follow a blind gorge almost to the sheer rock wall at its end, then veer left and upward, crawling and squeezing between immense boulders. It was here that Anawari thought that he had lost his companion—one moment Kaltu was there, only a few meters ahead of him; the next, the old man had disappeared. Anawari panicked and began to shout and call aloud, whereupon Kaltu appeared from behind a great block of rock—here the two had to crawl some distance along a tunnel carved, beyond the memory of man, by an underground river, before emerging deeper in the hills. The travelers' route followed a rock shelter stretching for some distance alongside a sheer cliff, and when at last they sat to rest in the shade, Kaltu explained that the shelter was once a *milmilpa* (very sacred) place to all Aborigines, where only *wati,* elders, were permitted, to perform ceremonies. This had changed, however, not by the wish of spirit or man, but because the only way to reach *nangari,* hiding in the Ulumbara Caves, was to follow the sacred path where only the old and wise had walked for thousands of years past.

The Ulumbara Caves lay deep inside an immense monolith, almost a mountain in itself, and the entrance was well concealed in a wall of rocks and behind the skeleton of a huge dead gum tree. The opening was very narrow but widened quickly into a broad space—a cave larger than Anawari had ever seen—lit from above by the sun, which found its way through cracks and crannies, where patches of blue sky showed here and there.

97

Much had been told and even more expected of *nangari,* tribal healers, none of whom Anawari had ever come in contact with. However, the image of a tribal healer appeared in his dreams now and then. The man always had traditionally arranged hair with a wide string belt pushing the bushy growth backward from his forehead, where it was wound around an eagle's wing bone to form a thick tube hanging over the nape of his neck. His face was thickly coated in kangaroo fat, which glistened with reflected light. The face seemed familiar, though Anawari was under the impression it represented the combined images of many tribal elders he had dealt with. The *nangari* held out a pair of *kadaitja* shoes. "I made them for Namir but they should fit you—try." The words, half sung, sounded like some ceremony. The man, looking much younger than Nupuru, was smeared about the body with white and ocher. His free hand held a *tjuringa,* which he swung in the air as he chanted: "Our lost young man is back; *tjamu,* help me catch his *karan,* he needs a soul to hold a spear again."

Now, in the cave, Anawari looked around in search of that same familiar face of which he had dreamed.

A woman was lying on a stone slab in the cave. She got up slowly and as her face came into the light he saw—Gara's wife! Yes, she's here. Anawari felt pleasantly surprised that she had reached the safety of the caves from the desert plain. He stepped forward to offer his sympathy and give her news of her husband.

The woman backed to the wall, her face frozen in horror. Anawari assumed that her agony had increased and bent to pat her shoulder by way of comfort, but . . .

"Maluk! Maluk . . . " she cried weakly, cringing away until her body was huddled against the rock wall, moving a stiff hand to cover her face. A young girl rose from hiding behind a rock and, scuttling like a frightened animal, ran to fling her arms around the woman, sobbing hysterically. Anawari had never seen the girl before, but assumed from her extreme distress that she was the woman's older child rushing to comfort and be comforted. He looked around helplessly, hoping that *nangari* would come and restore calm, but instead, old Kaltu gestured for them to leave.

"I'm so sorry for this terrible misunderstanding"; Anawari was shocked into speech. "Please let me tell you . . . " but Kaltu turned his back before Anawari had finished the sentence, and walked toward the exit. "Please, can't anyone here make her understand? I'm taking care of her husband," Anawari begged. The woman wailed again as if seeking help from the rocks. He made one silent gesture of pleading but, repulsed, walked away silent and helpless.

A narrow passage sloped down into the interior of the cave and, as the space widened, led to a subterranean rock pool. Anawari walked around, slowly swinging the lightweight empty water bag. No sound came from anywhere, but the dim, damp air felt as though someone had just disturbed it. The light coming from a small gap among the rocks cut a line across the pool. Someone moved! No, it was only a shadow, a boulder half sunk in the dark, concluded Anawari. He would have been received by *nangari,* for sure, had it not been for the sudden appearance of the whites at the mountain. Was it just coincidental, or had something more sinister been trailing him? Without searching for an answer, Anawari concluded that it would be a long time before he could convince tribal elders to trust him again.

Anawari plunged the water bag into the pool to refill it. He had not seen Nupuru for several days. The old man often left camp and was off in the bush, sometimes for weeks. It might be ages before he saw him—perhaps it was better not to mention the visit to the cave.

On his way out, Anawari walked on tiptoe; the woman still lay huddled on the stone slab clutching the girl and sighing. He wanted to slip past unseen and without causing the unhappy pair any further pain.

CHAPTER 10

They reached the settlement the following evening, and though Anawari's first thought was to go to the office, he finally decided that Gara, sleeping on the Army bags in the storeroom, could be safely left till the morning. Fearing that if the captive were left in the compound, no one would give him water and food, Anawari had settled him among the boxes of biscuits all made in the shape of a cross, shown him the whereabouts of the tap, and set off on his journey—so now it seemed unnecessary to risk skulking about the hospital buildings after dark, and Anawari headed straight for home.

The house was in darkness, the streetlights switched off, and the blackness was almost tangible. Anawari dragged himself up the stairs and across the veranda until he felt the screen door under his fingers; as he pulled this open, something fell to the wooden floor with a clatter that echoed in the surrounding darkness, and when Anawari picked it up, he felt the cool touch of stone in his palm.

After he pulled the door to behind him, Anawari clicked on the light and lifted the flat stone in his hand toward the beam—*kulpitji!* He had seen such stones in the museum behind glass, and as pictures in books, but never before had he held one in his hand. So seldom had Anawari heard Aborigines speak of *kulpitji* that he believed the stones to be *milmilpa*, the most sacred object, and had dared not ask any tribal elder to tell him more, but he had once consulted the computer, and had been told that the *kulpitji* was a totemic symbol, handed down from the head of a clan to his successor when the younger became *wankar* and was about to assume full ritual responsibility. There was such a ring of authenticity to this answer that Anawari had put aside skepticism and for once believed the machine.

Engraved circular lines covered the surface of the *kulpitji*: Anawari went gently over each single curve of the design with the tips of his fingers then, tucking that same hand under his shirt, traced the marks on his chest. He could feel hardly any difference between the two patterns and was happy and proud, for though he had no way of knowing how the stone had found its way to his door, or from whom it came, it was clearly his to inherit. This object had been bequeathed to him, its sole and rightful custodian, and Anawari must now stand firm and do justice to the honor bestowed—but how? He knew nothing of the ritual appropriate to the keeping of a sacred stone, and even if he had been familiar with the code, how much of the bush lore could be applied in a suburban house? The previously delivered message stick was hidden under the laundry trough, but the *kulpitji* surely deserved more respect, and Anawari, having decided that his ritual inheritances should have a room to themselves, hit upon the cyclone shelter as the most appropriate place in the house, and the safest.

The underground shelter lay beneath the middle of the house— a box molded out of reinforced concrete without windows, and entered through a trapdoor in the floor—though Anawari had often wondered why such shelters were built at all. Cyclones were unknown so far inland, and the worst of the occasional dust storms did little damage to buildings . . . but perhaps the concrete room was not designed as a refuge from weather at all. Each house had a small information board instructing its occupants how best to utilize the shelter, and advising that under any "external" threat they should withdraw to it, where there was a standard emergency supply of tinned food and drink, chairs, candles, and a New Testament. On several occasions Anawari had taken the book to read, but had hardly finished the second chapter before he lost interest, and he wondered whether he should remove it for good, or leave it to share the room with the *kulpitji*. The conjunction of sacred objects from two cultures did not seem appropriate, but Anawari was too exhausted from his journey, and too shocked with the knowledge of his new ritual responsibility, to think clearly, so he decided to leave the decision until after a shower and a good night's sleep.

When he arrived at his office the following morning, Anawari was faced with another surprise—the sign board at the entrance to the Centre for Aboriginal Welfare had been removed and a new plaque reading "Centre for Social Development" stood in its stead, but Anawari did not expect that the change of name would also bring a change of duties. He and the computer would have to carry on with the usual tasks, and the Aborigines would see no difference—to read the white man's signs one must know the white man's alphabet—yet Anawari was annoyed that he had not been told about the forthcoming change and the reason for it, if there was one.

It concerned Anawari that the whole office might have been reorganized, for there was nothing to prevent Dr. Tinto, Superintendent Hunt, or the sergeant from altering any procedure in the computer or the filing system. Additional monitoring equipment could have been installed, without his knowledge, that perhaps encroached into the dark corner of the office that Anawari regarded as his only secure territory. That was his one patch of freedom, where he could exchange whispered words with Aboriginal visitors from the Menzies, McMahon, Whitlam, and Fraser camps with reasonable confidence that the words were not overheard by whites, and he did not wish to lose this privilege.

Anawari questioned Gara, who had kept himself well hidden, and heard that there had been some movements in the main office but that no one had been in the storeroom. "Good, good! We're still safe, then."

Having transferred Gara from the office into the compound, Anawari was about to carry food and water to him in the crate when the telephone shattered the unusual silence of the office.

"Ha! I've found you at last, my friend. My God, I thought you'd gone for good," Laura's voice came through the receiver.

" . . . Gone where?"

"Finished. I paged you everywhere."

"You don't have to worry about me. I was just wandering around a bit."

"Are you going to be in the office for a while?"

"Yes."

"I'll be down to see you then. It's about our old super."

Anawari wondered why no one was arriving for work—the building was never crowded, but now it gave the impression of an abandoned ship cast adrift on a sea of sand. On the opposite wing of the hospital, and next to the communication tower, the flag had been wound around its pole by the playful wind; perhaps the flag flew for the Queen's birthday, or maybe a new prime minister had been elected, but even if such was the case, Anawari felt certain it would have no effect on him, or on his workmate— the computer.

Gara's file must be put in order, immediately and with care, for though Anawari had learned much about the captive, only the most sketchy details—just enough to allay suspicion and correspond with existing data—should be fed into the computer, and Anawari was pleased at the opportunity to work at this without interruption.

The program was only half done, however, when Laura walked into the office. She moved slowly, looking somewhat different. How badly am I contaminated, thought Anawari, and without searching for an answer, asked if Namir had gone through the same troubles.

"We're getting contributions in honor of the boss"; she held a notebook and placed it on Anawari's desk. "I made a list of all the staff and you're included."

Anawari failed to grasp what she was talking about. "Is that some charity fund?"

"For our boss—see how generous everyone has been." While she slowly traced the list with a pencil, she whispered: "We'll see about contamination at the party. They kept away from Namir when he became contaminated."

You can be a reverend, a priest, or a saint—they'll melt you in the pot, just the same. When they are split, do our cells look any different? Hampered by anger, he asked, "What party?"

"Tomorrow night, down at the club; you know, to celebrate old Superintendent Hunt's knighthood. It was his O.B.E. when Namir was here. The Queen is kept busy pinning medals on our boss. Haven't you been invited?"

"No. What a bloody honor to have to celebrate. When was he knighted?"

"In the Queen's Christmas list. There is a half-page picture of him in the paper."

Hell, yes! It was Christmas Day and Anawari could not help grinning to himself—the Reverend Anawari Mallee, servant of the Christian God, had quite forgotten Christmas Day. Oh well— if God was watching, He had seen Anawari doing "good works" this day, whether in God's name or not.

"What will you be getting for him? A pair of steel traps, or some fishing gear?" Anawari bit his tongue, remembering, too late, the presence of the computer.

"Ann's getting us something very exciting from Canberra."

Anawari felt suddenly sick at the way the white mob stuck together; despite his relationship with Ann, he could never be one with them.

"How much will I put you down for?"

The computer suddenly sprang, clattering, to life, but whether or not its hysterical outburst had been triggered by the conversation between Laura and Anawari, there was no way of

104

knowing. "What's the average donation so far?" asked Anawari loudly.

"We're all putting in one week's salary."

"Oh well, you can put me down for the same, I suppose." Anawari turned to attend to the computer, then, realizing that this could be the right moment to persuade Laura into letting him have his photograph, he faced her again, smiling. If only he could have another look at the number of that picture, Anawari was sure he would have easy access to all the information that the computer had filed away on him, so far. "Listen! You know that old photo of mine stuck on the wall above Ann's work-table. . . . It's the only one left and I want to make a few copies. . . ."

"What a pity you didn't think of doing it earlier. I've just posted it away."

"Posted it? Where?"

"To Ann; she rang me. Apparently she needs it for the press." Laura was already at the door on her way out. "Thanks for the donation. I knew I could count on you."

Alone again, Anawari faced the computer, then patted it as one would to reassure an animal. "Well, old friend, we're going to have a party, just the two of us, while everybody else is out enjoying Christmas." In the bottom of his desk drawer Anawari spread the list of all possible two-figure combinations, ready for quick concealment if he was disturbed. First he punched the 505 code and then, descending from 99, began to add the extension numbers.

Not all the numbers brought results; some were reserved for additional programming, a few bounced back, rejected by the machine, and most referred to various projects that were of no interest to Anawari, but number 75 scored a direct hit at last, revealing a file on one of the Twins. Anawari played with the computer for a little, picking a sequence here and there from the girl's life, before he came across a conversation between her and Superintendent Hunt:

H: You've got to help me get that bloody Father Namir.

T: Has he gone bush?

H: He's just left Menzies Camp with some boongs . . . all heading for the ranges.

T: Don't you want him to lead us to that tribal witch doctor?

H: I thought so, but look . . . that bloody major from the Special Unit is on his way here to seize him.

T: It must be a mistake, surely. Why would the Special Unit intervene?

H: It must have something to do with the rain. The country is stricken with that bloody drought. I just had word from the surveyor chap down on the border. The major's on the way here; he'll be landing with his helicopter to grab him before they reach the hills.

T: You want us to catch him before that?

H: We'd better move quickly, get that boong processed and bottled with the rest of his lot.

Anawari patted the computer encouragingly and whispered: "Good on you, pal"; he was almost certain now that he had hit on the number range allocated for Dr. Tinto's staff, and by continuing the descending figures, he expected to reveal many more files.

Then the door opened, and Dr. Tinto let himself in. Though his heart leaped and began to beat loud and fast, Anawari kept his presence of mind; closing the drawer with his knee, he greeted his visitor with a casual wave of one hand and with the other punched a tattoo that cut off the program and initiated another. Then, with the air of a man enjoying every moment of his work, he rose to shake the doctor's hand.

"I thought you'd be down at Menzies with a Bible in your hand, telling the natives about the Virgin Mary and the three wise men."

106

"They know too much already, Doc; they've had forty thousand years of learning time, remember."

"Maybe, but they've never developed any technology—not even the simplest bronze implement."

"A pity they didn't learn to split atoms. I . . . " Anawari heard the bitterness in his own voice, but it was too late—an ugly shadow moved over Dr. Tinto's face and his eyes narrowed. He'll have me yet, Anawari thought to himself and shuddered suddenly. "I'm more than halfway through compiling the data on that man in the compound. You shall have it very soon." Anawari rifled through Gara's file as if checking it and added, "Yes, only a few more entries and it'll be completed."

"I'm to be called as soon as you have it ready, and"—with a sharp look at Anawari—"I expect a signed statement from you, outlining the cause of the delay." Dr. Tinto walked out, leaving the door open behind him.

CHAPTER 11

t was past noon. Anawari had eaten no breakfast and heard rumbling noises in his stomach, so he tidied his desk and was about to leave for lunch when Superintendent Hunt passed by outside the window and a moment later walked into the office. "How's everything going here, sonny?"

Anawari had a kind of sympathy—no, more than that, an affinity—toward old folk, which he had recognized as a longing to know his own parentage, and a constant awareness that any one of these elderly people might be his parent, without either party recognizing the other. As a student Anawari had spent his weekends hanging around the Salvation Army and St. Vincent de Paul shelters, but everyone he met there was white; on many Sunday mornings he had sneaked out of the dormitory while the other boys slept, and though the holy brothers had punished him severely for his unauthorized absences, Anawari still thought it worth the penances to explore, to search, and even if not to find his own folk, at least to keep alive the hope that one day he might do so.

"You have it all very tidy and neat here." The superintendent bumped a briefcase down on the desk.

Anawari felt quite certain that Hunt could not be his father, but even had he been, Anawari would have been able to find no room in his heart for one tiny fragment of sympathy toward the old man.

"Jolly good; maybe a bit of dust here and there, but then I suppose that can blow out of one's own background." Hunt was really enjoying poking about, peeping into filing cabinets and behind computer installations.

With the urgency of youth Anawari had searched relentlessly for his family; deep in his heritage lay the belief that older people have more virtue and a deeper understanding than the young, and Anawari yearned for the support of someone with these attributes. Not far from the school, at the end of a blind alley and near a rubbish dump, Anawari found a woman sheltering under some discarded corrugated iron sheets that had once been a shed; she was half naked and partly covered by hessian bags so thick with coal dust that Anawari had persuaded himself that she was one of his own race. . . .

"I'm afraid you've been rather too generous lately with the handouts; I'm told there are great heaps of empty boxes and bags." Hunt was frowning.

. . . It seemed that the woman could not speak. She lay quite stiff, but her wide-open eyes clearly tried to tell him something. Anawari thought she was perhaps drunk, for at that time he had no experience of any other reason why someone should lie immobile in the wreck of a ruined shed, but still he had come the following morning with a piece of buttered bread and a cup of milk, smuggled from the kitchen, in his schoolbag. The woman had not moved; her mouth sagged partly open, and when Anawari poured in some milk, she gagged but seemed to swallow it. When Anawari pushed a piece of bread between her teeth, however, the woman could not chew, and the bread had just stayed there, sticking out from her mouth. . . .

"We'd better have those biscuits locked away somewhere; it's the drought, we can't afford such extravagance."

. . . Anawari had tried to come to the shed the following day, but had been caught in the act of struggling through the dormitory window, so it was three mornings later before he ran down the alley again, carrying a whole bottle of milk. The woman no longer needed milk, however; the piece of bread was still in her mouth, and as Anawari approached, a rat scuttled away. The woman's eyes were still open but stared, expressionless, and a swarm of flies buzzed in the air. He spoke of it later to his mate and . . .

"Are you with me, sonny?" The old man was peering into Anawari's face.

"Yes, Mister Hunt," Anawari thought it better not to use "Sir" just yet.

"Then do as I say. Take your shirt off and stand there, on the other side of the counter. I want you to behave as though you are one of the blacks who's called in for, er, welfare. . . . "

"Is there anything wrong, Sir?"

"No. Well, I hope not. It's just a routine check. Every member of staff has to undergo a periodic examination, you know."

Only now did Anawari notice that Hunt's briefcase was open, and that he held a sheaf of papers in his hand. "Come now, don't hang back; it's all for the good of your health, sonny." Hunt changed his glasses, consulted the papers, and then reset the dial on the computer board.

Anawari's one hope was to stand at a sufficient distance so as to be out of focus in Hunt's reading glasses. He pulled his shirt off behind the screen, as instructed, but carried it with him pressed to his chest, and leaned against the counter as far from the superintendent as he dared without seeming suspicious. "Have you had a good helping of turkey and plum pudding today?" he asked.

"Indeed, no! The state of emergency is on, all because of that bloody drought. This check must be done. Actually I had planned to do it after the holiday, but quite unexpectedly I find I must fly south the day after tomorrow." As he spoke the superintendent fiddled with various buttons on the computer. "Well . . . that'll be all for now, thank you."

Anawari hurried to dress before the old man changed his glasses again.

During the afternoon of that same Christmas Day, Anawari struck another pot of gold; he had the computer tuned in on Ann's file when an unusually long monologue came spewing out: "Due to the nuclear development in the area of the ranges, the local tribal people have absorbed a far greater dose of radioactivity than it has been previously known a single human organism could tolerate and still continue to function. It should be remembered here that the local tribes are the direct genetic and cultural descendants of a unique race which, generation after generation, has existed for at last forty thousand years. These are the only people known to science capable of assimilating such high degrees of radioactivity. . . . "

Anawari at first assumed that this scientific oration must be something of Dr. Tinto's that the computer had mistakenly printed into Ann's file, but no, . . . whatever distaste Anawari felt for the computer he must admit that the machine was supremely efficient.

"The metabolism of these people has reached a crucial stage of genetic disorder, and therefore provides the ideal proving ground for my theory on the splitting of the human cell, so hastening the transition of the race. . . . "

Ann had spent evening after evening in her office typing Dr. Tinto's papers, and from what she had told him then, it seemed that the work was a detailed scientific essay suitable for presentation to experts at a symposium, or some other learned gathering. These comments were brief and simplified, however, so Anawari concluded they were nothing but an annual report to the appropriate government instrumentality. He let the computer run on for a time and then picked out another sequence:

"We rounded up ninety-five percent of the natives in the area and fed the best specimens into our system. . . . "

Sweat rolled down Anawari's face; he felt racked with exhaustion and his hand was stiff against the button as he brought the machine to a halt. He felt he needed time to pull himself together. Outside, a small willy-willy swept across the compound, stirring up the dust and flinging it against the windows, and through the murk Anawari glimpsed the sergeant hesitate at the door of his office before hunching his shoulders and braving the buffeting wind. Anawari, anxious to have the unpleasantness over and done with, set the machine running again.

"The divided Aboriginal cell formed two new units—a *positive* half containing all worthwhile properties of the race, and a *negative* half. After a successful crossing of the positive half with a one-quarter bovine cell, we bred a camel, an economically viable creature adapted to the desert environment; during the prolonged droughts it could be milked, ridden, skinned, and eaten. The negative half, crossed with a one-quarter dingo cell, an animal which is in spiritual and totemic harmony with the local tribesmen, produced *Oecophylla smaragdina*—a green ant which survives without water. . . . " Through the haze of dust left in the wake of the willy-willy, Anawari saw the sergeant scuffling with Gara, and he raced out to investigate.

It was not clear to Anawari what had caused the incident; the sergeant had Gara's left hand chained to one of his own, while with the other he clutched a swatch of the captive's hair and by jerking it kept smashing Gara's face against the cage.

"Hey there! Hold on a minute, please! Let's sort this out in a civilized manner," called Anawari.

"This bloody black savage jammed my hand in the door of the cage." His shrill trembling voice betrayed that the sergeant had quite lost control of himself.

It appeared that Gara had positioned his hand between the bars of the open cage door so that, as he was being locked to the sergeant's wrist, a sharp tug brought his captor's fingers and the slamming door into painful contact, and elicited a roar of pain and fury. "It was just an accident—I'm sure he intended no harm, Sergeant. He must have caught his hand in the door." Anawari placated the angry man, who sucked the bruised fingers and rubbed them by turn.

"Oh yes? I know better; this bugger gave me hell up in the desert. Just wait until I get him inside the cell! Come on, you bloody boong."

Anawari shuffled his feet uneasily. "I must ask you a favor, Sergeant—look, I'm still working on this bloke's file and I've come up against a few difficulties. Dr. Tinto's on my back to get the job finished and . . . "

112

"That bloody doctor is right up everyone's backside, here." A taste of bitterness flavored the sergeant's words.

" . . . and I have to get the captive to cooperate if I'm ever to finish the job for the Doc."

"You'll never get this beast to cooperate, mate."

"Well, I'm paid to try. As soon as I finish he'll be handed back to you. He's your catch, after all."

"It'd just better be that way, hm?"

"Thanks, Sarge! Now you leave him there in the cage, and I'll nick back and get the computer ready." Anawari wanted to sort out the mess scattered in the office before he let anyone in; he had left the computer running and the drawer, with the list of possible numbers in it, wide open. On his return, however, Anawari found the machine silent, as though an electrical fuse had blown, or maybe the power had been cut off. The desk drawer was closed and when Anawari snatched it open he could see no list of numbers: he stared around in the vain hope that the paper might have blown away in some strange circumstances, and then he noticed that the door, which Dr. Tinto had earlier left open, was now closed.

Anawari let his body slide slowly into a chair. "It looks as if I'm really caught this time." Outside, the storm was gathering momentum, and the more savage gusts of wind howled their challenge to the building walls. "What a pity my computer game did not last a bit longer." He had not yet fully realized the implications of the information squeezed from the machine, but Anawari's intuition recognized evil and destruction in the cold, scientific words he had read. An old man had told him once, "A fish rots from the head," and he himself had long been in this particular fish head—one small bacteria in the mass of decay, and so accustomed to the company of other microbes, and to the scent of putrefaction, that living a new life on his own might prove harder than he could bear.

A whistle shrilled outside; Anawari listened a moment and heard the sound again. Quickly he scurried out into the pall of dust and saw the cage, with Gara in it, dangling in the air a few feet from the ground, and crouched on top of it the sergeant, blowing the whistle in a fury of anger. Anawari leaped up beside him.

"I'm not going to let this one go so easily."

"They can't sneak a captive away from you like this. It's a disgrace, Sarge."

"He's bloody well mine. That doctor's mob . . . "

High above their heads the arm of the crane appeared through the dust, reeling in the steel rope. The cage, with both men on top of it, spun in the air past the windows of the top floor and once over the edge of the wall hung suspended above the hospital roof. The sergeant blew his whistle even harder, and Anawari joined him, first by shouting at the top of his voice, and then by whistling with two fingers thrust into his mouth. The crane stopped, and as the cage spun in the air, it struck the corner of the incinerator's chimney and came to a shuddering halt. Anawari, clinging to his precarious vantage point, surveyed the scene; the roof of the hospital looked like nothing more than the deck of a great ship that had sailed into a stormy sea and been left abandoned by its crew. The boom of the crane swiveled suddenly, throwng the two men off balance but bringing the cage to a position above the compound before lowering it to the ground again. "Well, you might be 'Sir' or 'Doctor' but justice prevails in the end," remarked the sergeant.

"It certainly seems so," said Anawari politely. "I'd better take our friend, here, inside—we really have to keep a close watch on him now. Are you coming in too?"

"No fear! I'd rather go and enjoy what's left of Christmas. You'll take good care of my prisoner, won't you?"

"My word, I'll do that alright."

Because of the storm, darkness closed in unexpectedly early, and Anawari, not wishing to illuminate the office, led Gara through the semidarkness to where they could sit on army bags and talk, leaning toward each other as they spoke so that their whispered words could be heard. "I've to get you out of here."

"But where can I go?"

114

Anawari spoke impatiently: "Did you see that chimney on the hospital roof? It puffs smoke into the air now and then; you saw that? Well whenever it does, it's one of our fellows going up in smoke—I'm just beginning to understand what this place really is."

Gara was silent.

"*Nangari*'s caring for your wife. She's going to be all right, so I heard."

"But they'll only catch me again if I go back to the desert."

"Yes, well what about that place where they dig for gem-stones?"

"I worked there before I went back to the bush—it's far to the south—many, many *gabi* away. I'd never get there on foot."

Anawari had heard of many tribes that crossed deserts carrying their children and nursing the old people through the difficult journey, and though he doubted if he, himself, would survive such an ordeal, he felt that Gara had been divorced from the white man's way of life long enough to exist out there, where most animals and plants had given up. "Your wife comes from the south also?"

"Yes, from the Tjuta tribe; we have one child still—a girl."

"Which is your tribe then?"

Gara felt uncertain; it was hard to find where one belonged when the country had turned into dust and the tribe had vanished. A handful of the people who survived had fled north into Pipilia, River Gum country, hoping that *tjamu*, spirits, would bring about some miracle whereby the whites would go away, and so would the drought.

"That mine at Bidi is on the way to Lake Takapiri country."

Gara looked vague. "Namir used to go there often."

Anawari whispered, "*Namir,* what does the word mean in tribal lingo?"

"A notch on a spear—the identification mark of a hunter."

Silence fell again in the darkness. When leaving on holiday Ann had left her car parked under the high pillars of the house foundations, and Anawari had never bothered to check how much

115

petrol there was in the tank, but now he needed to know. Still, even if the car could carry them only a few kilometers, they would be away by the time the whites from the settlement had discovered their absence, and if luck was with them, there might be petrol enough to take them a long way, if not to Bidi.

We'll wait for darkness to settle, thought Anawari.

Now Anawari and Gara must wait; wait for the night to become dark enough to conceal two dark men.

CHAPTER 12

n the black world, as in the white one, friends and foes do meet, often even after years of absence. They come back from the edge of oblivion, not to behave any more wisely but to admit to growing different. Anawari did not have to worry about that; for the first time in his memory he found himself on the run and knew he would stay alive only as long as he kept away from the world he had deserted.

They drove along an old bush track through scrub country, vast and empty. In the morning, while the shadows were long, they saw a pair of kangaroos trying to rear up and look around; but unable to stand on two legs alone, their skinny bodies kept sliding down. Anawari attributed this to the lack of a tail, where instead of a solid limb there was only a stumpy growth showing from under the skin—too light to balance the body.

"Animals eat no sand," muttered Anawari, wondering what the kangaroos could live on in country that might not have seen rain in their lifetime. He wondered it again later on, when they came across a featherless *takapiri,* emu, dust bathing in the middle of the track. The bird must have been deaf, for it failed to hear the car horn. The travelers had to stop and remove the *takapiri* out of the way, for the track, narrowed by the rising tide of sand, hardly gave enough room for a car to move along.

The track must follow an old stock route, thought Anawari

later on when they pulled up by a derelict bore. The bore, almost buried by sand, had held no water for years, and the troughs that once provided drinking water for drovers and their stock were almost eaten through by rust.

Anawari felt jubilant seeing the white man's beloved metal and labor dissolving into sand, and he barely heard Gara's suggestion that there might be some water farther along the track. His imagination carried him away: "The country will bloom again." Now that the whites are falling back and the wilderness is reclaiming the old stock route, life may begin in earnest. There will be no more deformed young children, tailless kangaroos, and emus without feathers.

As they drove off, leaving behind a long serpent of billowing dust, in his mind Anawari saw green country ahead, lushly green and alive as it had been millenia ago in the postglacial age. A wide river made its way through a forest of towering gum trees, leaving behind strings of billabongs, dormant water shaded by fronds— palms or tree ferns, Anawari could not tell. The country rose gently toward the horizon with a flock of cockatoos flying over the green canopy. Just the right place to begin a new tribe, he thought. The country reminded him of a painting of a rain forest by the Napoleonic explorer Baudin, though in his mind it was greener and much thicker. That Baudin, or someone from his expedition, had also painted the Aborigines; beautiful they appeared, with bright faces and muscles full of strength. Seen in the bush, they would have looked even more impressive, though only pictures survived of those tribal people. Down in that lush green country, on the banks of the river and the shores of that lake, he would form a new tribe. Gara would be with him. They would first have to build *wiltja* from saplings and roof it with bark. The other fellows would be around in time to join the new tribe— Namir, Ruwe, Ily, and others. Good old Nupuru should be about too, to show them how to make a stone ax, choose the right tree for carving a boomerang, and then smooth the newly made tools with *kanti*, stone flakes. "Those Pungal, how long have they been about in tribal tales?" Gara did not know that either, but noted

118

that the myths and legends could date before the creation or the Ice Age or be even older. He, too, thought that old scars die hard, and by scorching the country with a nuclear blast, the whites had unearthed the fear of the Pungal, who had spread terror in mythical times.

"What shall we name our tribe?" Anawari was about to ask, when he suddenly noticed a large shadow on the red sand moving parallel to the car. The shadow looked like one cast down from a bird. Perhaps that featherless emu they passed on the road had taken to the air—*takapiri* do fly in Aboriginal mythology. She too would be heading toward that lush green valley ahead, the kangaroos without tails would be moving there, and so would that scarred dingo flapping his wounded ear all the way—every wounded soul would flock down to that new country. "Do you know how to make a *woomera*, a spear thrower?" Gara admitted to not being the best craftsman but he made all his own tools. Wood and stone tools had served the Aborigines for two thousand generations, remembered Anawari. "They will serve us just as well." No one will miss Dr. Tinto and his microscope. The shadow of the bird was now visible on the other side of the track, moving over the bushes, but Anawari felt there was something far more pressing to be considered than a flying companion. "Do you know all about *magarada*, the peace-making ceremony?" He assumed that the ceremony belonged to the tribes farther north, but he expected that the desert people would have something similar to settle their disputes. "Well, who needs the sergeant and his helicopter, then?" The shadow had disappeared for a while and he thought that the bold emu must be lagging behind—the car moves faster than that poor soul—at least while the petrol lasts. "What about *inma,* the rainmaking ceremony?" They would have to make rain often for the country to stay lush green, otherwise the drought could set in and trees could die, just as had happened when the whites began to blast their nuclear bombs. "Old Nupuru taught me about *inma.* . . ." The new country would need consistent rain to sustain the lush greenery and it might be handy to know the customs, for that ceremony has been about ever since mythical times. "He

119

taught me all about . . ." Gara's eyes were riveted to the helicopter seen through the windscreen. The machine hovered ahead of the car till Anawari slowed down and pulled up by the track. "What a pity that green country of ours did not last," he told Gara.

He thought of it again some hours later while watching his old schoolmate Ily searching among his papers for a photo taken about a decade before when they all had deserted the school and run to the bush to set up a new tribe. They would all be there with little caps and school badges with the large letters, *Nobis crus progressus est* (the Cross is progress). Yes, all are there: Jungkun, Antakin, Namir, Ily, Zambo, he—Anawari, Ruwe, Yapy—the new generation of Janizary, as that old missionary Rotar used to say, who would come back to the bush with sword and tyranny—not quite, though. Janizary!

Looking at the old photo Anawari hoped he might be able to persuade some of his old schoolmates to join him. Perhaps they all might follow him in time, providing that they are about. Romanticizing is destructive, Ily thought. He disliked the bush and had acquired a great admiration for machines, a particular group of them that had flocked together weeks earlier somewhere in Europe, sped down the Middle East, and beat their way across the Indian subcontinent, tearing along muddy roads and rolling over villagers' chooks brave enough to have ventured out. "The Great Rally of the World!" In his tent Ily had mounted a map with a striking red line that cut across the continents and the seas as it progressed toward Australia. The line had actually hit Darwin already and in a few days the great metal horde would roll down, tearing along bush tracks at first then arrowing through the red sand on its way to Sydney. "They equate this with Captain Cook's arrival at Botany Bay," said Ily, overwhelmed.

Sport or fanaticism—it mattered little to Anawari. He would even have pretended to place a bet on one of the metal racing beasts, had he been more fortunate. When picked up by the helicopter, he told Ily that he had been heading toward the Eastern Coast, but had lost the track and his fuel had dwindled almost to the last drop. He mentioned how lucky the drivers of the Great

Rally must have been for having their tank full, at which his old schoolmate had remarked: "It's worth every drop—the epic!" When he had met them earlier, Ily had explained that he was out in the desert with his helicopter to see whether there had been any rain, for a dust storm had shown up earlier on his radar. The dust storm swooped down on the area, shifting sand from one part of the country to another, piling up new dunes, and burying the skeletons of dead trees. "Not one drop of rain fell." He felt pleased, as anyone would who had invested so much hope in the rally. He hardly spoke of his assignment surveying the northern border of the Nuclear Development Area, apart from telling Anawari that instead of heading to the Eastern Coast, he had been driving south, following an old stock route that had been closed ever since the Nuclear Authority had moved into the area. Had they not met, Anawari would have soon crossed the boundary and faded into the desert where the nuclear blasts had melted the sand.

The Northern Border, stretching for a thousand miles along the twenty-sixth parallel, was seldom marked on the ground. The conditions were to change though, when Ily and his three sur-veying mates were to pass on along that line. He had shown a plan for the erection of "the fence." Anawari had expected to see posts and mesh wire as in the fence he had seen earlier stretching across the whole continent to prevent dingoes from moving north to south. Instead of a conventional fence the plan showed only vantage points here and there—metal towers stretching endlessly across a sea of sand. On the towers perched something that looked hardly bigger than a billy can. It had a pair of prickly ears and long feelers like those seen in flying foxes. Ily explained that the scanner had nocturnal eyes that could detect an object in a heavy dust storm. During the test run it had picked up a human track fifty miles away. When analyzed by the computer, the track turned out to be from Father Rotar. Anawari wanted to know what the man was doing in the border area, but Ily felt uncertain. The scanner had not been designed to ask questions; he predicted, however, that the missionary was out in the desert to meet an old friend, a medicine man called Nupuru. Forgetting for a moment that he was on the run, Anawari wanted to know whether Rotar had assumed the task of prophet, a sort of desert monk who is to be handed down secrets from the spiritual world and who is to lead the decimated tribes into the new world.

Ily admitted that Rotar would be rightly placed, for that man was favored by the spirits. He had inherited scores of families from his blood brothers who were deceased and his influence spread over a whole block of desert tribes, even though the people had long been displaced from their traditional environment and the land. However well Rotar was placed, Ily did not seem so pleased with him: "He should try earnestly to bring some rain—dead country is useless to the blacks and whites alike." Though he felt very bitter about the prolonged drought, Ily thought that the rain should stay away for a few more days until the racing rally was over. "We have waited for years—a few days would make no difference." He cursed the dust storm, which when sweeping through the camp a day earlier had hit the communication tower with lightning and burned his transmitter. "Just think of that rally—you would not like to miss the event of a lifetime." His camp had been out of communication for a while, but thanks to an old airplane, word could get in and out. "Lucky there's an airport nearby," said Anawari, wondering if perhaps he had already entered the Nuclear Area. Ily explained that the airplane had been used as a target during nuclear testings, as was the helicopter he flew about in: "Some of the machines got away with barely a scratch—you only have to blow off the dust and hop in the seat." One of Ily's men had flown that airplane around for some time, and today he and others had flown to Bidi for supplies.

The old schoolmates hardly spoke of their tribal ancestry for a while. However, after they had helped to repair the damaged aerial and left Gara to stack the new pegs for supporting ropes, they retired into the shade for a chat. Ily explained that he would have gone south for a medical consultation if it had not been for the Great Rally. "I doubt the psychiatrist could help much—it is about that bloody dingo." For a moment Anawari thought that Ily had

122

been bitten by a wild dog and thought that one would go to the GP for that. No dingo bit Ily, but one kept appearing in his dream. "It comes regularly; I can set my watch by him." Anawari failed to see why anyone would be upset about seeing an animal in his sleep. The dingo was often a tribal totem, or if domesticated could be one of your dead relatives reincarnated, which is to say that chips do not fall far from the log. "It looks very scared, that bastard," complained Ily. Anawari explained that he had seen a dingo like that one in the daytime in the bush, but had avoided telling him the exact spot. "One can turn a dingo into his best friend, just as they do a dog." Drops of sweat rolled down Ily's temples. "You're kidding—what about those fangs?" He explained that his night visitor had four of them; they were long and twisted like a pig's tail. The dingo growled, brought his head under Ily's nose, and clattered his teeth. "Indeed, you should see your . . . " Anawari was to say *nangari*, but bit his tongue quickly, " . . . see your psychiatrist."

Later, when calmed, Ily advised Anawari how to keep clear of the Nuclear Development Area. "You can often see a greenish smear at night. Make sure you head away from it." Anawari explained that he had seen the glow on the horizon and had thought it to be a settlement or some kind of night mirage. "It's there all right—the blasting site. I adjust my surveying instruments by that—it's so constant." Anawari was at first speechless at the thought that he could have unknowingly walked into a nuclear crater, then asked, "What if the light goes out?" Ily laughed. "Don't you worry, mate; that beacon will glow for thousands of generations yet."

After leaving, Anawari noticed that the tank of his car was almost empty, but he saw a smile on Gara's face. "We'll reach Bidi all right—I knocked off two cans of petrol from that bloke— that should do for helping him with that aerial." From Ily he had also knocked off a map of the Nuclear Development Area, a map that Anawari had never seen before. Scattered across the paper lay red dots, presumably nuclear testing sites. The dots looked like some malignant insect clustered around the salty Lake Emu and, from there, swarming out along the valley of a river to spread throughout the desert. Emu is *takapiri,* Anawari reminded himself. In the lake lay an island shaped like a boomerang and pointing to the river mouth. With his eyes closed Anawari tried to memorize the position of the island and the rigid line of the lake's shore, not that he would ever get there but he thought that one should always remember the place where evil had wallowed. The place lay some distance from the Northern Border, along which stretched a string of crosses marking the electronic beacons that he had seen earlier on Ily's working paper. "It might come in handy one day, this map," he told Gara.

Later on as they drove into the empty vastness, he saw the dingo again, a mirage of him only somewhere in the space toward the horizon. The animal turned toward them, looked for a while, and then flipped his ear. Anawari thought, Something very odd with that Ily; he never mentioned Namir once.

PART TWO

CHAPTER 13

The township slept; it was an eerie time in the depths of the night when it seemed as if the whites had gone for good, abandoning their mechanical toys. The half-eaten moon hurried to drift over the western edge of the sky, and left behind it an immensity of semidarkness and silence broken only, at irregular intervals, by a mysterious sound that came throbbing from the distance, and ebbed away again into nothingness, unexplained. Anawari knew it to be the stars conversing, however, and wondered if these stellar chats were held only at night; perhaps the stars talked during the day as well, but the din made by the noisy whites drowned any soft voice from the skies. "Don't go to sleep," said Gara. "Michael, the boss, should be here soon."

They sat on a pile of earth flung out from a mineshaft, a rough and uneven resting place but familiar enough to Anawari—he had known no softer bed for months, and could readily have fallen asleep if it were not for the cold wind. It felt as though the gusts were coming from the end of the world and gathering speed across the wide desert plains before finally lashing against the mound of mining waste. Anawari wondered if the stars, too, had such cold and wind-swept places, but in his heart he needed no answer, for the universe is a white man's theory based on science and logic, but with no ears for the music of the firmament. Anawari had learned much, in school, of the white man's conquest of the skies, when the lust for possession led even into the cosmos, but he knew, as the tribal people did, that each star is a spirit. Every fellow who, at some time or another, has found life on Earth to be a bitter struggle finally leaves all his troubles behind him and rises high in the sky; and those distant murmurs to be heard on cloudless nights are those spirit stars whispering to each other, and perhaps even laughing at the white man digging up the whole Earth in his selfish madness.

"Michael, the boss, he should have been here by now. He has to drive us to the new diggings tonight—we can't move in the daylight." Between words Gara's teeth could be heard chattering with cold, like nuts in an empty bucket.

"If he doesn't turn up we're stuck out here in the open—we'll be caught—for sure—soon after daybreak." Anawari was worried.

"Well, we just have to hope he comes."

"Isn't there anywhere to hide?"

"No. Not really; there's nothing but heaps of mining waste around here. We'll be easily seen in the morning when the miners start work digging again."

"And there's no way of going back into the shaft, I suppose, since the boss took away the winch and the ropes?"

Gara's hunched silhouette, pacing back and forth over the edge of the hummock, showed clearly against the glow of the distant moonset. It was a pity that the greatcoat had not lasted longer; Anawari had last seen it some months before, already disintegrating into tatters but not discarded, for clothes, although worn out, are not lightly thrown away when there is nothing to replace them. Though past wearing, the coat had been kept as their only item of bedding, and it would probably still have been in use had not an unlucky accident landed it in the bucket, to be winched to the surface and buried forever under a mounting pile of earth.

"For how long did you say you know this bloke Michael?"

Gara was more concerned with the cold than with the conversation: his teeth rattled as he forced words between them. "He helped me get back here from Europe—Manolo is his real name."

128

Anawari realized that he had heard that already. Gara and Michael knew each other while still in Europe, and it was due to that acquaintance that Gara had reached Australia, traveling with the papers of Michael's brother, a Spaniard, who had disappeared in the Foreign Legion. "I owe Manolo a lot," Gara mentioned some days ago, though Anawari failed to see why someone should be so obliged for being brought back to a country wiped out by a nuclear blast. On reaching Australia the two old friends worked for a while at Bidi digging gemstone, where, according to Gara, "The stones felt less tough and the ground was not so deep." That changed some years ago when the desert mining settlement fell under the jurisdiction of the Nuclear Development Authority, for at the diggings, down below a layer of shining stone, they struck something even more precious—uranium. The sleepy township fringed by hills of dug-out dirt lay outside the Nuclear Development Area; it nevertheless became a jowl of the ever expanding Nuclear Empire. According to Michael a bucket full of the uranium rocks could wipe off part of Europe from the map. He and the other miners had to buy twice as much gelignite as before, for the new rocks felt tough indeed. Everyone on the diggings had a quota for how much ore to extract, and dared not to fail, for the uranium measured far more than a human soul. The miners tripled the lengths of their ropes, and as the shaft sank deeper into the ground and the quotas increased, they went so high, that after a day of struggle a man often wondered whether to come out or stay in the shaft forever.

Anawari was about to ask Gara how long ago since he had come back from Europe but realized that the question would mean little to his companion. It seemed that time—or anyway the measurement of it—had lost meaning and purpose, and that weeks, months, and years had somehow blurred into oblivion and left only yesterday, today, and tomorrow; anything beyond these had long since ceased being counted. There was one specific span of years, however, probably a sizable chunk of his life, to which Gara referred simply as "the time before this one"; he spoke almost as if it were another dimension into which he had been sucked, against his will and that of his spiritual ancestors, but by the malice of white men, as inexorable as a whirling willy-willy wind.

Now as he watched Gara pacing and shivering in the cold wind, Anawari muttered, "Poor fellow." The man has come halfway across the world to his ancestral country to find it has perished. Left behind are clusters of marking sites where the blast has melted sand, and greenish smear—no man survives that, perhaps not even the spirits. "Poor brave fellow." Some days ago when they complained about rocks being too tough, Michael had smiled saying that no job could be hard enough for a Janizary. Ever since they had come to the mining settlement, the word "Janizary" had been much on the mind of every one of them. Talking about them some days earlier Gara had explained that so fearless were these Janizaries in fighting for their Ottoman masters that they thrust a spit through the bodies of their victims and left them to die slowly stuck on a pole. One of their victims was Milinko, Gara's great-grandfather on his paternal side, whose name he admiringly pronounced with a long vowel. The man, himself a Janizary, had deserted from the Ottoman guard and fled back to his village in the Serbian hills, only to be caught years later by his own regiment. When they stuck him on a pole in the village, he became known as *kara* Milinko, *kara*, black, because of a crow that had perched on his head digging out his eyes. The pole under him came alive and grew into a huge oak tree and into the legend of Milinkovo, as the village became known later. Under that century-old tree, craggy and torn by time and storms, Gara's father, Stevan, came down to rest on his return from a distant world— the gold diggings of Australia. In his arm he held a little boy wrapped in a hessian bag, which after the long journey still smelled of salt from the sea. They called the boy Gara, not only because it means spearhead and was what his tribal mother would have liked to call him, but in the village lingo *gara* is someone half dark.

Gara was now busily shoveling loose earth with his bare hands to form a hollow in which to shelter from the wind, and though the result gave small comfort, the exercise warmed him a little.

Anawari wondered what gave this fugitive the strength in his bid to quit the white man's world, for though he surely would perservere, there was nearly no place left where a man could fly to be free. The whites had spread everywhere like a plague of ants, and when not one tree or rock was left unconsumed, man too must be doomed. It dawned on him that it might have been on a diggings like this, on the side of a hummock of freshly dug mining waste, that Gara had been conceived. Anawari suddenly envied him for that, for he felt it was something a man could be much more proud of than being brought up by the holy brothers. Mining in the 1930s had centered somewhere north of Lake Takapiri, and Anawari predicted the diggings could have been situated about where Boomerang Island points inland toward the river valley, for it was alluvial gold that the prospectors were after. We could well be relatives. The idea that he might be related to Gara, even tribally, excited him, though the chances of finding that out looked grim. There are only clusters of red dots marking that area now; not only the country, but humans too are wiped out. Those who may have survived and can remember who is related to whom will not be around for long. Frightened by the blasting of the country or by the rolling mist that followed, *karan* had deserted the human body and wandered off to the desert, and eventually to the sky. The Milky Way up there is so long—a huge swarm of tiny midgets. Yes, the sky looks crowded. So many of our folk have gone. Anawari gazed above, moving his eyes slowly and studying each star in turn; the larger ones that glittered so brightly were the *nangari*—the white men had sent plenty of medicine men to shine up there. Anawari bowed his head a moment in ceremonial respect to all those men who had left their earthly troubles here, below. His eyes swept the Southern Cross and then stopped at one star, not big, but brilliantly clear and set well apart from the rest. Anawari had particularly watched this star since . . . he was not sure now when he had first seen it, but it could not have been during the summer camping holiday when the holy brothers had taught the Boy Scout troop the skills of orientation. The Southern Cross, the most outstanding group,

131

was used to determine the cardinal compass points, and each night the boys had stared into the sky for hours. Anawari had a clear mental picture of the setting of the Cross from that time, but no—there was no lonely star to be seen then—it must have appeared in the sky some time after that. In later years Anawari grew to think that the star must be one of his *tjamu*—his tribal ancestors, perhaps even his father—and night after night he had stood gazing at it. When still living in the settlement, Anawari would sit on the veranda for hours, not only looking at the star but even concentrating his thoughts toward it, and though Ann complained at first—"It's a pity you Abos never learned to make rockets; you could visit your ancestors without waiting to die"— she finally accepted the habit as a harmless one, and even bought Anawari books on astronomy, and a small telescope, for his birthday.

Anawari's eyes became riveted to the lonely star again, noticing that it now did not appear so lonely as he had thought before. Around it sat many smaller ones forming a galaxy in the shape of—a dingo's head! Yes, it is indeed; a pair of prickly ears stretch out almost to the Southern Cross, while the snout points down toward the earth. The head must be slightly tilted sideways, to show the Lonely Star the wound below the flapping ear. Anawari was convinced that it must be the Dingo Clan up there—a group of desert tribes with a common spiritual ancestor. The smaller stars were said to be children, and he often found himself wanting to smile and wave to them. Now one of these, low on the horizon, seemed to come forward from the mist blinking and quivering, and Anawari trembled at the notion that it was Gara's child, found dead in the desert, but now forever in the sky to torture his conscience. Anawari turned his head away, but found he could not resist another glance—the star was now two stars, and coming even closer. "Gara! Look! He's coming."

Gara's hand grabbed Anawari's shoulder, waking him from the dream. "Careful, don't fall off the back of the truck." They were on the move. In spite of the roughness of the road, Anawari had been asleep. "Where's he taking us? Did he tell you?"

"To Coronation Downs; it's another diggings."

"Very far?"

"Not really—it's on the other side of the township."

"That'd be somewhere near the ridge where Patupiri lives, would it?"

"Yes, not far away."

"Will he be there, do you think?"

"I hope so; I haven't seen him for years. We must try and sneak out one day to look for him."

Anawari kept silent for a time, thinking how much like pulling a tooth it was, drawing information from his companion. The two men were crouched under the canopy of the truck, while around them echoed the mixed sounds of the roaring engine, the rattling vehicle chassis, and the howling wind, punctuated by the slap of a piece of rope that had come unfastened and, now and then, lashed the taut canvas overhead. "Is there anything wrong? Did he say why he was so late?" Anawari jerked his head toward the truck's cabin although he knew well that the gesture could not be seen.

"They're looking for us."

This time Anawari was not sure whether the sound of chattering teeth came from Gara's mouth or from his own. He heard that chattering again when later somewhere on the road running through the mining township the truck came to a stop, but Anawari, hemmed in by tools, buckets, winch, boxes, drums—all the mining paraphernalia on the move from one diggings to another—could not see out to discover the reason for their halt. He could hear voices raised in excitement or anger but so blended that none could be clearly heard. Anawari felt along the edge of the truck's canopy until his fingers met with a loose piece of canvas, which he stealthily pried outward until he could peer out. Close by stood a monument, positioned in the center of what appeared to be a crossroads—a life-sized statue of a prospector with water bag and billy in one hand, and a rock in the other. That must be the man who discovered uranium. Who else would be on the pedestal here? concluded Anawari. From the small square around the statue four

133

dirt roads radiated, and down the widest of these—probably the town's main street—roared a mob of people, shouting and brandishing picks, shovels, bars—seemingly anything there was time to snatch up in an emergency; several shots rang out, probably only fired overhead into the dark sky, but nonetheless frightening.

The mob gathered in the main square; one man moved to the front of the crowd and, climbing onto the pedestal of the prospector, turned to the others and shouted some slogan unintelligible to Anawari. The crowd howled with excitement. Anawari felt Gara's hand on his shoulder trying to pull him back from the peephole but he shrugged it away—he had never before seen a crowd so inflamed with insane excitement. As the orator had some trouble keeping his balance on the edge of the pedestal, he put his arm around the prospector and clung there shouting even louder to the crowd: "Catch the boongs!" His cry was repeated several times, and on each instance the mob howled in response. The speaker's voice struck a chord in Anawari's memory, and when a car's headlights lit the scene, he recognized Sir Midas Hunt himself raising his clenched fists to add to the emotion evoked by his cries. Finally the old man, transported by hysteria, stumbled forward, slipped away from the stalwart prospector, and plunged, arms flailing, into the crowd; he reappeared a moment later unharmed, however, levered back to his vantage point on the pole of a garishly painted banner. Anawari craned his neck to see what message the pennant bore, but as it swayed and flapped in front of Hunt he could read only the words WATER . . . and BRING RAIN NOW.

On the edge of the crowd behind Hunt, in a haze of dust, two men appeared carrying burning branches, and in the firelight Anawari saw an effigy of himself dangling from a makeshift gallows. The figure must have been soaked in kerosene, for as soon as the fire touched, it ignited in a ball of flame, illuminating the circle of angry faces and the upraised picks and shovels.

At the death of the effigy flames the mob dispersed. Anawari missed seeing Hunt dismount from the prospector's pedestal, and as he looked about for the old man, he saw, at the petrol station, posters of himself covering an entire wall. The pictures plastered there were copies of the familiar one Ann had kept above her workbench, but much enlarged, and emblazoned with the words WANTED FOR TREASON below. There was something else written in smaller print, which one could not read at that distance—a reward was offered perhaps, but though Anawari rubbed his eyes and stared, the words became no clearer. At that moment the junction must have been opened again to traffic and the truck jerked forward.

By the time they reached the diggings and stopped again, the moon had set, leaving no trace in the dark sky. "All right, come out boys—we're here." Michael's usually hearty voice was hoarse and tremulous—the voice of a man who had just passed through hell.

"That was pretty close, meeting that mob back there," said Anawari.

"They're after you, all right—I thought we'd all had it."

Anawari did not think this man would inform on him, but could see nothing of his facial expression in the darkness. He and Gara had dug for Michael many months since, but they had seldom spoken—there was little time for exchanging pleasantries and few, in such a situation, wish to dwell on the past. Though the old friends had a lot to reminisce about, how they had successfully slipped from Europe into Australia without the real identity of Gara being detected, that was put aside for some better time, if that time was ever to come. "Let's squeeze through the needle's eye first, then chat later," Gara had said once. Anawari felt childishly frightened that he did not even know the full name of this man on whose mercy his life might depend.

"Get all that gear down off the truck, will you?" The words were hurried now, as Michael grabbed some tools himself and flung them to the ground; his voice jerked out through the clatter of hastily unloaded gear but never stopped to check that the instructions had been heard and understood. "The shaft has been drilled already; you only have to set the winch and get the hell underground."

135

Anawari reassured himself that Michael would not inform on them. With a new shaft drilled they would have to go down, deepen it further, and then on reaching the uranium layer burrow horizontally, following the trace of the ore. As long as they winched the buckets out and as long as Michael met his quota, there should be no need for concern. Something else might occur; Anawari felt uneasy hiding in a sleepy mining settlement that owed its life to the N.D.A. Some *panya*—yes, that is the tribal word for man-hunt—would start if the drought persisted or the ore ran out. Well, that might have started already, judging by the sound of the mob at the Prospector's Square. The whites are like Pungal, those malevolent mythical beings—they would drink blood in the absence of water, first someone else's blood then their own. Before that happened, Anawari hoped that he would be warned by Nu-puru, in a dream perhaps. The old tribal healer might be in the sky with other souls there, but *nangari* never really dies; he can appear in any shape he wishes and wander through the country, even though it has long been turned into a plain of sand.

Michael dashed back to start the engine of the truck and spoke through the open window of the driver's cabin: "Make sure you have enough water with you down there, and don't come out from underground unless you really must. Those men don't muck around, and they've got some pretty fancy gear they can use to sneak in and surprise you. You could be caught and finished off before you even know it."

Before he knew it? Anawari doubted that, for he felt he knew it all—and from both vantage points—the hunter's and that of his quarry. It was months, now, since he had first climbed under-ground and crawled away from the main shaft, digging out a narrow tunnel hardly wide enough for his body to squeeze through. He dragged a plastic trough, tied to one leg, and when this was full of excavated earth, he tugged it back through the wombat burrow to the main bucket at the bottom of the shaft, and winched it to the surface. Although there was neither enough room to move, nor air to breathe, yet there, with tons of rock and soil above him, Anawari felt far more secure than he ever could have aboveground.

The only longing to trouble his mind, from time to time, was a persistent desire that after digging his burrow and dragging that trough behind him day after day, he would at last reach the end of the tunnel and spring out into a strange country where the white man had never been. Sometimes he felt this dream was pure foolishness, but at other times, he remembered and believed the stories he had heard from Nupuru. He often spoke of tribal ancestral heroes who, in times long ago, when the world was very different, traveled under the ground to spring up again far away in another country, and safely out of reach of any pursuer. So while he dug for uranium, that persistent memory never quite left him, Anawari, in peace, and a spark of hope remained that he, too, might be given the luck and the magic to find his way under the ground to that other world.

CHAPTER 14

Something must have happened. Michael had failed to make the calls customary every day at the diggings, to bring petrol for the winch, to renew the supply of food and water, and to collect any uranium dug; since the move to Coronation Downs, a whole week had passed without one call. The two men had rationed the drinking water, at first; then, instead of swallowing, had merely wet their mouths, but finally the last drop had been shaken from the container and a whole day had been spent without any water at all. Anawari feared that if nothing happened shortly, they would become too weak to set out and search for drinking water. "I wonder if there are any trees around—we might crush their leaves; you told me you've squeezed a bit of moisture out of them before."

"No. There's not a single tree left standing for miles around—there's not even any scrub left."

"What about their roots?"

"Yes, you can get quite a good drink from them."

"Should we go up and look around?"

Gara tried to wet his dry lips, but his tongue moved over them without leaving any mark. "There's nothing but rocks around, I tell you. The whites saw to that."

Hills of excavated earth lay all over the valley like the leavings of a monstrous mole that had moved under the ground, and heaved to the surface, here and there, heaps of mining waste. These had lain bare and pale in the rain that in a year might fall once—or two or even three times—and suffered the constant beating of the wind until they were compacted and stone hard; their light-colored surfaces reflected the blazing sun all day, and the whole valley became a vast boiling pot.

At one end of the valley rose a sharp escarpment from which razor-backed ridges reached toward the lower country like fingers, and the higher ridge, enclosing the valley, gave protection to the township hidden from view on its farther side. Here and there on the steep slope were dark patches, each marking the entrance to a tunnel—Gara had explained that much of the ridge's interior had already been dragged away to be thoroughly searched for the precious rocks—and it was into these caverns that the two must sneak to look for Patupiri. He had spoken of this often, and worried that if the visit was delayed too long, the old man might not still be there. "We'll have to get some water before we go in there looking for him."

"What about"—Anawari felt a tearing of the dry and cracked skin of his lips, and made his statement in fewer words—"raid that water plant."

Not far away, and deeper into the valley, an area of land had been saved from excavation, and there, behind wire mesh, two corrugated-iron sheds housed a plant for converting salty bore water into palatable drinking water. Whenever he was above-ground, Anawari had found himself irresistibly drawn to gaze toward this, their closest link with other human beings. The scene was quite clear, even at that distance—a dusty road, cars rolling downhill to the plant and queuing along one side of the farthest shed, and people moving to and fro carrying containers. During the last few thirsty days, that scene had materialized whenever Anawari dozed, and it was so vivid that he could see himself in that queue, and could hear cool water splashing into the brightly colored container in his hand.

Gara struggled to form clumsy words: "It's not guarded but . . . every white has a gun hidden somewhere. They fear for their rocks—no fear of blacks."

"We'd better try to creep in as soon as it's dark then."

The attendant at the plant quit the place not long after dark, locked both gates, hurried to his car, and drove off; Anawari and Gara, watching from behind the hummock beside a nearby diggings, waited until the car lights disappeared over the ridge before walking toward the fence. Much of the plant lay in darkness relieved only by the moon, for the two lights left alight—one at the gate and the other over the attendant's office doorway—both shone on the front part of the building and not in the compound. Anawari blessed the luck that he and Gara had by creeping in from the dark side, and then realized that his companion probably had prior knowledge of which lights would be left alight at night, and had planned their approach accordingly. As Anawari watched, Gara paced along the fence from the corner post . . . eight, nine, ten . . . then knelt, loosened a twist of wire, and pushed open a square of the chain-wire mesh. He had certainly been there before, and knew his way about, while Anawari could only follow and admire. A vertical pipe, with flexible hose dangling from it in an arc, stood silhouetted against the milky sky, and Anawari could, suddenly, control himself no longer. His mouth was burning— he must have water and he charged forward, frantically searching for a tap that would start the flow from the mouth of the hose. Stumbling, Anawari bruised his shins and cut his hand, but found nothing, and in desperation began crashing against the pipe with his shoulder, his face upturned to catch any falling drops.

"Hey, hey, take it easy," called Gara.

"There's no bloody water. They've cut it off, the bastards." Anawari was weeping now.

"Yes, it's all locked, but come here."

"We'll have to break in, I'm dying."

"The main valve's chained—you'd do no better inside. Just come here will you?" Gara pulled Anawari several steps, then guided his hand downward into the dark and his fingers touched

140

water at last. As Anawari plunged his head and shoulders into the coolness, sucking life back into his body, he became aware of the shape and size of the water container. "This feels like some sort of trough."

"Yes, they keep it filled for animals."

"There are no animals around here."

"It's for dogs—the pets the whites keep. When they come here for water, they let the dogs drink and bathe in that trough."

Anawari spat the water from his mouth, and then slowly drank again as he realized that even if he had known the state of the water before he took his first mouthful, it would not have prevented him from drinking.

"Patupiri comes here to drink too; and every other one of us around."

Anawari had a container sunk into the trough to fill and he waited for the bubbling noises to stop before he spoke: "We could have come here earlier, then?"

They had walked across the compound and were approaching the hole in the fence when Gara said, "When they're after any of our folk, this is where they set the trap."

Goose pimples rose on Anawari's skin as he squeezed through the gap in the wire, moving as breathlessly as if he were treading a minefield. He fervently hoped that it would not be necessary to make the trip again.

The two men had to move slowly and cautiously back over the diggings in the darkness; Gara walked ahead poking a long rod into the ground in front of him, at every step, to detect any mine shafts. There was no path to follow, and each move must be made only after careful investigation, for one mistake could send a man pitching into the abyss of a shaft with no time to think, let alone cry out.

Anawari thought he could hear a ticking like that of a watch, though neither he nor Gara wore one, and the ticking sounded as if it were splitting one last second from another, at the end of someone's life. Perhaps it was time gone mad, and what little there might be left of life was being chipped audibly away, second

141

by second, until when the ticking stopped—that would be the end. Anawari looked toward the sky and fastened his eyes on the Dingo's Head near the Southern Cross. The two prickly ears seemed to have moved; below them the Lonely Star, brighter than before, beamed like a torch down into the darkness. "You'll take care of me, won't you?" He had never asked for help before, either for himself or for his people, but now that life had become so precarious, he clung to it with an urgency that permitted acceptance of any available favors. "Surely I haven't come this far for nothing," he whispered to the sky again. Anawari had been told by Nupuru that every man is born at the wish of his spiritual ancestor—perhaps a kangaroo, or an emu, a lizard, or a fly, but always something to be found in your own country—which will follow him for the rest of his life, and watch over his destiny. As Anawari trod haltingly through the darkness, a night bird dived and flashed suddenly above his head, then swooped away again. It came a second time, a moment later, and though Anawari could catch only a glimpse in the dark, he guessed that the bird was very small, for its wings made no beating sound, and its flight was swift through the air like a thrown spear. Anawari strode confidently forward after that, for he was somehow sure that this was his *tjamu* from the sky reassuring him that now that he had found water, he would be allowed time to drink it.

When Anawari and Gara stopped to rest again, it was well past midnight; the moon had moved some distance toward the horizon and Gara had to admit that they had lost their way back to the mine shaft. Around them lay a sea of piles of mining waste, all alike in size, shape, and color, and all as faceless as eggs. The hope of wandering around and, following a hunch, of picking the right shaft had long ago faded and now it was safer not even to look at the mocking mullock heaps, in order to stay sane.

Silent now, Anawari was resting, leaning back against the slope of a mound and searching the sky again for the Southern Cross, when a beam of strange violet light sprang from beyond the ridge, sliced across the valley, and then moved, clockwise, to sweep the entire area. It was much too penetrating to be a reflected light,

Anawari decided, for though less dazzling, it seemed effective at a great distance.

"It's getting closer. Get down!" called Gara, who had crouched behind some discarded fuel drums and was now beckoning Anawari to join him.

As Anawari flung himself down, the beam, like a strip of purplish mist, passed overhead, cast its violet glow on the bank above, and drifted down the valley, followed by another beam, this time glowing rusty red and thrusting rhythmically as if it were controlled by some electronic impulse. "Have you ever seen anything like this before?" he asked.

"No, and I don't like it."

"I wonder what good it does."

"It must do something!"

"Yes, it hunts."

"Blacks?"

"Who else would the whites be tracking out in this country? You heard what Michael said about the smart gear they can use to get you, nowadays."

Anawari wondered if the beam was able to pinpoint the presence of a man, for, if so, it must also be able to distinguish between black man and white, unless a different-colored ray was used to hunt white ore-thieves. It seemed that sophisticated technology had made the black tracker obsolete and it would no longer be possible for a tribal black on the run to evade capture. Anawari had heard, once, of a runaway who remained free for months, leading the white hunters and their best Aboriginal trackers all over the country, and though the fugitive must have been caught at last, he at least had the pride of the chase to keep in his heart. Maybe that had been the last great chase before the machine took over—and brought despair, for a machine will give no quarter. A man on the run from men could always hope that a tracker— one of your own folk—might spare you, or that the whites would become tired and give up the hunt, but a machine allows you no time for hope, and can pin you down before you even have time to run. Who had told him about that hunt? It must have been Ily

143

when he visited him in the desert camp. Old Ily and his pack of electronic scanners. How did they interest him in such an assignment? It would not be just because he had married the daughter of a prominent politician. He may have tracked that fellow Rotar with his electronic toys. The fool, he would not hesitate to turn the scanners on Nupuru, if one can track the spirit. "Should we move?" he asked.

"Where could we go?"

"What about going to the water plant, and trying to pick up the track from there?"

"We'd be caught by the daylight."

"Yes, I suppose so. And right in the middle of the diggings."

Seen across the field of paler heaps of mining dirt, the dark silhouette of the ridge, against the setting moon, seemed less like a mountain than an immense dark cloud, drawn from some unknown corner of outer space and pausing a moment before it rolled its dark mass over the plain below.

"What about trying our luck up there?" suggested Anawari.

"We'll have to try it; there are plenty of places to hide in the tunnels up there, and . . . tomorrow night we can go back down to the plant and pick up the track again."

"And we can look for Patupiri in the tunnels too."

"We'd better leave that for another trip—one thing at a time, mate."

As they rose to begin their walk, Anawari spoke: "I just hope we make contact with Michael again soon."

"We have to! If we're cut off from him we're finished for sure."

At Gara's words Anawari was filled with a deep pity for this poor man, dispossessed of his most valuable heritage—his unity with the very land beneath his feet. Anawari had never heard of an Aborigine becoming lost and being unable to find a place to call home, for even those separated from their tribal life had with the country an affinity that made them confident and invulnerable in the bush. Without having to memorize landmarks, or search for a familiar sign to guide him on the right track, the Aborigine seemed possessed of the power to roam for hundreds of kilometers

144

through open, featureless desert, and yet return to the exact spot from which he had set out; the tribal elders are sure that a man's own ancestral spirit (that the white man calls a totem) watches over him wherever he goes, and sees that he stays on the right track. Nupuru had told Anawari long ago about the track marked by the spiritual ancestors at the time of creation, a track that leads from one waterhole to the next, all the way across the Great Desert and beyond—to the far West Coast of Australia. The old man had traveled that path, on a journey a thousand kilometers long, as a young man in flight from the Great Massacre when a white punitive party had moved into Para country and shot every black on sight. Nupuru had regarded himself lucky to lose only a slice of his scalp—hewn off by an axe blow—and with a few others, whose lives had also been spared, he had taken the mythical road and put the desert between them and the white murderers; and at the end of the journey, which must have taken years, perhaps half a lifetime, the fugitives found that the whites had settled on the other side of the desert as well. Anawari knew, now, that since then, whenever white settlers had become aggressive, or Aborigines had feared that a punitive movement was developing, they had withdrawn into the desert and, following the legendary path, had abandoned their tribal lands to the white man. Now even the desert was desirable, for its gems, and men like Gara knew no refuge from the invader's greed.

"Don't lag behind—come on. Dawn will be breaking soon." Gara's voice came from some distance ahead and Anawari hurried to draw level. They had been on the move for some time now, the ground had begun to rise, and only a few scattered heaps of waste earth lay here and there. Anawari drew his thoughts back to the white man's rape of the bush and ruination of the Aboriginal heritage. Two years ago he had thought to write a book—maybe Nupuru's story—but the size of the topic and its abstract quality had seemed beyond his powers of authorship, and he had doubted his ability to tell whites of their mistakes in an effective way. Now he was relieved that he had not published the black man's secrets— if the whites knew that an Aborigine is led across the desert by

145

his ancestor's spirit, there would always be a chance that they might find their own way of contacting the Aboriginal spirits and . . . but no . . . surely no tribal ancestor would allow himself to be corrupted, even if he were offered a whole truckload of grog and tobacco. Once they were in contact with the spirit world, though, the prying whites would not leave it at that, Anawari felt sure, and he was glad that he could not be blamed for the inception of some electronic gadget or other magic gear designed to harass the spirits. Some of the spiritual secrets might have already leaked out, of course, and the whites' hurry to dig up the whole countryside may be part of a plan to confuse the spirits by converting their traditional places into unrecognizable wastes, like this mining field.

"Don't lag so far behind," called Gara again.

"I'm so tired."

"Didn't your father ever take you on walkabout in the desert?"

"No—no such luck."

His mother might have taken him, though, and he might have crossed the desert while still in her womb; though this imaginary walkabout had only just formed in his mind, Anawari felt as proud as though it were an established fact, and he stepped out boldly, his fatigue quite gone, to march beside Gara.

When they stopped again to rest, the travelers had climbed higher and the incline was much sharper. It seemed unwise to go farther in the dark, for each misplaced step set rocks rolling noisily downhill into the valley below, so the two weary climbers paused to wait for the break of dawn.

"Have you ever got lost before?" asked Anawari.

"I did when I was here with Namir—didn't I tell you all about it?" The two men often used to meet at the digging, and when he was lost once, Namir was directed onto the right track by that elder, Patupiri.

"That only works when you are of the same tribe, I gather." Anawari felt uncertain as to whether they should be talking about these things.

"Yes, it does—a fellow communicates with tribal elders or

146

nangari that way even if they are skies apart. A white man here wanted to learn that too."

"A prospector?"

As he lay, Gara pushed some stones away to make himself more comfortable. "No, he hung around. . . . they called him Major. He tried to bargain, to swap, I mean."

"Swap—what?"

"Namir was to be flown south to his tribe if he told them the secret of communicating with *nangari*."

One of Anawari's ears rang insistently.

"Old Patupiri did not like that. He feared that if the whites learned how to talk to us that way, they would lead every fellow into the waterless desert, instead of getting them out of trouble. He became so angry." The old man actually worried that once they learned how to communicate with tribal spirits, the whites would be out to steal the secrets of rain. They had taken land, but land without water; the country would do no one good. The whites drink heavily; they sweat so often. In the old days they moved about by riding on horses, and the animals drank far more than humans; now they move about by riding on their machines, but they too need water. "Let them dry like dead trees or fall back to their own country," Patupiri had told Namir and asked him to stay away from the whites. Anawari felt proud of his old schoolmate and wished that Ily had turned that way too instead of growing obsessed with the white man's machines. It surprised him that the whites, in pursuit of the tribal secrets, did not try Rotar, being *wati:* he would know how to communicate with spirits and how one makes rain. "Rotar let them down badly," explained Gara. That was long before the N.D.A. moved into the tribal area. To prevent the abduction of tribal children, missionary Rotar joined desert tribes, thus inheriting many wives and children. The whites did not like abducting children from a missionary; besides it was impossible to tell which of the children were under his paternal jurisdiction, so no abducting took place from the desert tribes, at least till the Nuclear Development Authority had moved in. Gara claimed that Rotar had a greater soul

147

than the whole white man's world. He was expelled to Europe as the Nuclear Development moved in, but made his way back. That was where Gara met him—on a flight from Europe to Australia. On that same flight was a girl; Gara wasn't sure about her name, but while he was held captive in the hospital, he had seen her there through the window. Laura!—Anawari thought that she had grown fond of Namir and would not betray him, though he felt uncertain how well she had known Rotar.

Anawari lay on his back, among the stones, and gazed again into the sky. He would have written that book just for the black people if he had not foolishly confided his idea to Ann; she had become so caught up with the project—brought home a tape recorder and urged Anawari, night and day, to put his spiritual feelings on tape—that his wish to write had evaporated. "Every black man in the world . . . all of mankind . . . would benefit from this knowledge. People could travel overseas or into outer space—wherever their ancestors wanted them to be," Ann had enthused. "Not a single black man would ever again die of thirst— do it, please, for black mankind; the whole world will be grateful."

But in spite of, or perhaps because of, Ann's exhortations, Anawari had found himself unable to express his inner knowledge in the white man's language, and so he could lie there under the desert sky, knowing that, deliberately or not, he had kept the tribal secret safe.

That night as he lay among the stones on the slope of the hill, the Skeleton Woman came to see him. "I shall make fire soon— desert frost will be about." She struggled with words, for part of her face was stiff and one of her eyes kept still. She had lost most of her hair and the little of it that remained reminded Anawari of scattered clumps of mulga grass he had seen in the desert. He had asked himself how it was that the silver grass was still about when the drought had wiped out trees. Had it not been for those patches of mulga grass, the country would have looked bald, like

148

a shorn beast. "They need grass to make the rain," the Skeleton Woman explained. Anawari reminded himself that he had been told while still a toddler that the mulga grass looks much like gray clouds laden with rain, and later as he grew up, he had learned that during *inma,* the rainmaking ceremony, *maban,* or the magic seashell, should be passed over the tips of the mulga grass: that and much more would help bring the rain. "*Gapi wia,*" the Skeleton Woman told him in the dream; she held a *karupa* made of a cross and kept jabbing the ground. Scars covering her body had puckered as though they too had dried out like everything else in the country. "*Gapi wia,*" she struggled to say again with her partly paralyzed face. Anawari thought of telling her that there could be no water among the rocks. There are many shafts sunk down in the valley, as deep as your eyes can reach, but none of them have come up with a single drop of water. As she struggled to bring out her words again, Anawari realized that she was addressing a little boy who stood behind her nagging for a drink. The boy grew angry and threw a stone. The stone fell on the slope just above Anawari; it triggered some loose rocks, which rolled down on him. "Don't hurt your *kurta,*" the woman told the boy while trying to help Anawari, who was partly buried. The boy tossed another stone; it went much higher up though and, striking the top of the hill, set off an avalanche of boulders. They rolled down onto the mining settlement and soon, out of the whole place, only the prospector's statue was visible; it stood up from the pile of rocks holding out a water bag. The woman finally came to make a fire and rubbed two wooden sticks, one against the other, hard, until wisps of smoke appeared. "I shall make *nyuma* for you and your *kurta,* as soon as the ashes are hot." He felt uncertain whether she was speaking to him or to the little boy, for *kurta* means brother. Does she know there are no *kaltu* seeds about to grind flour?

CHAPTER 15

Anawari woke with the first hint of day, and for a moment or two watched the night mist drifting away over the farthest lip of the valley. Above towered jagged walls of bare rock, and one huge block, separated from the main mass by some great prehistoric upheaval, appeared poised in dilemma whether to dash itself onto the rocks below or to subside among its fellows on the hillside.

Farther along the ridge . . . Anawari's eyes were riveted and his breath cut short, for less than a hundred meters away, on the edge of a flat rock, stood something he could not identify but that he instinctively realized was hostile, whether it was machine, man, or bird. The head resembled that of a monstrous and unnatural eagle, which, in lieu of eyes, sported a pair of steel shutters of overlapping armor plate like a knight's visor, and as Anawari stared, the monster blinked with the fluttering sound of a dragonfly's wings. The terrible eyelids slid open, at last, and forth came two beams of light, violet and red, casting back and forth across the valley as Anawari had watched them doing in the darkness. For a moment he wondered whether it was the same monster he had seen perching on the post to scan the Northern Border. Perhaps they had been hatched from the same design, but the one employed there seemed to be immobile and much smaller. Did

Ily know he had second best? The blacks always do, even if one marries the daughter of a prominent politician. Gara stirred and made a move as if to rise, but Anawari pushed him roughly down again and, pinning his companion to the ground with his own body, cringed back behind a sheltering rock.

When Anawari had recovered enough to rise to a gap in the rock, he saw that the monster had moved closer to the edge of the precipice and spread gleaming wings; like a caricature of a bird the thing launched itself into the air then, folding the wings slightly backward for greater mobility, swooped out over the valley at great speed.

"It's some kind of tracker; a steel bird of prey." Gara's voice was hushed.

"A monstrous hunting bird." Anawari had a sudden and vivid mental picture of a white man at the controls behind the armor plate of the man-made eagle, and as the object zoomed toward the horizon, he fancied that he could even see a pair of talons looming ready to snatch the blacks.

"He must have followed the road from the township, and crossed the ridge over there, behind those hills." Gara pointed.

"He's on our track, you mean?"

"Well, that's the way Michael brought us here in the truck."

"Let's get out of here, then, before that tracking devil comes back."

They moved on, one behind the other with Gara leading at first, while Anawari kept watch on the valley for the return of the tracker, then Gara watching while Anawari caught up, always following a line of pale mining waste long ago tunneled out of the hill, and which would lead them directly inside the ridge. They stopped to rest again at the mouth of the tunnel, which commanded a broad view of the valley, and though the tracker itself could not be seen, a shadow flitted now and then among the mullock heaps below, accompanied by a distant whispering, more like the sound of electronic equipment than that of any flying machine.

"That tracker is onto our shaft, I reckon," observed Gara.

"Lucky we got out of there, then."

"Lucky? For how long, I wonder?"

"For just as long as the luck holds, I suppose."

"And that won't be very long; every day a man is taken, sometimes a whole tribe, in this country."

"Oh well, even if we have to go tomorrow, let's hope we leave by the will of our spirit ancestors and not by being kicked out before our time by the whites."

"And who do we cry to for help? The country all around has been turned into a stony desert. Where are our animal ancestors who should keep us safe, and guide us to a proper death?" Gara's cry was anguished.

The sound of the tracking machine grew suddenly loud, as if heading toward them, but faded away again.

Anawari was amazed at the accuracy of the machine following the fugitive's movements, but deduced that, as it was now circling where they had been, the machine followed some clue other than a human presence—perhaps . . . but of course . . . radioactivity. Both he and Gara were contaminated—Gara severely so since being held as a detainee down at Lake Takapiri to help with the nuclear testing—and could be easily followed and pinpointed at a far greater distance than eyes could ever see, if the equipment was suitable. Anawari was engulfed with bitterness that the white man's contamination that had failed to kill them before might yet be the means of leading him and Gara to their death. The white man seemed endlessly skillful at turning even his failures into new successes against the blacks. Anawari reminded himself to ask Gara again what exactly had happened during the detention. He had tried twice till now to talk about that and got only one word: "Hell." Anawari assumed that Gara had been held at the Takapiri, for in his dream he often had long struggles to reach the shore and cursed the salty mud: "It gulps you." While muttering, he struggled with his limbs and groped at the ground, trying to pull himself out of that hell.

*　　　*　　　*

Though he could not be sure, Anawari guessed that he and Gara must have been inside the hill two or three days now; several times they had felt sleepy and had rested on the floor of the tunnel—Anawari supposed that it was nighttime then, but he did not have a wristwatch with which to tell the right hour, and when the patch of light behind them had faded as they moved deeper inside the ridge, the thick darkness made time meaningless. "Are any of our people here?" he had asked.

"Quite a crowd—all trapped inside." Gara had explained further how Namir used to sit among the boulders up on the ridge and listen to the tribal women wailing, through the crevices in the rocks, from the ground far below. "You could free every black soul howling for help"; the major tried to talk him into a deal. The white man often came to the ridge to see him, bringing a flask of water and a packet of biscuits each time. "The blacks are calling on you to lead them out."

Did he hear that in a dream, or . . . perhaps he really had been told. Anawari had a sudden pang of fear that he had lost his memory, for he could remember very little of what had happened during the last few days—but then there was nearly nothing to remember, surrounded by darkness and moving along the walls only by feeling them with the tips of his fingers. He had, however, a very vivid memory of the moment they had entered the mountain, tiptoeing cautiously as though walking into some strange world where the next step or two might lead into a trap. After moving some distance the men's mood changed, though, and the darkness became a warm refuge from the rest of the world, in which they felt more secure the deeper they went. "I wouldn't mind peeping out, just for a moment or two," mused Anawari.

"Why? The world outside would have changed, d'you think?"

"Well, we could dream that the whites had left, forever, so long ago that even their machines have rusted away to dust."

"Yes! The lizards, ants, waterholes—everything had come back to life again." Gara's voice grew more cheerful as he joined the game of make-believe.

"Our *tjamu* from the sky have come down to make a new world."

"The *nangari* are back, with their sacred *tjurunga*; and they are busy chanting."

"They have made a whole tribe of men live again. We must go and see them."

The game of make-believe lasted only a short time, for Gara's voice grew dry: "I've had these dreams before." He and a handful of others that had fled the testing area had come to Bidi and sneaked inside the belly of the mountain to lick their wounds. Anawari thought that the mountain would be a perfect place to hide; in darkness, one could not tell the color of your skin, nor could they track your contaminated body with that monstrous eagle machine, for the mountain is radioactive as well. "Hiding inside mother's womb," Anawari was about to say, but became aware that man does not eat rocks, nor could one squeeze a drop of water from them. Man can hide inside as long as he is useful to others, as he and Gara did down at the diggings. Soon that would end and the soul would desert the withering body, leaving behind a dry skeleton. That must have worried Gara too. "I have the feeling that we're going around in circles. You still have the water container?" he asked.

"Yes, and there's still a fair bit in it—I don't seem to get very thirsty in here."

"Neither do I."

Presently the tunnel began to ascend sharply and narrowed to a burrow, through which the travelers had to crawl with scarcely enough space to move their struggling limbs. Progress was slow and silent as the two men inched forward, feeling their way with their fingers and constantly fearful of losing each other in the dark, until Anawari discovered that they could maintain contact if he held onto Gara's foot and followed as he moved forward. They advanced for a while, then Gara suddenly stopped, and Anawari guessed that some obstacle, perhaps a rock, was blocking the way.

"If it's a rock, pass it back to me if you can, or roll it in front of you." Gara did not answer, but Anawari could hear heavy breathing and scuffling sounds, and the feet so close to Anawari's head jerked and writhed.

"What is it? What's the matter?"

"It's all right . . . only this bloody . . . " Gara's voice stopped suddenly as he began to move again, and Anawari followed close behind. His fingers immediately touched loose stones, and as he explored the size and shape of the obstacle Anawari recognized it as a trough full of rocks, seemingly abandoned there by someone too tired to drag it farther along the burrow. Anawari pulled a few rocks off the top, pushed them behind him, and then crawled over the trough, anxiously stretching forward to regain contact with Gara and urgently thrusting his body over the rough floor of the tunnel. A chain ran from the edge of the trough into the dust, and Anawari's fingers slipped over the cold metal links, one by one, to where it ended at . . . what? A sharp stump? No . . . Anawari hesitated, not wishing to believe what his senses were telling him, but . . . yes, his hand passed over a thigh bone. Drops of sweat rolled from his forehead, and over his closed eyelids; Anawari took a deep breath and made a sudden lunge forward; his elbow struck a row of human ribs and the sound of crackling old bones echoed in his ears. With a moan he threw himself forward again, slid scrabbling over a skull and plunged into the dark ahead in pursuit of Gara.

The burrow soon began to descend and to widen, and what had seemed the worst was turning out for the best. Presently the passage became large enough for the two men to crawl side by side, and a little farther on, to stand erect. As Anawari leaned, in relief, against the rocky wall he felt a whisper of coolness touch his sweaty temples. "Hey! I feel a draft."

"Yes, I can feel it too."

"So there has to be an opening somewhere nearby."

"I shouldn't think it's too far away—that poor bloke back there was dragging his trough in this direction."

They were suddenly silent again, at the thought of that trapped and lonely skeleton. The end of the tunnel was indeed not far ahead, but when the travelers reached it at last, they faced a tumbled pile of boulders that blocked the entrance. Daylight filtered through gaps between several rocks, and Gara, following the dazzling beams, crawled under one immense slab, over another, and called to Anawari: "Come on, squeeze in here. There's enough room for both of us."

The men lay there awhile among the rocks, just breathing the warm dry air and blinking at the sun, but at last they turned their attention to the township, to their left—at the foot of the cliff but seeming close enough to touch. The prospector's monument at the road junction was certainly less impressive from that height, but Anawari could see its detail as clearly as if he held it in the palm of his hand and . . . next to the monument a group of men were mounting a huge poster upon a scaffold and the giant lettering read, clearly, WANTED FOR TREASON; Anawari did not need to read more and asked quickly: "Do they ever come up here?"

"The whites don't know about this passage. It was blasted out by Namir. The major gave him the gelignite. When the rocks blew up, the whole ridge trembled like a mortally wounded serpent."

"Is there a way to climb down the cliff?"

"No one has ever done it except . . . Patupiri. . . . He has a secret pathway so he can sneak down to the water plant and back but"—Gara paused as if making a decision—"but he never showed anyone else his private track . . . not anyone."

Anawari was about to ask if Gara knew Patupiri's whereabouts when he was interrupted. "Wait here a moment. I have something to show you." Gara slid from the rock crevice and disappeared among the shadows. Anawari pulled himself forward to the edge of a jutting slab of rock to gain a better view of the valley to his right, for from his vantage point on the knuckle of the ridge's pointing finger, with the escarpment behind him, he could see both the diggings and the township. He still wanted to know how and why he and Gara had lost their way back from the water plant that night, but though the shaft they were seeking must have been almost directly below him, Anawari could not distinguish it from any other and was left staring helplessly into the distance.

"Look at this." Gara had crawled back into the slab and clenched in his hand was the biggest chunk of opal Anawari had ever seen.

"Where did that srping from?"

"I buried it among the rocks years ago." Anawari assumed that the opal had come into Gara's hands not long after he and Michael had arrived in the desert from Europe, when Bidi had been no more than a dusty little settlement of people searching for gemstones. A man could have made his fortune with an opal of that size, but Gara was searching for his country and people, and the size made no difference. Anawari was told that he had actually brought that stone with him from Lake Takapiri, where it had been in tribal hands for generations. It had been about for so long that the stone's surface had been made smooth by human hands. Anawari felt apologetic for thinking of it as a mere lump of opal that could bring a fortune to the owner, when he was told that the stone was *tjurunga*—a sacred emblem that had much to do with initiation and other tribal rites, as well as bringing the rain. While working in the settlement Anawari had seen an emblem like that, a diagram of one on the computer screens; the white man's machine referred to it as a *kulpitji* and as the most precious ritual object associated with the power of bringing the rain. The computer here interpreted an old legend about the stone once being part of the arm of an Aboriginal girl who made the first rain and brought about a string of waterholes across the desert. That must have been Witjinti, Corkwood Girl, assumed Anawari; the computer called her "Glorious maiden who performed the miracle of rain," and spoke of her not so much as a mythical ancestor but as a creator, who in some prehistoric time brought life back to the desert. Gara did not say much about *tjurunga* except that the stone, originally oval in shape, had an end missing. Anawari touched the rough surface and felt loose fragments crumbling under his fingers. Under the nuclear blast the boulders must have crumpled into sand, he thought and, sliding his fingers over *tju-*

157

runga, said, "Hold on to that; it will be needed one day." As he spoke, Anawari turned his gaze back to the valley and . . . there it was—the dreadful tracker—fluttering its gleaming, monstrous wings above a mine shaft, to the accompaniment of that strange electronic murmur.

The diggings suddenly echoed with a voice, amplified to a high volume: "Anawari Mallee . . . come out from below with your hands up. I call on you in the name of the Queen, three times over. . . ."

The tracker backed some distance from the shaft, blinked one of its hooded eyes, and directed its violet beam onto the target. In a trice a stream of glittering silver objects exploded from under the monster's belly and darted down the purple path to their objective. As a great cloud of mixed smoke and dust burst from the shaft under attack and then subsided again, leaving a gaping crater, the gang erecting the poster at the junction pointed at the man-made cloud, cheered, and threw their helmets in the air. People rushed from their houses forming a merry crowd in the main street and cheering a truck that was being pushed toward the junction by more helmeted men. As the procession reached the prospector, Anawari could see that the truck carried a gallows, from which the figure of a man dangled grotesquely. "It's Michael—they got him—they got him!" Anawari put his hands over his ears to shut out his own babbling voice. He stared at the crowd for a while, unable to say much more or move until he felt Gara tugging at his arm. "You're in view of that bloody monster." They crawled back from the slab, squeezed through the crevice, and stepped back into the dark, and this time the enveloping blackness seemed even warmer, softer, and safer than before. Much later Gara whispered: "They got that poor fellow. Do you think it might be a ploy to get us out?" Anawari said nothing; he felt unable to think in the dark.

Anawari remembered seeing an echidna once, curled in a crevice in a rock. Yes, it was on that camping excursion with his schoolmates. The boys thought the animal was stuck and tried to get it out, but as soon as it was free, the echidna began to dig and was soon under the ground in front of their very eyes. Does Namir remember it any longer? wondered Anawari. He asked, "Did any of the people come out through that opening?"

"When you are black, you would rather stay in the dark. Patupiri often told us that."

It was worth trying, and Anawari felt somewhat proud of his schoolmate although he was still unable to trace just how dearly Namir had had to pay for it. In going from one world to another the prize is trivial to those who struggle to come out unscathed and . . . yes, how else could you grow into *wati,* a wise man.

CHAPTER 16

Moving again through the interior of the hill, Anawari, leading the way, thought he saw a fire—only a glimmer or a flicker now and then in the far distance though, and so infrequent and feeble that he thought it better not to mention anything to Gara, behind him, until he could be sure he was not imagining things.

The light was not steady like that of a lantern or a torch, but danced and trembled on the surface of the rocks before its reflection was snatched away by the depth of the darkness, leaving no trace; then a moment or two later it could be seen again, always some distance ahead, as if it were showing the way. Anawari was still thinking of that different world that he and Gara had conjured in their minds, and so confident was he that the flickering flame would lead them to the place that he did not pause to question its virtues.

"It's really quite pleasantly warm in here," came Gara's voice from the rear.

"Yes, and so calm, it's like being in a dream."

"The dark seems to wrap around me . . . like a blanket . . . I feel as if I'm in a safe place . . . my own home."

Anawari looked back for a moment. "Have you ever been afraid of the dark?"

"Once, yes—but that was in Milinkovo." Gara would have

long forgotten about that, if it had not been for the woman who had brought him up, for he remembered everything about her. She had let him sit by an open fire every evening and had often spread a rug over the ground for him to rest and watch the flames playing with shadows in the semidark room. She never let that fire die out for years, except one night during the war when a bomb hit the oak tree outside and brought part of the house down. That night the ashes went cold, for his "mother" felt too scared to rekindle the fire. Gara did not sleep that night, fearing that she would never light it again; the dark around him would harden like a rock and the daylight would vanish forever. Gara was fond of his village mother. The fire worshiper, tough like flint, he often thought. She made him a long shirt, which she had woven herself from flax that grew behind the house. There must have been enough flax for only one shirt, for once each week he had to go naked until noon while she washed and dried it by the fire. The women from the village used to tease her that Gara had been left behind as an informer by the gypsies who had camped one night under the oak tree, and that the gypsies would be back one day to ransack the house. Gara often feared that someone might steal the fire and ever since his toddling days he had tried to rub two sticks of wood against each other, hoping that smoke would appear, if not flame. He often went to sleep with his fire-making sticks. He lay them down on the rug, hoping that by the following morning the sticks might have been taught by the nearby fire how to begin burning. Some years later his father showed him how to hold the two wooden sticks properly, when taking him for the first time to the nearest township. They went there together every market day, for his father was the only man who knew the magic of making fire and didn't want people to buy matches anymore. He called his fire *waru* and he often muttered that word while squatting on a rug at the marketplace, whirling the sticks till the smoke rose. However, his father was away during the war, and that was when Gara feared eternal dark would descend upon him, for he had not yet mastered the skill of making *waru*.

Walking in the dark through the tunnel under the mountain,

Anawari wondered how different his life would have been if he, too, had been allowed to grow up by the fire. The whites had always maintained that the tribal children had to be taken from the bush, so as not to grow up under the evil spell of the campfire; even the computer in his office was programmed to comment on that. Perhaps there is something magic, not so much in fire but in *waru,* for it must have been that, more than anything else, that had brought Gara back from a half world away to the bush. Gara, on the other hand, tried to convince him that while he grew up in that Serbian village, the people thought him no more than a little gypsy. "You can tell their children by the way they stare into the fire, just as their horses do," the village people told his mother. They often reminded her to make sure that the jar full of gold that her husband had brought back from Australia was safely tucked away, for the gypsies would loot the house. Someone did indeed come and dig a hole under the oak, just where the fork of the tree marked the ground with its shadow at noon on St. Peter's Day. Instead of the gold, the robbers dug out an old stump, leaving the villagers to talk about the stump being the remains of the post on which old Milinko had been stuck by the Janizaries. Gara doubted there would have been any gold about, for his "mother" went on picking blackberries along the hedges in the village for two whole successive summers to buy him a book. "You must learn to read if you're going to find that place again." She thought that Australia was somewhere along a distant lonely road, and to get there one must be able to follow the road signs for the right turnoff. Gara liked his father; he knew how to make *waru*—the only one in the white man's world to do so, and that was greater than a pot of gold.

The track began to wind steeply downward and after a time broadened out, but there was no longer any need to cling to the rocky walls for guidance, for the way was smooth, now, and well defined. Whenever Anawari strayed from the well-trodden path, he felt squeaking charcoal underfoot, or the smooth touch of ashes, and he wondered at the number of dead campfires that must lie there; but then, he mused, if every Aborigine who had ever lived and trodden this path should wish to leave a memento of their passing, cold ashes would well serve the purpose. A dead camp-fire endures far longer than human remains and, to those who understand, can tell the story of one's ancestors and their habits; so as Anawari felt the soft ash between his toes, he fancied he was stepping over the coals of every fire lit by every one of his forebears in a lifetime.

The impenetrable darkness had gradually melted into a gray haze, and though Anawari could not pinpoint the source of this subdued glow, he could feel a warmth on his skin as comforting as morning sunlight. Now, instead of cold rock under his hand, Anawari could feel the rough bark of living trees—overhead arched a canopy of rustling leaves, and though the scattered ashes could now be clearly seen, neither Gara nor Anawari could feel the roughness against the soles of their feet. In front of them, quite unexpectedly, sat an old man. Against a piece of wood laid flat on the ground he was spinning the pointed end of a smooth stick, turning it back and forth between his palms in an effort to produce a glimmer of fire. The man raised his head as the travelers drew near. "I've made so many, many fires in my lifetime but . . . now . . . it will not light anymore."

Anawari could not guess at the age of the man, whose long hair and beard concealed most of his face; his voice . . . was the voice heard in the dream of the *kadaitja* shoes, and not only then. . . . Anawari felt that that same familiar voice had been around whispering to him much longer than he could remember. He looked at the old man struggling to start the fire and said calmly: "We should have brought you some wood. I'm sorry; I didn't know you made a camp." Anawari felt he had somehow failed.

"Is there still wood to be found outside then?" The long hair shook from side to side in disbelief.

Gara moved closer to the old man. "I had hoped you would still be around."

"A man stays with his people. Where else would I be? Look, some of them still have their fires alight." The old fellow raised his arms with outspread fingers, and Anawari noticed for the first time that, in the shadows behind him, glowed thousands upon thousands of flickering specks like countless stars quivering in the evening sky.

"How is my daughter?" The old man's eyes shone in the dark.

Gara bowed his head. "She is a good wife and mother."

"Did you make her a new *wana*?"

"One needs wood for that—drought grows no trees."

"There'll be no rain."

"For how much longer?"

The old man blinked. "The whites have to leave the country first; it'll rain soon after. Sand can wait for that, there's hardly anything else about."

Gara must have thought so too, for he nodded his head then said, "I have brought him to you."

The eyes of the old man shone toward Anawari. "I waited for you to come." Nupuru, yes, it was he—seeing the old friend brought no surprise, however. Ever since that dream when he met the tribal *nangari*, Anawari had a fair idea who the legendary healer might be, though to admit it even to himself would have meant the betrayal of the sacred secrets one is entrusted with while heading to be initiated into manhood.

"He could not find his tribe." Gara spoke now in Para tribal dialect.

"He has met his skin sister though."

Anawari understood this was final confirmation of what he already knew. He had come from *pulkarin,* the fertility rock, from which every *karan* is born. The people of the desert tree tribes do not breed from the semen of man as the whites do, but originate from the sacred rock in the country and need only a woman to mother them. There is always a head of the family to which the woman belongs, a man to protect you and to hunt as you grow up, to tell you that you owe your life to that sacred place of the country. If there is no tribal father about, then your uncle will teach you the ritual secrets of life and see that you grow into *wati,* full man. Anawari felt uncertain if this was traditional practice, but it was often so with his generation.

Nupuru spoke again: "You have seen your mother."

She must have been the old man's sister, assumed Anawari; perhaps a skin sister—it makes no difference—without him how else would one learn where one had come from and who had mothered him? The picture of the skeleton woman from the dead camp flashed through Anawari's mind. Perhaps better that he did not meet her alive, for the pain might have been too great to bear. He held his breath for a while trying to comprehend fully how he must have been seen in the eyes of his tribal relatives—a club in the hand of the Pungals? Though the new invaders were of human size and pretended not to be cannibals, the blacks were hunted as prey just the same while their tribal country was pounded into dust. He . . . yes, he had been part of that brutal machine that gulped the tribes.

"She often asked about you." Nupuru's eyes blinked while his face remained calm.

How many children did his mother have? Anawari restrained himself from asking though, knowing that Nupuru, like any other *nangari* and like all *tjamu*—spritual ancestors—would say no more or less than what their ritual code told them to say. He knew, since he was on the way back, that as he progressed into tribal manhood, there would be the proper time and occasion to learn not only about his family but of every black brother in the country.

"You know some of them already," the old man reminded him.

Suddenly Anawari remembered a scene from the settlement soon after he had first joined the staff of the William Wilberforce Hospital. He was sitting with Nupuru under a tree and had begun to write in the sand as if his hand belonged to someone else: "Namir, Enowari, Ily . . . ," feeling doubt that the names could be those of his tribal brothers and . . . only now did he realize that his own name was there—spelled differently, of course, but *A* and *E* were almost interchangeable in the Aborginal tongue.

Anawari felt, once more, the guiding hand of his ancestors, for the name had been picked by chance from a book he had read in school while preparing to be the *maijada,* the ringmaster of that unfinished circus of an initiation ceremony they had tried to organize there. The book was the diary of an early explorer who owed his survival, on a desert crossing, to a native named Anawari, who had helped him find water and led him to safety. Since he had mixed with tribal people, Anawari had noticed that the sounds of *A* or *E* beginning a word were nearly indistinguishable—forming a sound not recognized by the European ear—so the explorer had obviously made a phonetic mistake; anyway, in his excitement at leading the white man's path into a new and vast country, the proper name of one black man would have held no importance for him.

"So you are *wankar,* a half man now."

Anawari caught the old man's eyes fixed on the tribal marks on his chest. "I have done my best to free my spirit of the white man's influence. I have been too far away, for too long."

"Even the dead come back. There's no room for any of us in the white man's world." A dingo lay beside Nupuru, resting his head on the old man's thigh. It hardly took any notice of the visitors and looked almost asleep; the animal raised his eyelids only once, from behind which shone beady eyes like two torches. Anawari wanted to say a soft word or two, as one would greet a dog, but reminded himself that the dingo was not only Nupuru's personal "dreaming" totem—every man or spirit has one to accompany him about—but a replica of his life, the skin that man can slip in and out of, providing he has the magic power of *nangari* to do so. Long after man goes and the wind grinds his bones into sand, his "dreaming" would still be about; not only in the sky, but down on earth—a shadow of it would be seen moving about the country. No white man could kill that. "How long must I say *wankar?*" asked Anawari. He was told to grow further; man has to wait for a better time, just as trees wait for rain. To thrive, one needs to have one's country about, ground to stand on, and space to grow into. Nupuru, that wise old man, spoke often of

166

humans being no better or worse than plants. "We all depend on rain." Anawari understood that once people turned into trees, they would be grouped into tribes again—Ghost Gum, Blood Gum, River Gum, and Box Gum—just as they had been before, and it would matter little whether you grew under skin or bark as long as you thrived. The trees are not able to walk though, and that prompted him to ask, "How do they run from the whites?" Nupuru seemed tired now, for his head drooped and the sticks in his hands were spinning no longer. In the sweep of darkness behind him, many of the fires made a last flickering glow, shrank to tiny specks, and were engulfed in blackness. Very few were still left; Anawari began to count them and dozed off.

He must have slept a little, and when he woke, even the few fires still glowing had grown small and pale. "I must get back to my country," Anawari was thinking aloud. Nupuru raised his head and a strange light shone in his eyes: "Watch out for *walpa*— it has wiped out everything." He flung his arms wide and before them spread a panoramic view of vast scrub country. A dreadful noise roared from beyond the horizon—an unrecognizable sound but one that pressed against Anawari's eardrums and filled him with fear. A great light flashed as if the sun itself had burst open and spewed its molten contents in a shower of crystal sparks that spread faster than eyes could follow. The plants turned into ashes instantly, and the earth lost its color. A frightened lizard dashed into the crevice of a boulder, but the rock lost its shape and slid into a pile of sand. At the lake, the line of the water retreated fast, but caught by the light, it too lost its color. The arm of the lake, which resembled an emu's neck, broke in half, the upper part with a dangling head on its end trembled for a while, but that too soon became obliterated. Farther on, Boomerang Island quivered under the heat; then the sand ignited. From the molten country there mushroomed a cloud; whirled by the storm it grew, gulping the sky. Human figures appeared silhouetted by the white billowing mass. Could anyone survive? wondered Anawari and tried to count the silhouettes whirling in the cloud. There should be more people about, many more—a whole tribe of them; no,

167

scores of tribes. While at the settlement he had often looked at the map of Central Australia that hung on the wall in Ann's study. The map had a red shaded section covering the area between the 27th and 31st parallels—almost entirely desert. When he had asked Ann about the area, "Oh, that's the nuclear testing and such" had been the airy answer. And such! Such diabolical hell! Anawari mentally compared the area of a typical tribal territory with that of the green strip and calculated that there was space enough left to accommodate a half dozen more. Six tribes . . . at least six tribes and maybe more . . . just blown away like dust. *Walpa . . . Walpa* oh *Walpa.* He wished that he had a map of the area at hand. "How far's that bloody Walpa from the lake?" It was pitch dark in the tunnel, and Anawari touched Gara to make sure that he was listening. "I mean the place, not a storm."

Gara must have dozed off, for it took him a while to answer: "It seems to be some kind of code word for a whole chain of nuclear testing sites at the lake area; they're marked on the map. You keep that map?" Gara explained that for most desert tribes *walpa* means not only storm but heavenly downpour. The wind often marks the breaking of a long drought and the beginning of the growing season, for after it comes about, the desert blooms, turning from red into green. It is the best time for plants and people the country can come up with. While the waterholes are still full and *kaltu* seed is ripening to be ground into *nyuma*, the families gather to initiate the tribal youths and betroth those born recently. *Walpa*, or *waralpa* as it is known in some dialects, means "life, the beginning of." "That was when the tribes were about." Gara spoke as though the happy days belonged to some mythical past and the desert were destined for no rain. Anawari on his part remembered traveling through Walpa when on holidays with Ann. They headed south along the dirt track; there was nothing of that blooming forest to be seen then, nor did they see the nuclear blasts. Actually he complained about continuously seeing an endless plain of sand, and Ann reminded him twice that he had been born in the bush and the sand is native to Australia as much as the color of his skin. The Landrover they were traveling in broke down, and Anawari began asking himself how long it takes a man to die of thirst in the desert. He should not have panicked, for soon after the car broke down, a group of security men turned up and escorted them in quite a military fashion to the nearest post. They were placed in a locked room, and were obviously regarded with suspicion by the security men until Ann did some fast talking and convinced the officers that they were just an innocent couple on their holiday trip.

The Landrover and all the baggage had been searched so thoroughly that not a pin escaped scrutiny; the security men had checked Ann's handbag and even peeped into her lipstick holder; Anawari had to undress, twice, in front of the inspecting officers and to raise his hands to prove that nothing was hidden in his armpits—he should have suspected something more than a harmless testing area, then. Gara's voice came questioning: "You're not thinking of shooting through to Takapiri?" Anawari wondered what a man would live on if he got there—grains of sand and salty water would not be much comfort. There must be some people, though, still fleeing from there or sneaking back to that area. Why else would Ily survey the Northern Border and install his electronic trackers? "I went through that place once." Released at last, Anawari and Ann were ordered to drive out of the area making no stops, but it was a long stretch of bumpy dirt road, and Anawari was, inevitably, forced to stop to urinate. Before he had even zipped up his fly, a car had pulled up behind, and security men had leaped out and manhandled him back into the Landrover. It took the rest of that day and part of the night to drive off the restricted area.

"Walpa, *Tjamu-ngura,* the country I was born in," Anawari whispered, and suddenly felt sure that he would be there again.

Later, much later, while lying on the ground in the pitch dark, Anawari saw Namir at last. Yes, it was him, sitting on the rim of a mushroom-shaped cloud, holding the two halves of a broken boomerang in his hands. From inside the cloud comes a husky voice: "Keep calling that spook of yours. Doesn't he want to help you out?" Namir claps the pieces of boomerang together and mumbles some words. The husky voice becomes urgent: "There's no food or water around here; even the scorpions have perished. That ancestor of yours better bring some rain. There hasn't been a drop for ages. C'mon man, make him come. He can give us some clue how to get the rain." The cloud began to spin faster and a moment later it formed the shape of Namir's face, lit by a great sulphur light, but the husky voice went on: "A good rain would shower off that radioactive dust from you—people do die from that dirt." The cloud whirled but the shape of Namir's face remained.

Anawari's voice quivered in the dark: "Had Patupiri, Nupuru, I mean, tried to help the poor fellow?"

"No. Whatever he is—spirit or human—the old man knew all about traps." Gara was silent for a while. "The whites won't snatch our secrets from him so easily."

The still darkness settled again, as though both Anawari and Gara had run out of words.

Man and trees are not far apart. Though the plants do not walk as fast as humans, they have their secret way of getting about. Trees have tough twisted limbs that root into the ground or hug the rocks, for earth is their home too. No tree grows without skin; cut that and the tree bleeds. When hurt, plants feel pain, just as humans do. When losing a limb one calls for help. At dusk you can hear the howls of a hollow log echoing through the bush; the howls go on till midnight, often for days, just like the howl of a trapped dingo, to tell the world about the anguish of dying alone. When calling for help, the trees stretch their long arms and wrestle with long fingers, for no soul in the bush dies silently.

Trunks let their wounds be licked by the breeze, for no tree has yet grown a lolling tongue like that of a dingo. The wound heals slowly; it takes years and a stretch of long drought in between to recover, though the droughts bring no help! On the heath, bare wood cracks just as every dry crust does. When in distress, trees drop their leaves, and if the pain does not go away, they weather like all wounded souls for they too have karan that leaves the decomposing body and flees to the bush.

The trees do not die so easily though, they have been in the country for too long to learn their way about. Man seldom sees them walking about, but they do. For how else did they spread throughout the world, sneaking into every valley and climbing up steep ridges? They know how to cross wide rivers, and what's more cross the desert from one end to the other.

Only an everlasting soul and enduring limbs could make that. Journeying across the sandy vastness, the trees stopped to camp, always at a waterhole, horizons apart. Following their path, man could cross the desert also, but only if he believed in trees.

CHAPTER 17

On the eastern flank of the ridge Anawari and Gara found another exit, but it was secured with heavy steel bars concreted into the rock walls, and with a small gate firmly chained to the main metal structure. There was no way out now, but the place must have carried much traffic, once, for around the rocks and away out of sight, toward Coronation Downs, wound a well-worn track. The valley itself lay hidden farther down the ridge, but within sight on the rocky slopes were dotted heaps of excavated mining waste marking the far eastern flank of the diggings.

As the men approached the gate, a pair of wings, presumably those of a bat, fluttered over their heads out of the darkness; but what appeared instead was a finch, which hovered in the air a moment, alighted before the bars of the gate, and turned around to look at the travelers. Anawari realized, then, that the bird could not pass between the bars with open wings so it must land and walk out, and he was surprised that a finch would come into the dimness of the tunnel often enough to be familiar with such a procedure; it seemed quite unafraid and cocked its head on one side, watching with wide-open eyes.

Anawari racked his brains for the Para tribal word for "finch," then tried to remember the word in any associated dialect he knew, but it eluded him. Feeling foolish he asked, "What do you call that bird?"

"I don't know." Gara turned his face away as if embarrassed.

Then Anawari remembered that many local tribesmen would not willingly speak the name of any living creature which they believed had assumed the spirit of a dead relative. *Nyinyi!* . . . that was it! Anawari remembered, but left the word unspoken. He was still uncertain whether the word was from Para, Pipalia, or the dialect of some neighboring tribe, but surely the origin of a name must be of little importance; in a land and time where spirits can freely call on their descendants, the usage of a word could be of mere significance . . . but . . . on the other hand . . . if a man is still *wankar* and has yet to grow to manhood, it might be safer not to think or say words with which he is not fully acquainted, and which might be misunderstood and give offense. The finch hopped between the steel bars, took off, and swooped from view, but Gara scarcely glanced after the bird; his eyes were fixed on the gate. "They've only just been here."

"Who?"

"The whites. Look." Gara was staring at the shining galvanized chain and glittering new brass padlock fastening the gate; they could not have been there longer than a few days. Anawari's eyes followed the track beyond the bars to where, some distance away, the roof of a Landrover could just be seen behind some rocks. Both men backed hastily from the gateway into the darkness of the tunnel. "Don't run away, I've brought you some food!" Hunt's voice boomed over a megaphone.

The fugitives held their breath.

"We all have to eat, now and then—even insects do. I have left you a bowl of food. See it? Right there at the gate—can you see it?"

Only now Anawari noticed a plastic dish of salted fish pushed under the gate—the bastard's up to his old tricks! Anawari licked his lips.

"Try it. It's very tasty tucker, really. Fish is the traditional food for most of your brothers in the coastal area."

Gara pressed his body back against the rocks, his breath coming in harsh and uneven gasps. He crouched lower and lower, cowering as if he expected to be fired upon, and Anawari realized that he should take the same precautions or else he would be in the direct line of fire from the parked car. Anawari felt sure, however, that it was too soon for Hunt to stage a direct attack; during the old man's long dealings with the blacks he had learned to apply techniques far more sophisticated than the bullet, and though these might appear less brutal, they brought him to the same deadly goal in the end.

"Don't be shy, lads; there's plenty more food where that came from."

The distant whispering of the tracker fluttered in the air and through the bars at the mouth of the tunnel the machine could be seen circling above the valley. It paused, a moment later the earth trembled slightly, and then a puff of smoke and dust rose into the air. The ensuing silence did not last long; the electronic murmur began again and though the dreadful bird could not be seen, repeated tremors and puffs of dusty smoke revealed its progress and activity.

"That monster's blasting every shaft down there," whispered Gara.

"It looks like it. He must have realized he didn't get us in that first raid."

"What about him?" Gara glanced toward the bowl of food at the gate.

The bowl of food had puzzled Anawari too, but now it became clear that whoever rode on the monster was working independently of Hunt and the others, driven perhaps by his own greed for personal gain. . . . Yes, the whites must be in conflict among themselves over who would collect the catch, and it may have been thanks to rivalry among the pursuers that the two of them had stayed alive so far—if thanks should be given for a life so ground to dust and compressed by fear as theirs had become.

"Perhaps you don't like the fish? Should I get you witchetty grubs or lizards then? Some really traditional tucker?"

The earth trembled again even more violently than before, specks of dirt fell from above into the semidarkness, and at the exit a cloud of disturbed dust flew into the air.

"You'll have to come out sooner or later you know," echoed Hunt's voice.

"The old bastard could be right," muttered Anawari, for one could stay inside a hollow hill for just so long before one must either walk out, or else pass silently over to join the others who have gone before. Once Anawari had, from the back veranda of his home in the settlement, watched a man sitting on the sand in a clearing in the scrub a short distance away. The sun was blazing and the ground must have been scorching hot, yet the man did not move nor did he show any sign of discomfort, and later in the day he could still be seen, in the same upright position resembling a post plunged into the sand. Anawari took him a jug of water but the man gave no sign that he was even aware of Anawari's presence; his face, turned to the sun, had a greasy coating of *ngintaka,* the fat from a goanna, which gave a clue to his totemic affiliation, and his expression was one of content and calm, as if he had receded into a dream. The only movement to be seen about the rigid figure was a pulse in the temple, weak, certainly, but still beating on; in the evening, when Anawari went into the scrub again he found the jug and its contents untouched and the man in exactly the same pose, but . . . the pulse had stopped. When Anawari related the incident to Nupuru, he had learned from the elder that the man's *karan* had left him, so it was necessary that he should also put his body to rest, and though Anawari had applauded this dignified way of death at the time, he now felt himself inadequate in the strength and determination needed to carry out this tradition.

The amplified voice bellowed again: "There's hardly any water left in that container, is there? Don't hesitate to ask when you need some more; you will certainly not be able to go down to the water plant again yourselves. Oh yes! I know about that little jaunt. I followed you all the way on a clever little screen I have right in my car. The special substance dissolved in that water trough made it even easier to track you after that. This machine really is so very handy, it shows even how much pee there is in your bladder."

A new blast, blowing yet another shaft in the valley, took Anawari by surprise; at its sudden eruption he threw himself into a rocky corner of the tunnel, struck his arm on a sharp protrusion, and lay there feeling a warm line of blood sliding down from the gash.

"That's a nasty cut you've got there," called Hunt. "Why not come out for treatment? People die from blood poisoning, you know. It's nothing new. Don't go crawling back into that nasty darkness. The scorpions will get you in there, or red-back spiders . . . snakes . . . Black Plague . . . any one of those horrible things we liberated your people from."

Anawari looked around and found that Gara had already left; he crawled a little way, then stood upright and scurried deeper into the tunnel. Behind him the voice from the megaphone persisted: "Don't go back in there. You have been in the dark for all those milleniums. The darkness has followed the whole of your race. All your five hundred and fifty tribes have gone that way. Come out and be the last survivor."

As Anawari moved further into the tunnel, the sound of the megaphone receded until it was only a muffled echo, the sense and meaning of which had been stolen by the darkness all around.

When Anawari emerged again from underground, deep night had fallen; this tunnel sprang out on the western slope of the ridge, giving a view of only that part of the township surrounding the Prospector Square, where a large crowd of people milled about under the glaring lights. To see the main street and much of the township, obscured by the lower cliffs of the ridge, Anawari would have had to venture out onto the rocky slope to reach a better vantage point, but he found the way was blocked. Heavy chain-wire mesh was stretched across the tunnel mouth, its intricate patterns silhouetted against the night sky, and though

Anawari shook and clawed at the steel web, the supporting structure, which was driven deep into the surrounding rocks, scarcely moved under his onslaught. He leaned there, pressing his face against the cold metal and breathing deeply of the fresh air driving in from the world outside.

In Prospector Square the lights suddenly went out and a moment later a burst of cheering broke from the gathered crowd.

"Good evening, Your Excellency, and my dear fellow citizens . . . " The amplified voice of a speaker echoed in the darkness. ". . . it is my great honor and, indeed, a rare human privilege, to be given the opportunity to deliver the Colonel Arthur Memorial Lecture." Anawari recognized the voice as that of Dr. Tinto, and was wondering if his old enemy was actually there, or if the voice had been recorded, when he saw a gigantic picture of the doctor projected clearly, high in the darkness. It was impossible to tell whether the picture was being thrown onto a screen mounted on the ridge or was cleverly reflected onto the very sky itself, but however it was done, Anawari was sure that the doctor was not very far away, for every detail, down to the single hairs of his eyebrows, could be clearly seen.

"I wish to present to you all, tonight, a new inhabitant of Australia—a friendly harmless, little fellow—Abo-ant."

The viewing angle of the camera changed and Ann appeared on the screen carrying a tray covered with a flag and on which lay a stainless steel box. Dr. Tinto, with a swift sweep of his hand, much like the gesture of a magician, took up the box and tapped at its lid with his finger ends while he talked. At last a small glass tube was taken out of the box, its contents tipped onto the Doctor's palm—and the camera zoomed in to focus on an ant. The tiny creature was confused by the strange environment and did not seem eager to crawl about and display itself, but its feelers, Anawari saw, flicked and quivered in all directions trying to analyze this new set of sensations.

Anawari regretted that Gara was not there to share the first glimpse of their future brother, and though they had become parted, Anawari hoped that his erstwhile companion might be

177

watching the screen from the mouth of some other tunnel. The two of them used to chat occasionally about what was going on in the William Wilberforce Hospital and Dr. Tinto's work on manipulating genes. Neither of them knew enough about science to predict what the doctor was after, except that they were black and that their souls differed from the souls of the whites. They had been robbed of their country; now their souls were to be looted too. "When a body rots the flies flock." Gara often used to repeat a saying from the village where he grew up. The people died there as everywhere else, especially during the wars, but evil never went on such a rampage as to gulp both—the country and the people. He told Anawari that when an Aborigine sees a nuclear blast or the rolling mist that follows, *karan* deserts him and flies to the bush, leaving the empty body to weather. It might take many days for a man to wear out with pain, but he grows weaker. Gara, too, felt that way after being held as a detainee on Boomerang Island, but thanks to Nupuru, who caught *karan* in the bush and put it back into his body, he survived. Nupuru helped others as well, being *nangari,* the tribal healer; he was the only one capable of doing so, though single-handedly, neither man nor spirit could save the whole tribe.

The ant tried to crawl but halted, suddenly frightened of what was ahead. Ignoring his captive the doctor went on: "I'll now demonstrate how my discovery will benefit us all. The ants eat little and don't drink—once man evolves into this shape, we won't be dependent on rain any longer. So eat your hearts out, you rain lords." With the tip of the pincers, Dr. Tinto tried to steer his captive. "This creature—Abo-ant, if he had retained his human shape, would have consumed, daily, half a wallaby and a gallon of water." Ann stood behind Dr. Tinto holding the tray again, but this time it bore a bowl full of wheat and a glittering-bladed cleaver. "This is a single grain of wheat. I hope you all can see it. There are about two thousand of those in a single kilo. Now let us cut the wheat in four parts. . . . " The doctor pressed down on the shining blade. "And here, we take one quarter of the grain and cut that in four pieces. We now have here one sixteenth of the grain, and though you can scarcely see it, this tiny particle is enough food for this wonderful creature for two days. A single bag of wheat could feed a whole race of them for a year—providing, of course, that there is proper birth control. Later I will show you our Abo-ant hatchery, where the inmates live happily without water, but first, let us hear a message from our sponsor. . . ."

Anawari did not wish to see the advertisement, but though he turned away and walked back into the tunnel, the soapy voice reached after him and echoed against the rocks.

The sound faded away so suddenly that Anawari could not decide whether the amplifying system had broken down or the path had wound such a serpentine course that the voice simply could no longer reach him to harass and to sicken. Cold air flowed like an unseen river, and shivering, Anawari moved deeper into the labyrinth, hoping to find not only refuge from the bone-chilling draft, but the comforting company of his lost companion Gara.

CHAPTER 18

What is this? The dark seems to have seeped away, and underfoot are drifts of dust such as are left behind a great dry storm. Dust is piled around uprooted scrub and under the leafless trees from which the anger of the wind has stripped even the bark. A white woman dressed in a nurse's uniform emblazoned with a large Red Cross badge is casting with a fishing rod toward a wall of massive rocks before her. Anawari sees now that it is a noose—gear such as is used to catch stray dogs—that the woman wields. Now she moves cautiously forward, peeps into a crevice, and then swings the noose again into the depths of the rock shelter where a woman cringes in the dimmest corner, huddled among the rocks.

A black woman cradles a *kanilypa,* a shallow trough, on one arm, but the small child lying inside it is only partly seen because she presses it so vehemently against her breast, and with her free hand tries to ward off the white woman predator. The loop of a lasso snakes over the mother, slides down her naked shoulders and then tightens viciously around her body, jerking the *kanilypa* from her grasp. The screaming child slips down its mother's body and clings for a moment to her *mawulyari,* a belt made from spun human hair and animal fur, but the fingers are too weak to hold for long and the infant tumbles in the dust.

A white man wearing a clergyman's collar skillfully manipulates a long-handled net between the rocks, and deftly sweeps up the child; the tribal woman struggles forward and the child's fingers, clawing through the imprisoning mesh, catch hold of its mother's *mawulyari* belt but the rope around the woman's bosom fastens tighter and the rod thrust in her face forces her backward against the rocks.

The clergyman fetches the child out from the net, hands it to the nurse, and together they hurry to push the child into a cage on the back of a truck—where it adds its cries to those of a dozen or more other naked infants screaming in despair and lashing about with their feet and fists. A sheet of canvas is thrown over the cage, but it does nothing to muffle the cacophony of crying.

The nurse lifts a microphone from the dashboard of the truck. "Project Janizary to Tracker; Janizary to Tracker, Janizary to Tracker . . . " The voice sounds like Ann's; yes, it is her voice though she looks much younger and her expression is the stiff cold face of duty. "Any new sightings for us, Tracker?" she speaks into the microphone.

"Another mob of women and children on the run, some miles northward from the lake," crackles a voice from the radio loudspeaker. "They seem to have stopped at a dry riverbed, probably digging for water."

"Will it be easy for us to locate them?"

"Head straight north. I'll drop a few smoke markers from the helicopter—follow those and you can't go wrong."

The woman like Ann hesitates for a moment. "Are there any men with spears hanging about?"

"Don't you worry, sweetie. They're all gone."

"Fled? Run away, you mean?"

"Well . . . yes, you could say 'fled.' Actually they'll flee to their spirit world when that blast goes off—all rounded up at Boomerang Island. We . . ." The voice stops, and only the sound of the helicopter rattling persistently can be heard from the radio.

Ann grows impatient and thumps it a few times, but as this has no effect, she begins to scan the sky as if expecting that the machine, like some unpredictable phantom, will appear on the horizon beyond the desert.

"Here we are again. Sorry for cutting you off, sweetie. We had some trouble down at the lake." He went on explaining how a group of detainees broke loose while being transported to Boomerang Island. The Aborigines overpowered the guards and once free headed to Pulkarin Rock, a hill not far away. The man explained in detail how every unit had been alerted before the fatal rebellion came to an end. "They must have sensed what awaited them on that island—even animals do that."

The woman wondered if testing would now be postponed for a while since a consignment of detainees had been lost. "How can you tell how good the blast is with no people on that island?" The cries of the imprisoned children rose to a crescendo—cries of a great flock of terrified birds that had descended upon the country. The leaves on the scrub halted for a while, as did the grains of drifting sand; the insects fell silent and reptiles froze, for the cry told of the curse cast not upon man alone, but also on the country—not even the rocks beneath would come out unscathed.

The man yelled over the radio, "Can you shut those little devils up?"

At the top of her voice the woman explained that they had no control over the children's cries—they went on and off at will. She and Padre Hunt had been given sets of earmuffs and were equipped to handle the menace of the noise. "Once they're away from the bush the crying will cease; the padre thinks so."

"Sweetie, tell Padre Hunt that they want him down at Pulkarin Rock to say a final blessing over those Abos before they're bulldozed into the pit. I'll fetch him later."

So that really is Hunt! His face is some years younger than the face Anawari knows and hates, and is not black, as it seemed at first, but only painted so as to resemble an Aborigine; the dark disguise has cracked and flaked around the chaplain's mouth and eyes, and sweat has left pale tracks on his cheeks. So that is how my colleague looked in the old days. In all those five-hundred-fifty tribes they could not find a black face to trust.

A group of black women gather around the truck, wailing as they try to open the cage or jump on board with it. Hunt pulls out a hose, similar to that of a fire extinguisher, and directs it toward the mothers, enveloping them in a cloud of choking fume; most fall immediately to the ground but a few cling tenaciously to the cage, and as the truck gathers speed, their thin black legs can be seen dangling in the dust boiling behind its wheels.

A moment later, the women are seen walking in a group above the line of billowing dust left behind the truck. They wail—their faces stripped of skin and flesh. They all now look like the woman seen at the dead camp. Anawari yells, "Stop! Please stop!" and realizes that his voice has not been heard; he cries out again, but however loud are his screams, they are slammed back into his face as if deflected by an invisible barrier. Perhaps the truck's windows are closed; Anawari smashes his fist against the glass in a desperate effort to destroy the barrier—Ann sits behind the driving wheel hardly a foot away, Anawari hits the window again but the glass stands firm under his bleeding knuckles; he loses his hold of the truck and flies off into the dust of the road. . . .

When he awoke, Anawari found himself lying face down on rocky ground and too stiff to move; in his mind's eye he saw the truckload of caged children disappearing into the distance, and though the face of the driver could not be seen, large red lettering on the vehicle's door was clearly legible. It read PROJECT JANIZARY.

Anawari remembered well that the wire gate at the tunnel's mouth had been closed—he had wrenched and pushed ineffectually at it the night before—but now, on the following day, when he crawled back there, he found it unlocked and standing partly open. Anawari could not summon strength enough to wonder who might have been there, and when he tried to rise from where he had slept, a sharp pain gripping his temples forced him to sink back onto the stony floor.

The sun shining from outside printed the pattern of the wire mesh on Anawari's skin; his right wrist was swollen, bruised, and marked with angry red scratches. Anawari gingerly explored his face—dried blood had congealed around one eye, sealing it firmly shut, his nose was swollen and tender to the touch, and from his aching jaw Anawari felt a strip of torn skin hanging loose.

"You can come out now, the gate is open. Can you hear me?" It was Ann's voice calling so clearly that she might be standing a few feet away, but Anawari guessed that it was amplified, in order to increase the emotional impact on him.

"There'll be no harm done to you, I have been asked to assure you of that—maybe some judicial formalities, but you mustn't worry about that—no harm, as I said."

Anawari tried to raise his head so that he could see over the edge of the cliff descending from the exit, but the ache in his neck so discouraged him that he paused and then decided that satisfying useless curiosity was not worth the pain and effort involved.

"I can see you sitting there, darling. Come on out, now, please; we've had our differences but . . . let's not carry this too far."

Then Anawari saw the helicopter squatting on a plateau beyond some lower region that was out of his line of vision, but certainly not too far away to exterminate him with a single shot. Anawari's first thought was to crawl back into the darkness but on reconsidering he decided that the possibility of execution was a remote one; the whites would want to perform their rituals according to law—rituals more complex and convoluted than most men can understand but still apparently satisfying to those who enacted them. For example: The men like Kaltu or any other elder would be far more content in their spiritual world than confined in a camp, and one planting of typhoid or cholera virus in the Red Cross blankets, or a single dose of strychnine in the water supply, would grant their wish. Such things had happened before; there was nothing new about a tribe becoming extinct; but no! These whites wanted the Aborigines to go one by one, on a predetermined schedule and preferably with the appearance that tribal man was the cause of his own destruction. For a moment it seemed to

Anawari as though some conspiracy existed between the white man and the spirits to organize the departure of the Aboriginal race in an orderly fashion, by booking each man for his appropriate hour of embarkation. A picture of the man with the goanna-oiled face, whom Anawari had seen die so serenely in the scrub, came vividly to mind; what a dignified way to go, indeed, and yet so few had managed to achieve such a noble end.

"Can't you hear the blasting of the shafts, one by one? Darling, they'll be here, shortly, blasting the ridge as well. Come out, darling, please. I don't want them to get you."

"Let the fools blow the whole earth to shreds," muttered Anawari, envying Gara who had the sense to stay deep in the tunnel and die the way he chose without letting whites have any part in the process; he, too, should have stayed in there. Nyinyi, the finch, flew in from somewhere and landed on the gate, fluttering from wire to wire as if searching for an appropriate place to perch, but then it flew so suddenly away again, having scarcely glanced at Anawari, that he was concerned he might have done something to offend the spirit bird. Anawari watched Nyinyi with longing and envy as it soared, then slid upon the wind across the slopes and disappeared over the edge of the cliff.

The sound of the helicopter reverberated within Anawari's stone chamber. The machine was gone from the top of the mesa but though it sounded so close, Anawari could not see it from where he was huddled. He watched the sky, but the machine did not appear over the hill as he expected, and the mind-splitting rattling noise did not vary in intensity—the helicopter must have been hovering somewhere almost directly overhead. The sound hammered again at Anawari's temples, driving him to desperation with combined fury and pain but he was helpless, for to scream or to run away would be equally useless.

Quite suddenly Ann appeared, spinning in the air at the end of a descending rope. She stopped some distance above the ground and peeped into the mouth of the tunnel before signaling to the helicopter pilot to continue winching her down, and was then deposited on a flat patch of rock just a few meters from the gate.

Ann did not free herself from the dangling rope, however; instead she unhooked a bag with a long rod stretching out from it.

"You have far more sense than to do anything foolish, I trust." She paused, looked intently at Anawari. "Even an animal appreciates help when it is offered." She wore that old shell pendant dangling from her neck.

Taped across Ann's back and chest were two white posters bearing large Red Cross insignia. "Here we go with the rituals!" Anawari murmured; he was sure that a camera hidden in Ann's bag, or maybe in the helicopter, was already focused to zoom in and catch his every move and gesture for relay via satellite and computer to every television screen in the land. Anawari wondered how the story would be marketed—"Emancipation of a Native," perhaps, or "Salvation of a Soul"; or it might be sold as "Human Endeavor," "Rescue of Rainmaker's Disciple," "Livingstone I Presume"—he was familiar with a number of the standard promotion gimmicks. Of course, there might very well have been new phrases invented by the computer brains to stir up public emotions and released since Anawari had turned his back on the white man's wonderful ways.

From the bag Ann took several biscuits and a few oranges, placed them in a small net bag fastened to the end of a long rod, and pushed the contrivance through the gateway. "Have this food. It will put strength into you."

The voice sounded so formal that Anawari guessed it to be a recording prepared for telecasting to the fascinated viewers. The biscuits were the familiar brand in the shape of a cross, the oranges looked to be from the same crop as those kept in the basket at the Welfare Centre, and Anawari backed away; but his distaste was less for the suspect food than for the apparatus on which it hung, and which reminded him uncomfortably of the previous night's dream. In expectation of a lasso darting out to clasp him around the shoulders, Anawari shuffled backward and flattened his body against the wall of rock.

"You poor soul, you need some covering." Ann pulled the rod

expertly back and hooked some old clothing to it. "Look here now, we call this a T-shirt, you put it over your head . . . like this . . . you see? Now, this piece—this is a pair of shorts. You must slide your legs through these two openings, you see? You can do it, I'm sure." The rod came swaying toward Anawari—again with the clothes attached—but he raised his hands in front of his face to ward it off. "Yes, yes, I know you want to thank us but . . . don't try to talk, it will make you feel worse. Goodness, what a nasty wound you have on your face . . . you really mustn't talk."

Ann was making quite sure that Anawari had no chance to speak and spoil the whole show, in which she played the star part of the noble savior, or did she expect him to act too? Perhaps the script called for him to hesitate until Ann came closer and then, in a sudden outburst of fury, to rip off her clothes and rape her; the viewers would certainly enjoy seeing that in full color on the small screen in their very own homes. Maybe Anawari's role called for him to hold Ann hostage for a while so that the viewing public could thrill to the glories of her self-sacrificing endeavor. But in the end, of course, the "baddie" would surrender and walk meekly out through the gate as though overcome by Ann's force of will—it was a great pity that the television audience would miss all that, for Anawari had no intention of costarring in such a farce.

"Oh, dear me, they've smashed your face with a club, have they? That's such a savage tool you people call *irama*; it must have been quite a tribal brawl you got into." Ann passed through the gate, walking cautiously and carrying a first-aid kit conspicuously in her hand, with the rope still attached to the helicopter winch paying out slowly behind her as she moved. "What a savage mob. They must have positively danced on you. Let me wash off the filth—there's a pile of germs in those wounds. Do you know, five hundred and fifty of your tribes have perished because the poor ignorant natives didn't know about antiseptic. Yes! Truly!"

Anawari had seen many would-be saviors in his time—the one he was watching now performed worse than any of them.

187

In the beginning the world was divided into water and sand—that happened before trees came about. They rose from the sea, so our tjamu say. They came out together with narngi, frogs, to search for food on the land. While they were out, a dust storm caught them in flat open country; narngi hopped back to the sea, but the trees lost their way and as night fell made their camp on the floor of a large claypan. When in an unknown country one grows scared; the plants cling together to stay brave and spread their roots into the warm sand, so that the leaves will not grow stiff on chilly nights. None knew about waru, fire, then, for the plants do not believe that you will get any warmth from burning your own limbs.

While camping, the trees feared that the sand might creep in during the night and cover the claypan. What is the good of sleeping anyway, if you are to wake up buried up to your neck? The trees kept awake by clattering their branches, as men would do nowadays by clapping their boomerang against their spear, for no soul likes to be swallowed silently by the desert.

At floor of a claypan
gum trees gathered for camp
    Into ground
    cling on
    with your claws
The chant brought about birds, for the birds have beady eyes and are the first to see that grains of sand have stopped moving. The birds also have sharp calls to wake up every soul to come out and hold back the tide of the desert.

The trees have long since spread across the country, though some of them are still there camping in that claypan halfway across the desert to the sea. When last there, I saw a whole grove of them—all tribal elders—shedding an old limb or two occasionally, but still holding on. The sand has banked up against some of the trunks, but no desert could gulp a tall fellow grown up to the armpit of the sky. On their top branches perch cockatoos on the lookout; the birds screech as soon as they see a storm. When warned, their fellow trees prop up on their wooden crutches and aim toward the sky. It takes more than a sandstorm to swallow them.

CHAPTER 19

Much must have occurred while Anawari was unconscious or, at least, too dazed to be aware, for his next lucid moments found him lying in the bottom of a cage on the back of a moving truck, and wearing a pair of striped shorts and a light yellowish T-shirt, in which Ann must have dressed him, for he could not recall putting them on himself.

Across the front of the T-shirt were printed words now so faded as to be almost indecipherable, but when he pulled the material outward from his body, Anawari found he could read SAVE LONDON FROM SI—"sinking," he supposed—and the line below spelled GIVE GEN . . . generously. Yes, Ann had tried to con him once into being the convenor of the Save London Appeal. What a pity—his lips twitched in an ironical grimace—if I had gone on a trip to London, I could have written to Ruwe in the Himalayas from there.

The striped shorts occupied Anawari's attention far more than the shirt, though they had no slogans printed on them, for they were most uncomfortable. Too loose in the waist, they were constantly slipping down, exposing a good deal of bare backside, but when Anawari tried to pull them up, he found it an impossible task unless he could stand up; the top of the cage, little more than two feet from the floor, forced him into a kneeling position with the back of his head cracking painfully against the steel bars each time the truck struck a bump in the road. Anawari gave up the struggle; perhaps there would be a more auspicious moment to pull up the shorts, and hopefully it would come before the nationwide television cameras started turning again.

Through the back window of the truck Anawari could see the driver's bare shoulders, caked with dust and sweat, and he tried to call out to the man to slow down, but all his aching jaws emitted was a whisper far too weak to be heard above the rattling of the bounding truck. Anawari's head still throbbed painfully in spite of the fresh bandage around his temples, and he pressed his palms to his forehead, trying to ease the maddening pulse. One end of the bandage had become loose, and flapped now and then across Anawari's one good eye, but he succeeded in imprisoning it under his clasping fingers so that his view of the road was unimpaired— it seemed best to know just where his captors were taking him.

As the truck rolled down the main street, faces could be seen peeping out from doorways or shop windows; a pair of eyes would dart a glance at Anawari, disappear quickly, and then reappear a moment later in company with a dozen others, but no one shouted or gestured at him. The people seemed surprised rather than angry, in fact, but Anawari supposed that this was only because his capture had not been announced, and had found them unprepared.

The truck kept moving, perhaps hurrying to whisk Anawari away from the township and the mob before the news of his capture could spread and then . . . What would they do with him? A sudden suspicion sprang into Anawari's mind and took his breath away for a second, but as he reconsidered, a smile twitched one corner of his mouth. So, what if they did take him back to the settlement. It would be the happiest thing they could do. Anawari fell to wondering in which of the four camps the whites would choose to place him, and to what tribe he would cleave for support, and his heart lifted in something like excitement in anticipation of seeing the old folk again. Although he well knew that there was little brightness in what life had to offer at any of the camps, the prospect of sharing his despair with others of his

own kind promised more comfort to Anawari now than an unnatural existence among the whites. Would I also go out in a puff
of smoke through the chimney of that hospital? Surely I am contaminated.

Surprisingly, the truck came to a halt in the parking area of a
pub near Prospector Square; the driver got out and slammed the
cab door shut. Anawari watched him walk heavily away—the
weight of two men carried by one pair of legs, and wearing only
a pair of unbecoming striped shorts. Above the waist, across the
flabby sweating sunburnt skin, stretched a brightly colored tattoo
reading "Get an Abo" embellished with hearts and roses, and as
Anawari watched the door of the hotel close behind the grotesque
figure, he tried to decide which had disgusted him more—the
obese bulk of the man, or the message on his back?

The material, design, and size of the driver's shorts and his own
were almost identical, and Anawari found a row of marks on the
waistband of those he wore, in evidence of the places where the
top button once had been. Such striped shorts must have been
made in one store only, and the previous owner had once filled
them—but later he must have begun to shrink and, as he grew
smaller and smaller each day, had moved the button—attached
to the cloth by a twist of wire—farther and farther across until . . . it
seemed that his stomach must have all but disappeared, and curved
inward to touch his backbone.

In one of the shorts pockets Anawari discovered a piece of
paper the shape of a business card, printed on one side with a
picture of a lighted candle encircled by barbed wire, and the words
AMNESTY INTERNATIONAL, and on the back . . . the pen marks were
almost indecipherable but when he exposed them to the full sunlight Anawari could just make out the blurred words: "This is to
certify that the prisoner Father Namir was interviewed, but failed
to qualify for any of the political categories. Field Officer . . . "
and signed by bold strokes of a purple pen.

Poor Namir—for a moment Anawari found some comfort in
the fact that his trouble might not be so distressing as his schoolmate's, if the second worst could be any consolation. He remem-

bered seeing the symbol of candle and wire before in a large newspaper advertisement, but long ago, and certainly before he had developed his cynicism regarding the whites; why would anyone build a jail for Aborigines and then come calling with offers of consolation? Maybe Namir appeared to some as being of mixed race and so had misled the "do-gooders" into mistaking him for a part-African or a European, and therefore deserving of compassion.

A man whose face was obscured under a solar topee strolled self-consciously about the parking area carrying a bag with the zip partly open. He placed the bag on the truck tray, leaned conspiratorially against the cage, and whispered: "I've got some of the stuff here."

He pulled the cork of a flagon hidden inside the bag, and pushed his finger into the container and then through the bars of the cage; a smell of wine, but strongly flavored with some other scent, assailed Anawari's nostrils.

"Smell that! The best booze you'll ever drink."

"No, thank you." Anawari held his nose.

"It's wine blended with petrol. New stuff developed especially to suit your mob. Try some!"

Anawari knew that many Aborigines sniffed petrol but doubted if any did so because of the smell or the taste; he had never tried it himself, but presumed that for many others, worse off than he had been, anything that would numb their minds and carry them off from awful reality might seem pleasurable. "Have you any water in that bag?" he asked.

"Sorry. I have no license to deal in water. But look here, this stuff will kill your thirst just the same."

"I have nothing to pay you with."

The man pressed his lips close to the bars. "A piece of opal will do me nicely, thanks."

"But I have none."

The man smiled. "Come on, now. You can be frank with me, mate—I know that you have worked for Michael, the Wog."

"We dug uranium only."

"C'mon now—there's still those shining opal lumps about. You must have struck some. Let's make a deal, hmmm?" It seemed incredible to the man that Anawari had smuggled no opal, but even if he had, where, in his meager clothing, could he have hidden it? And supposing there were treasure left hidden in the mine shaft, who would take his word for it?

The man in the topee grew restless. "Look here, mate, the Kangaroo Court is about to begin, and if they catch you sticking to those bloody stones, you'll have had it! Good and proper!"

"When is it to be held—this Kangaroo Court?"

"This afternoon. We haven't had a decent show like this since we dealt with Father Namir years ago. In the good old days there would be two or three trials a day. . . . We had more court hearings than we had church services in those days—three gallows working at the one time—really great. Now, of course, the Kangaroo Court and all that stuff is done by the machine. . . . Listen, are you absolutely sure that you have no opal?"

The man sounded so keen to make a deal that Anawari felt really sorry that he had nothing to offer. He recalled, with regret, the piece of opal Gara had shown him as they lay among the rocks at the tunnel's mouth. Would a piece as big as that save a man his skin? Anawari felt ashamed about thinking of trading off the sacred *tjurunga* to buy his freedom. Would that freedom be worth anything, anyway?

"You boys must have worked pretty hard. Michael, the Wog, never failed to meet his quota. The mob could be very nasty here after such a long drought, you know." The peddler said no word of what had happened to Michael.

The pain in Anawari's jaw had been steadily increasing until it finally excluded any other thought, but the man talked maddeningly on, gesturing toward a larger trailer caravan parked near the back door of the pub. "That computer there could be quite kind, I'm sure, if there was enough opal to share around; everyone would have to get a decent cut."

Anawari's words were muffled as he pressed his hands against the agony in his jaw: "Well actually, we had struck a good find

in that shaft but we had to get out suddenly, we hadn't time . . . "
The pain stabbed again and Anawari dropped his head to his knees.

The man's face was alight with greed. "Hang on, old man. I'll
get you some water." He ran quickly across the car park and
inside the trailer. Anawari put his hand against his forehead over
the clumsy bandage, trying to remember the position of the find,
how far it had been from the main shaft, and how good it had
really been—but then . . . did it really matter; a decent cut for
everyone? No! A mountain of solid opal would not buy him out
of this situation and the "decent cuts." Let that *tjurunga* lie in the
dust or be melted by some new nuclear blast rather than be des-
ecrated.

Anawari had only hearsay information about Kangaroo Courts
and had only once been present at a legal hearing—so long ago
that there was little left in his memory of that distant event—so
his preconceptions of "bush" trials were few and highly colored.
Most reports had been from Aborigines whose relatives were
brought before a Kangaroo Court and had not lived to tell the
story themselves, and Anawari wondered whether whites ever
met the same fate nowadays, or if it was a judicial privilege reserved for the black man.

Squeezed there, in the narrow confines of the cage in the blazing
sun, Anawari tried to recall everything that he had ever heard
about the Kangaroo Court in order to prepare himself in some
way for whatever was to come. Such bush trials, he knew, had
been commonplace in the far outback, wherever white settlers
ganged together, on cattle stations or remote settlements, to dis-
pose of those who displeased them; Aboriginal man had often
been charged for spearing a cow, for stealing a billy of water, or
for nothing more than being "without fixed address" or "without
adequate means of support"—accusations that could be leveled
with validity at every Aborigine. The nearest official court of law
often lay hundreds of miles away, few could see the need to send
a man to a proper hearing of which he would understand not a
single word, and so the locals took the law into their own hands
before anyone should have trouble with his conscience. Anawari

remembered an immense tree at least twelve feet in diameter at its base and partly hollow inside; he remembered scores of great iron staples—enough to accommodate the chains of a whole tribe as they waited their turn to be tried; he remembered the way the new young bark had bulged up around the rusting belts, marked here and there with fresh axe cuts clearing the way to allow a chain through the iron loop. How did he remember that? Where had he seen it? When . . . ?

"Do you plead guilty or not guilty?"

The voice came from the computer, revealed through an open panel in the side of the trailer. The machine paused, bleeping impatiently as it waited for him to confess. Inside the van, behind the computer, sat one of the Twins facing Anawari in the cage, and beside the trailer on a small platform, shaded by a canvas canopy, was an incongruous stage setting. Superintendent Hunt and Dr. Tinto were the central figures with the sergeant, who lolled as if disinterested—his elbows on his knees and his face buried in his hands as if he slept; next to the sergeant sat the other Twin, and to her left stood two empty chairs. Anawari knew who should occupy those chairs to complete the case of this drama, and he wondered which lady would be the first to arrive—Ann or Laura?

Behind the truck, on the farther side of the parking area, someone stamped on their accelerator and roared away with a scream of tires. "Silence . . . silence . . . silence!" The computer reacted quickly through its loudspeaker; the recorded sound of a judge's gavel slammed out, then hammered again . . . and again—a malfunction in the machine had made a mockery of solemn judicial authority, and Anawari could not help smiling as the Twin fiddled frantically with the computer buttons to silence the ridiculous drumming.

"Guilty or not guilty?"

Anawari opened and shut his mouth without forming any words. Where had I seen that huge tree?

"Cooperate or"—the computer whirred and chugged—"or . . . you will be held in contempt of the Crown."

The Twin sat straight and motionless. In front of her, scarcely a palm's breadth from her face, a dragonfly shimmered in the air, yet she did not even blink, reminding Anawari of the marble statue of the Queen in the main hall at school, to which as a student he had to bow every morning.

"You have been conspiring with your ancestors to withhold rain with the intention . . . intention . . . intention . . . " Only now, Anawari noticed the large trunk in front of the jury; the box looked slightly bigger now than when he had last seen it under his bed. Anawari wondered about the key hanging from the open lock, but soon realized that it, as well as the lock, had been made by the whites. "You have also been found in possession of a map marking secret nuclear sites, which you intended to destroy." Excited, the machine kept repeating for a while: "Destroy the whole country, the world, destroy . . . " Then it settled down to a routine run: "Guilty or not guilty?"

"Guilty. My client pleads guilty, your honor."

The man speaking on Anawari's behalf was the same gentleman who had tried to sell him the drink, wearing just the same clothes but with the addition of a barrister's wig—the only item of professional pageantry that could connect this farce with a proper court of law. It seemed that there were no set rules of procedure for the court save one—Anawari noticed that his "counsel" had a limited area in which to move, and that was a rectangular space, bounded by white lines, next to the truck and much similar to a spot marked out for car parking. The bush lawyer paced within his limited domain glancing from jury to computer to client, and so carried away was he by his own importance that he stepped, now and then, over the white-painted boundary line. Then the computer, programmed for perfection and incapable of inexactitude, emitted shrill piping noises to inform the lawyer that he had transgressed, and each time the warning bleeps sounded, the Twin in charge pulled a lever and produced a resounding thump on a drum.

The prosecution, on the other hand, had far more space in which to operate—an entire row of parking rectangles stretching from

197

the computer trailer to the jury platform, and running back against the hotel's toilet block. Counsel for the prosecution, the fat truck driver, was busy rushing from one member of the jury to the next giving each a long sheet of paper, which Anawari assumed to be a list of charges—and then running back to check with each juror that every single offense was noted and understood.

Anawari wished he could see the list; he had expected to be charged with treason, but it would seem that the whites and the computer had formed an alliance to include every possible offense imaginable—or was the list merely another stage property in this crazy play, made long and impressive-looking to increase its appearance of importance? Anawari watched the prosecutor hastening between members of the jury, marking the papers with a large pen, pointing out documents, one by one, into the machine. The flabby body was not built for such haste in the boiling sun, and before his task was halfway completed, the Crown prosecutor was seen to drag his bulk away from the court of law and disappear behind the wall marked GENTS.

. . . Where have I seen that tree?

The computer sprang suddenly to life and without any apparent reason bellowed, "Silence . . . silence . . . silence!" followed by imperious slammings of a judge's gavel; the call for silence was heard again and the same hammering was repeated over and over until Anawari had the feeling he was watching a dog chasing its own tail. The Twin knocked a few times on the top of the computer and the machine's erratic behavior stopped, but not permanently, for as the silence grew, under the hot sun in the parking area, the impatient computer grew restive. It coughed now and then as a hint to the court, then produced the sound of the gavel, and each time it was heard, the Twin pulled the lever and responded with a bang on the drum.

. . . Where was that huge tree? In his mind Anawari saw, again, the row of bolts and knew that, if he thought about it a little, he would remember exactly how many of them were nailed into the trunk; he felt that he must have not only seen the tree but touched it with his hands as well. If he had only been told about the tree, in a story, it would not have become so clearly etched in his mind, surely; and no dream ever remained in such detail after one woke— but there was more to this than just a huge hollow tree used for chaining blacks. Anawari's thoughts were drawn to the times he had wakened from a dream bathed in sweat, and so shattered by terror that he had spent the rest of the night staring into the darkness and trying to recall the precise nature of the dream that had disturbed him so much. Why was he remembering that? Had he dreamed of the tree, but wanted to forget? As Anawari delved deeper in his mind in pursuit of the distant dream, he suddenly saw Nupuru's face rising from the misty dark, and though Ana-wari clung to that friendly face, it lingered only a moment before dissolving again without having said anything to help solve the riddle of the tree. Without knowing why, Anawari suddenly wished he knew how many dogs Nupuru had; he had never counted them, but now he felt that his mind would rest easier if he had. It is believed that every dog has sprung into life from the soul of a dead relative and so, for the rest of its life, stays with you; a tribal elder would know each animal by name, from its human existence, but would not chat idly about it—not necessarily because he did not trust you, but because one should not talk about the deceased. How many dogs? How many . . . ? Would Namir and I become dogs too? And Ily, he should turn into one also.

Anawari's attention was attracted by a lorry pulling in next to him, to occupy that same rectangle where the bush lawyer had previously stood; the vehicle carried a cage of the same size and design as the one around him and . . . Gara was crouched there, locked inside; it was not the happiest place to find an old friend, and Anawari wondered whether he should smile, or demonstrate his regret that they should meet here in a Kangaroo Court. Anawari hissed to attract Gara's notice and then glanced quickly at the court—the computer lay in silence. In the shade, under the canopy, the entire jury was dozing in the heat, their heads dropping, in turn, foward and back, like dolls.

Anawari hissed again, then realizing that the truck beneath him had begun slowly to move, he hung onto the bars and called to his erstwhile companion; Gara's head turned slowly and Anawari saw his face, filled with the strange calm of a man who has nothing left but his soul, and even that overdue for departure to the spirit world. Anawari had seen such serenity only once before—on the face of the old man waiting to die out there in the bush.

As the truck moved farther, Gara's face was hidden by the lorry's cabin and only the top of his cage was visible, but beyond it the court was reconvening; the fat man was on his way back from the GENTS with his barrister's wig, soaked with water, dripping rivulets down his tattooed back. Anawari covered his face and blotted out the scene as he felt the jerk of the truck moving into top gear and gathering speed.

Only three, or perhaps four, miles had been covered when the truck slowed and then came to a halt, and, peering through the bars, Anawari saw a small airplane parked on the edge of a dusty airstrip. A tall moustached man lounging against the machine acknowledged the arrival of the truck and its burden with only a glance and a quirk of the lips, which Anawari could not define as either a smile or a sneer. Friend or foe? . . . It no longer seemed necessary to know, for Anawari, so strangely relaxed, felt that nothing held any importance for him anymore; he had grown to realize—was it hours or days ago?—that he had been in one kind of cage or another all his life.

The moustached man twitched again—no, he could not be a friend, even if he wished to be friendly, for in his new wisdom Anawari recognized the impossibility of the situation. There were whites who were genuinely saddened and concerned for Anawari's kind. They sympathized with a race uprooted from their tribes, transplanted into the white man's world, and left with little future and the almost unbearable burden of not knowing who they were, and why they were alive—but the best-intentioned help and care from those whites was aimed at assimilating the Aborigines into an alien world, which must end in destroying him totally. The white man cannot help but be a foe.

The driver of the truck sprang out, marched smartly to the moustached man, and stood to attention: "Major! Sir!"

Anawari had the feeling he was watching a story enacted on the cinema, and wished he could walk out on such a farfetched, unlikely tale.

"Let him out of the cage."

The driver was obviously doubtful. "Without drugs or handcuffs? What if he gets loose, Sir?"

"Oh, he's harmless enough," interrupted the major.

"But, Sir, he seems very savage to me. . . ."

"Go on, let him out. There's nowhere to run and he knows that as well as I do."

Anawari had heard that voice somewhere before, he was sure, but was it a friend of Ann's? . . . some visitor to the hospital? . . . or was one white man so much the footprint of another that their voices sounded identical?

Bolt cutters nipped the lock, but before the cage door fell open, the driver had dropped the tool, grabbed a gun, and begun backing slowly away.

"He's that same man we had before."

"Not exactly. We got the Reverend this time, not the Father. They are from the same tribe; perhaps the same mother as well."

"They look very alike, Sir."

"The one we had earlier was a disciple of Patupiri—the old man. This one here is taught by a Para medicine man. We should have tattooed numbers on their ears, perhaps as they do to captured dingoes."

For some time now Anawari had felt he was following Namir's track—the closer he came to his old mate, the more alike their faith looked. Should they ever meet, it was uncertain, however, if it would bring either of them any good.

"Come, climb aboard," called the major from the airplane— again the voice struck a chord in Anawari's memory, but even though he paused to stare at the major before he settled himself in the passenger's seat, Anawari could not be sure where, or even if, they had met before.

From the claypan the trees spread out to populate the country they had moved into, wondering about like a pack of dingoes, or tribal families for that matter, each having its own skin name. Having different bark and differently shaped leaves, each speaks his own lingo, for whether in the skin of a plant, animal, or human, you have to talk. The trees chat a lot to pass on news of well-moisturized soil or to tell one another to edge their leaves against the hot noon sun and not grow dry. That is why the trees hold on together. They move about in groves like dingoes in a pack, and if a tree is left alone, it will howl, for no soul likes to be stranded in a vast country on its own. Not all country is made of loamy, soft soil; coming up against rocky ground, the trees sharpened their roots and their limbs grew tougher. On reaching the ridges, the groves halted. No one yet knew how to climb up the bare boulders, and the trees that tried soon turned into reptiles—such was the crossing of the world. The trees regrouped in a gully, at the foot of the mountain. They climbed on each other; propped against the boulders, they aimed toward the sky. A whole grove of trees standing on each other stretched under the armpit of the sky. The trees grew prickly leaves, and if you tickle the soft belly of the clouds, the sky weeps—that is how the rain comes about and the plants grow taller.

In country of desert clans
trees grow sky tall fingers
Belly of clouds
laden with rain
—tickled by leaves

202

Looking over the ranges at last, the trees saw endless plains of sand dotted by claypans. Nothing can hold us any longer, they told themselves. Saturated by water, sand grows soft and the roots spread fast. Down from the ranges and across the plain, the country grew from red to green. No one thought of drought then or knew what it would be like to live through one.

PART THREE

CHAPTER 20

t was night when they landed, and Anawari saw nothing but darkness all around; however, when he awoke next morning a large glass window gave him a sweeping view of his surroundings. An immense plain stretched away below, smooth and pale like the surface of a calm desert coated with red. The sand looks strikingly red around here, he told himself. It was only when Anawari had jumped out of bed, walked onto the veranda and leaned over the railing that he realized that the plateau actually was water—the surface of a lake from which rose tendrils of morning mist. The house in which Anawari had spent the night stood on high ground that sloped sharply down to the water's edge—a ragged line that extended far beyond the point where his eyes could follow and that, in several places, penetrated deep into the body of the lake with spurs of land like bony human fingers. One arm of the water far longer than the others stretched far inland in the shape of an emu's neck and extended at the end forming the shape of the bird's head. Welcome home then, Anawari told himself. As the morning mist began to disperse, the outline of an immense boomerang rose from the water: Anawari waited for the morning sun to appear on the top of the dry tree trunks or nearby cliffs, but nothing showed and the blurred outline of the island looked as though the boomerang were floating on the murky water.

Between the nearest high ground and the slope upon which Anawari stood, a tongue of water had formed a small bay, and on the sloping shore of this, on the very brink of inundation, stood a belt of dying forest with its bare upper branches tinted red by the morning sun. The scene was one not unfamiliar to someone who had spent his life in the vastness of the Australian interior, witnessing the wind transforming tracts of gray-green scrub into a sea of red sand, and drought sucking the dry course of rivers already long dead and reduced to piles of gibber—yet this time Anawari had a feeling that the familiarity was more intimate; he sensed that he had been, sometime, on the lake's shore, and had seen the forest before it had become as petrified and ugly as it now looked.

Nyinyi flew from around the corner of the house and fluttered in the air a few feet away from Anawari. The bird seemed to be looking for somewhere to perch, but seeing no stump or scrub suitable, it rose again in the air and swooped in a straight line over the slope of the hill toward some dead gum trees. Anawari watched the bird as it headed toward the valley, knowing that finches usually move about in pairs but that the bird that is a spirit always flies alone.

The major's voice interrupted: "This must be a scene to gladden your heart. A missionary wrote once that a tribal fellow could suffer a stroke in his dream from catching a glimpse of his country."

Anawari turned to look at the man standing barely a foot away, and then he knew that it was the same pilot with whom he had shared a bottle of Bacardi at his old home in the settlement. Anawari wondered whether to address the man as "Ranger" again, or pretend that recognition had not dawned.

"I will take you on a guided tour through the whole area later. The old tribal magic should be there; no blast could wipe that out, so they say."

It was obviously time to ask the major why they were here, and yet Anawari hesitated, not only from habitual reticence, but because he was not aware that of the many questions he had asked of white men in his lifetime, nearly none had been answered with any truth.

"Breakfast won't be ready yet awhile, so in the meantime I'll brief you, Reverend. You don't mind me calling you that?" The major led the way into a room with partly the appearance of an office, and mostly of something else, which Anawari found himself unable to define. Not only did the character of the place confuse him but he was also at a loss to know what behavior was expected of him as a visitor. Anawari stood a while in the doorway looking at a map on the wall—an enlarged copy of the one seen with Ily, except it had a number of crosses in blue pen on Boomerang Island and Pulkarin Cliff on the mainland. On the old dusty map the markings looked recent and Anawari wondered if they had anything to do with the nuclear testing. The whites are still about, so he cautioned himself and, not wishing to be caught staring at the map, rested his eyes on a pair of *kulata,* long hunting spears, that hung crisscross above a single *kali,* boomerang. The spears must have been much used by their original owners, for the middle section of both still retained the shine left upon the surface of the wood by constant contact with a sweating palm. The major observed the spears also. "We recovered them from one of the first blasting sites. The sand had melted things there, but look—the spears have come out magically intact. Fascinating—wouldn't you say?" The man held an old boomerang and, swinging it about as an officer would do with a swagger stick, knocked it against the spears on the wall and let a clattering sound of dry hard wood echo throughout the room. "Look, some parts of the spears have aged more than others." The boomerang was now pointing to a spearhead to compare with the shaft of that same tool, which appeared much older. "Fascinating!" The man obviously knew little about *kulata* or pretended so; the spearheads, *wata,* were almost new, but those are replaceable parts which, with the aid of *kiti,* spinifex gum, are mounted on the main spear shaft and then bound fast with kangaroo or emu sinew that the hunter has softened by chewing and by running it between his teeth. A spearhead becomes quickly worn and is blunt after only one or two hunts, so it must be replaced often, but the main shaft is painstakingly fashioned from a flexible branch of the *urtjanpa* bush and is not so easily come by when the only tool to hand is a sharpened stone, so one might serve the hunter for many years.

The spear clattering went on. "We did send them to the Research Institute down at the N.D.A., but they had no answer. Fascinating! I wish your ancestor Nupuru was here to tell us more about this."

No man knew more about spears than Nupuru; when on that desert journey together, he had taught Anawari to make one. Inlaid into the bottom end of each *kulata* is a hollow tube called *palka*, which is carefully whittled to exactly fit into a *miru mukulpa*, the projecting heel on the hunter's spear-launching device. The throwing stick supports the spear, with delicate balance, on this pivot at its hindmost point; the hunter manipulates the throwing stick, and the spear flies, untrammeled, on its way. Just as one can judge the age of a man by the lines on his face, so one can judge the years of a spear by the depth and smoothness of the hollow end of its shaft.

"Would you like to have a go at throwing them?"

One never throws the spear of a dead hunter.

"Do sit down, old man. I'm sorry I can't offer you anything to smoke or drink—but I have to get you back in tune with your traditional habitat." The major tapped the boomerang several times against his thigh and said: "There seems to be much more to life than just molecules and atoms, as we know now. I have an immense task to find that out." The boomerang pointed to the empty space in the room and halted as though those extra components of life the whites were searching for had been located. "It would be much simpler if your ancestor Nupuru came forward and talked to us. But yours and my worlds prefer to remain secretive." Anawari felt uncertain about what the major was after, except that he behaved like a man ordered to map an unchartered desert and was about to ask for the way. At least he sounded sincere—in the beginning they often do. Once, what must have been generations ago, Nupuru found a white explorer stranded deep in the desert. With his packhorses dead and water a whole world away, the man opened a vein in one of his legs and tried to drink his blood instead. Nupuru cut a hole in *nalta*, a kurrajong trunk, and collected some sap, which brought the white man back to life. Then he led him across the desert to an everlasting *gabi* known only to tribal elders and spirits. Shady trees grew around the *gabi*, giving the traveler a nice place to recover, and the water was abundant with fish and birds, for it never dried. When he recovered, the white man told Nupuru, "It is so wonderful here—just the right place to build myself a new homestead." Anawari now had no fear of being robbed of the land, for his country had been lost already. The major kept talking about the area, frequently pointing the old boomerang to the island on the map and swinging it about in his hand, as though trying to chase some unseen intruders from the room. Anawari wanted to thank him for being rescued from the Kangaroo Court, but waited to hear first if he had been saved for better or worse. It mattered less now what the whites wanted of him. Ever since he had begun to rebel, his way of thinking and the words he used had changed—more so recently. Perhaps he had come close now to that gratifying moment when his shape would change as well. The desert tribes believe that people change into animals and plants; he too should be given that honor—good old Nupuru will see to that. Looking forward to that, Anawari had for some time hoped to return to his tribal bush, though he never expected to be brought back by the major or by any of the whites. Nupuru told him once, "Man never dies beyond his own country," and he believed that would happen to him too. Even at those times when he was particularly hard-pressed and it had seemed that the remainder of his life could be measured in minutes, still he had been convinced that there would be enough time granted him to make his way to *tjamu ngura*. It was that naked and humble hope, if nothing else, that had sent him crawling on, through the mess that others might call life. In the moments of darkest despair Anawari had clung to the thought that, even if his body was prevented from reaching his own country, his spirit would certainly get there.

"We have to get onto old Nupuru." The boomerang still swung about. Anawari guessed that he would be asked to spy on his medicine man; actually he had done that for years, informing on his tribal relatives, but now since the major did not request him to wear a clergyman's cloth, Anawari found the present situation complimentary. The major told him of the detainees held on Boomerang Island to test the impact of the nuclear blast. The boomerang in his hand pointed to the stretch of lake between the island and the testing sites on the mainland. "Hardly a whisker away." Which side is he on? thought Anawari, feeling that he was about to learn the fate of his tribal relatives. How many of them were there? He glanced through the window; the morning mist had cleared, revealing a stretch of bare land that looked like a barkless log thrown out into the lake. How many?

The major explained that some people survived miraculously just like the spears. "Fantastic, I would like to get to the bottom of that." Anawari understood that they were talking about the power of healing and suggested that *nangari* would know all about that. The major must have thought of Nupuru already and said, "That man performed quite a miracle here." He explained that after the nuclear explosion, people had seen Nupuru walking across the lake surface followed by the detainees. They had crossed from Boomerang Island to the mainland and disappeared into the desert. "They say it was like Moses leading his people across the sea— fantastic." The major lashed the boomerang against his thigh. Anawari still felt uncertain about what was wanted from him, though now that seemed of little importance. The whites must know that he had changed—man cannot hide the way he talks or thinks. When he was in the settlement, Laura had cautioned him twice, "Tread carefully." The trees and animals are cunning in hiding how they feel; he was not a tree yet, but that new leaf of life—it should not be far off now. On reaching his country, he had woken into, not the green place he had hoped for, but bare desert that even the insects had vacated. Left behind were the scattered skeletons of dead trees and grains of sand. It was still his country, and whenever he glanced through the window, he had convinced himself that his home had been found at last and he should hold on to it. Anawari watched the major looking at the map and wondered why the whites had to hold on to the place any longer. There were many parts of the desert beyond the horizon, far more hospitable, and there were skeletons of dead trees elsewhere, even taller than here. "You would not be taking me back to that hospital in the settlement?" he asked. The major was thinking of something else, for it took him a while to turn away from the map and swing the boomerang. "Heavens no—I have my own assignment, far more important than manipulating genes. Dear chap, if we do not come up with rain the desert will swallow us all." Anawari had often thought that the whites had inquisitive minds, scientifically speaking. He should tell that to the major—the man seemed too eccentric to be offended. Though as white as bone and with occasional freckles on his skin, the man reminded Anawari of a tribal soul. He had watched him looking at the map, although his mind seemed to have traveled far beyond the tree skeletons and the sand. Anawari had noticed something like that only in *nangari*. Feeling slightly embarrassed at having such a complimentary thought about the major, Anawari asked him about the crosses marked on the map. "The sacred tribal sites—I inserted them; close enough, let's hope." Anawari doubted that there would have been any site of traditional significance on Boomerang Island, for it was not accessible. The desert tree tribes knew of no canoes—one could neither swim nor paddle across the salty mud. During a prolonged drought, however, one could walk over the hardened salty crust after much of the lake had evaporated. The rains are uncommon in the desert; they come about several times in your whole memory, and life has to be organized in the absence of water. Looking at the Boomerang, Anawari thought that the major had inserted the crosses there to commemorate the detainees, the way they did at an Auschwitz or other places after the war had ended. It pleased him that at last

213

he had come across someone who would respect the dead, whatever their color or creed.

"Traditionally the place belonged to Ninya." According to the major, the original island dwellers were spirits and needed no canoes to reach the mainland. From what he had gathered from Father Rotar, the missionary, Ninya were light-skinned beings and might not be related to the Aborigines. They ventured out from Boomerang Island in search of tribal women. They normally appeared during cold mornings and caused frost mirages to trick the tribal elders into thinking that the trees had turned upside down. By studying Father Rotar's diary and other papers, the major had concluded that the frost mirages were to lure the tribal men into the bush to make *inma* ceremony, and while they were away, the Ninya would sneak into the camps and abduct the tribal women. Anawari did not reveal that he knew the story already and that he thought *inma* was a ceremony to bring about rain, not to drive away the mirage. He was told further that Ninya had no children since they had no *pulkarin,* fertility rock, of their own. The rock comprises *karanita*, essence of life from plants and humans, and has something to do with bringing the rain.

Later when leading him outside for breakfast, the major halted at the doorway. "Have you ever been shown *pulkarin,* by the way?" Anawari hedged, explaining that a man could know about the particulars of fertility only after being initiated into his tribe, but the tribes are around no longer. The major told him there was a *pulkarin* near the lake and a cliff was named after it, but the rock had not withstood the nuclear blast and had eroded into a heap of sand. "Do you think that might have something to do with this drought?" Anawari cautioned himself not to say what he thought: This man knows too much and is closing in on us.

Breakfast was cooking on an open fire built on the ground a little way from the house. The major poked a stick into the hot coals and rolled out a goanna, tapped the ash off, and then cutting it in half, handed a piece to Anawari on the point of the stick. "Here, catch! It is a great honor for an Aborigine to be offered a goanna, so Father Rotar believes." The major had gone into quite a search to locate the mysterious cave referred to in the missionary's diary as being on Boomerang Island, but had found no trace of any. Perhaps there were some subterranean passages that stretched under the lake and far into the desert, but that would have been during the mythical era and they left behind nothing more than the tales in the tribal folklore. Anawari thought, however, that the myth related to rain and the greening of the desert, and Rotar would have been perhaps the only outsider who understood it wholly. That might have been achieved by befriending Nupuru and marrying his tribal sister—a relationship that the whites had difficulty in comprehending, though the major seemed to understand that more than the others. "We should have named Boomerang Island after him but the river will do, tall trees grow on the banks there; he would have liked them." The river flowed into the lake near the opposite tip of the island. On an earlier map it was named Churchill after the British politician. Now, however, it bore the name of another white man, but one who had lived in the desert long enough to learn that to survive, man has to follow certain patterns of life that have been about ever since trees and rocks came into being. Anawari had often heard about Rotar from Gara, who hardly spoke of him as a missionary, but rather as a tribal elder who had grown to believe that man and trees had to share the desert if they were to survive. If they failed, the sand would claim the world around them. "He'll turn into a tree eventually, just as every tribal soul will do," Gara had suggested often, feeling uncertain whether the people would be any better off as plants in time of prolonged drought. Feeling for a moment that he was talking to Gara about Rotar, Anawari asked heatedly, "What did he look like, the old fellow?"

"Good tan, just like an average Mediterranean, but no way could he pass for an Aborigine." The major did not say if he had ever met Rotar, though he spoke of him at some length almost sympathetically: "That missionary used to wear *kadaitja* shoes. His friend Nupuru must have given him a pair. He's so obsessed with trees, talks about them often."

The goanna was hot; Anwari put it down on the ground, and

sat on a gibber waiting impatiently for the food to cool down, for not only was he starving, but he was more than eager that this breakfast ceremony, whatever its purpose, should be over and done with. The major went on to talk about his unsuccessful search for caves on the Boomerang. Anawari suggested cunningly that he should have brought Rotar to show him the caves; he learned that the missionary had been seen around for years. He was last sighted in the desert wearing his *kadaitja* shoes, and though a team of the best trackers had been on hand, they had failed to follow him. "He's very poetic in that diary—does not distinguish trees from humans." The major looked at Boomerang Island again. "That miraculous crossing showed even on film—bit foggy though. There's something there that defies the laws of physics." He explained that the lake was to be renamed after Nupuru, not because he led his people from that island, but because he saved the life of that white explorer. History should remember such a fine example of human coexistence regardless of color or creed. "Your ancestor should be pleased to have his name on the greatest waterhole in the country. Please do eat, it must be quite a while since your last meal."

The last hot meal Anawari had eaten was back at the settlement, but he had no conception of how much time had passed since then; he did know, however, that his old way of life there was gone, for better or worse, and had been replaced by a rediscovered world of his own, tougher and more uncertain, but no harder than that normally led by any of his tribal fellows. The major wrestled with a goanna leg. "That old man Patupiri died, I gather."

You have a lot to learn about us. Anawari felt certain that the major was not very cunning and said, "Old men do depart."

"A pity, I had a nice program lined up for him—to name that Emu Neck inlet down at the lake after him."

How is it that he has not learned that Patupiri and Nupuru are one man—Anawari felt proud of his old teacher; he had always admired him as a wizard, but even greater was his admiration of the old man's skill in outwitting the whites. When they were on that holiday, secretly in the desert together, Nupuru had showed him *kadaitja* shoes—and had said, "Leave no footprints, only a track to mislead those who are hunting you." He did not see the significance of ritual shoes at first, but later it had dawned on him that in the desert, people would recognize footprints, just as one would a photograph of a face, and the shoes were made in such a way as not to reveal to trackers the direction one was traveling. Feeling triumphant, Anawari glanced aside now to conceal his cunning words: "I never met the old man. He was a good ritual leader from what I have heard. Every Para soul will mourn him."

"*Tjuta* people should mourn him too. He must have been related to that tribe as well—he felt strongly about Namir and took him as a disciple."

So, the major knows we're from *tjuta*, Blood Gum Tree people, but thinks Patupiri is merely a leader of the local Para, Ghost Gum Tree people, and that is where he is bogged. If he had learned that the same man is Nupuru, he would have realized that the elder is the spiritual leader of a whole group of tribes stretching throughout the desert.

The major found a tiny bone in his food and spat it out of the corner of his mouth. "Not many Blood Gum people are left to mourn." Would he ever learn about Nupuru? Better not to; the old man is good at covering his tracks, wears *kadaitja* shoes, and has a pack of dogs that sense if the water is poisoned. He often leaves camp unexpectedly to spring in at another about a sky away and sweeps the desert from one end to another like a willy-willy. Even when he is not about, his presence is around, for he stands not as a man, but as a spirit, and is always at hand to heal wounds. I would not betray him for the whole white man's world, Anawari reassured himself and said, "They're still a few of us about though."

"Yes, luckily we gathered up a few of you when we swept this area before the tests. Some of your generation learned the best of both worlds. Think of Ily, for instance."

There was something in the major's words that puzzled Anawari; was he going to tell him what had happened to Namir, or lead him into a trap? By now, Anawari had learned that every word said to the whites is one too many, and he swallowed his food silently.

"That friend of yours, Gara—he's not from the Tjuta, Blood Gum tribe?"

He must know Gara's tribe, surely. "He's black, speaks our lingo."

"He's not particularly dark, is he?"

I too look less dark than the others; so does Ily. "Well . . . color varies, of course, but even if he does have a drop or two of white blood—our *nangari* would put tribal *karan* in him and"—Anawari's voice dropped—"for that he has paid a terrible price." The major was obviously leading up to something; Anawari tensed himself and laid his half-eaten food aside. "Look, I don't know what is expected of me here, but I do wish you had not swapped us and given Gara to that bunch of brutes. That man has had a rough enough . . ."

The major sounded apologetic. "Don't worry, he has been in bigger trouble before—always falls on his feet."

Anawari snapped quickly, "It sounds as though you know all about us."

The major paused before answering: "We are only researching, of course. Besides, there are not too many of you left to choose from—Namir, you and . . . Ily could be next. Let's hope you do not fail."

Anawari was at a loss to follow the rules of his devious game. The major told him that Ily was completing a "fantastic job" on the Northern Border, which no white surveyor would have been able to accomplish. Though born of a mother who hardly knew more than stubbing mulga roots with her *karupa* in search of witchetty grubs, he had nevertheless inherited traditional skills to orient himself in the inhospitable desert, where many surveyors before him had failed. Anawari assumed it must have been the major who had put Ily on that project, just as he had manipulated Namir and was now trying him as well in order to get his hands on Nupuru. One does not catch a dingo by setting a smelly bait.

"That *pulkarin* boulder disintegrated under the blast, yet the people fled." The major had pulled off another goanna's leg, and was waving it about, uneaten, to punctuate his words. He took a bite, chewed silently a moment, then stood up and pointed the bone down the Pulkarin Valley. "The man who walked over the lake could surely make the rain. We should not have disturbed that bloody boulder."

A dingo doesn't wag his tail to a stranger, thought Anawari. He sensed that he was to be sent down to Pulkarin Valley and left in the bush to live the way his ancestors had for generations. There would be no hope of squeezing water from skeletons of dry trees or from grains of sand. However, at Lake Takapiri miracles do happen, and he assumed the tribal ancestors would be about to lead him out of his despair. Let's hope that the dingo won't wag its tail, he told himself. As he and the major walked slowly back toward the Landrover parked on the slope above the house, Anawari had a strong presentiment that he and the world that had brought him up were about to part forever. It had fed him false belief in love and endeavor, had pushed him down into an abyss for the pleasure of watching him struggling to drag his naked life along with him, and now had come the parting of the ways; and yet any bitterness Anawari might have felt seemed to have evaporated here in the hot, dry air. Anawari did not remember the day he was taken from the arms of his mother, but he nevertheless had lived with a deep awareness that, from that very moment, he carried an invisible scar that, as he grew, did not fade but became more painful, until finally it bled and could no longer be hidden.

Anawari could see, now, that no single human being could be called to account for the blunders of the past—for the conflict between white race and black was between two entirely separate entities, so different in all but a common desire for existence that destruction of one or the other was inevitable. There was not room for both. "Come on, hop in." The major held the car door open, and Anawari slid his body slowly into the seat; it could all be a trick, but how could he possibly refuse to play along? Even if this meant an end, Anawari promised himself to make that end a noble one. The major smiled forcefully. "Ann sends you her regards; she really fell for you, you know. Mind you, she has developed quite an interest in Ily lately."

What a wily fellow this man had turned out to be—he must know that such talk would disgust Anawari. Through the car window Anawari saw the sun glinting on the dead trees, so white against the red earth, like skeletons, and though filled with curiosity as to why he was to be pushed into this eerie world, destroyed so long ago, he soon tired of the puzzle and let the white man's strange ritual proceed unquestioned. "This is the place you took Namir to?"

Not much showed on the face of the major. "It was very wicked of his spiritual master to let him down. Let's hope Nupuru would not do that to you also."

"You've got to catch the old man first, before you can bring him here."

"A man like him is skilled in telepathy; so well, I believe, that he can be at the other end of the country and still tell you what to do. Haven't you experienced that?"

The major was concentrating hard on what he was saying and the car bounced over a large gibber. It took him some time to regain control of the steering wheel again. "What a fascinating world of communication—no nuclear blast destroys that."

A willy-willy crossed the sun-baked earth, raising a tall column of red dust. The wind, sweeping the desert like an eerie tail hanging down from the sky, moved parallel to the car. Suddenly, Anawari saw the finch again; caught in the whirling wind, the bird sank into the dust mass to rise a moment later, struggling to break away from the immense force of the wind. "Your lot never get tired of games." While he spoke, Anawari still tried to follow the finch.

"It's pure science, this is what we're concerned with. It'll benefit the whole of mankind."

They always say that, did so when they mustered children from the bush, did so when they confined the tribal people on that island down there, did so when they blasted the country. The willy-willy swung toward the cluster of dead trees and veiled a large dry skeleton. Under the onslaught of the wind, the trunk gave up and pieces of disintegrating limbs flew out of the whirl-pool of dust, scattering over the desert. Bones and dust, there seems to be nothing else. Tjuta, my country, I have come back to you, sighed Anawari.

During long droughts trees shed their leaves and clatter their teeth through-out the night. Stripped of bark, trees bathe in the moonlight—in waterless country no trees grow to the length of a spear. That is how the first boomerang came about—a piece of wood bent by drought.

With the first boomerang at hand, the trees tossed it about to chase away grains of sand, but they learned that to make the desert retreat you need good rain. The world knew of no nangari or his magic shell to bring about clouds, so the trees went on cropping boomerangs, and when throwing them away rattled their dry leaves to help the tools fly farther. One of them flew beyond the desert, hit a cloud on the horizon, and dragging it back, broke the drought.

   Gum trees grow boomerangs
   long enough to fetch the rain
     Flying boomerangs
     drag clouds
     inland from sea

When it came, the first rain descended in torrents for a whole moon, turning the desert plain into a lake. The trees did not mind having the country engulfed in a flood. Once soaked, the sand stays wet in the ground below. Without the water about, trees would grow no limbs, nor would there be any young shoots stretching out toward the sky to tickle the soft bellies of the clouds. No rain comes uninvited; the clouds live in a distant sea and when wandering into the desert they carry water about in their big bellies. The trees have a way of telling how full each belly is and by tickling them can make the clouds empty their bladders. Full clouds do not venture into the country so often, and once the rain is about, the trees drink a lot. They store the water in their roots, in the pith of their stems or under the bark, and keep that to give man a drink when he is about.

CHAPTER 21

The last rain had probably fallen several years before, and when it did, the Rotar flowing through Pulkarin Valley must have been a mighty sight; the riverbanks of rusty red soil lay such a distance apart that a hunter might take an hour to walk between them where, in the now dry bed, the river had shaped its own world out of huge heaps of stone. Great boulders had been worn away, buried in the sand, and then, undermined by the water currents, were reshaped again. The stones had been on the move since time immemorial and needed only a rain or two more to reach their destiny on the bottom of the lake, thought Anawari.

"The country is all yours now," the major had said before dumping him in the wilderness. "It's up to *nanagari* now to care for you." He was now more occupied thinking of the Rotar than his own survival. The whites believe that everything should have a name of its own, but in a country with only a single river, the tribesmen needed only one word—*gabitjara*, moving water—to describe it, just as the white man has only one word each for the sun or the moon. Yet he held no bitterness about the river being named Rotar; the man must be his skin father and a good friend of Nupuru. He wished only the river was not dry—some water about, even occasional pools, if not a constant flow, would heal the scarred country. Plants are hit hard by the drought, just as humans are, he told himself.

Among the piles of stones a forest of immense gum trees had once flourished, drawing moisture from deep in the sandy ground for years after the rare falls of rain, and about their lifeless trunks lay an entanglement of spinifex, leaves, branches, pebbles, and even bones carried from upstream by the flood and stranded there when the water level fell once more. Anawari stopped at one of those embankments, where a log had become jammed between two trunks long ago and subsequently had been piled with a whole hill of flotsam; Anawari examined it as though he needed to know every detail of the tangled mass, and to calculate the size and extent of the force that had shaped it, but when he asked himself why he should be doing this, he felt a great questioning emptiness inside him. The river scene was familiar to him, somehow, from a dream or a story, and he felt an innate recognition of its importance, but it troubled him deeply that he lacked the knowledge or the instinct to know why it was so important, or even what to do next.

It came to Anawari, then, that his interest in the trees was connected with the need for water—though there was no clue to suggest just how long ago rain had fallen, it was not likely that the trees had died from drought, for such giants could survive for many years without a drop of rain. Anawari felt that his great-grandfather and even those who had lived many generations before that had probably rested in the shade of that same tree he now faced, for he had read that some gums could live on for thousands of years. Now Anawari was sorry that it had been in the white man's books he had read of a tree that was home to his *tjamu*. These trees must have been cursed, that they should die in their prime, showing no signs of decay or evidence to tell that some had died before others—all must have perished in one terrible sweep. Since trees live for centuries and often meant the only shelter for an Aboriginal family, Anawari saw them as a part of the tribal pattern, woven into the vast breadth of the semidesert; but trees were set on the earth not just for the sake of growing and sheltering, but also to feed the soul with their spectacular silhouette of leaves, twigs, and trunks thrown sharply against the sunburned soil and moving in a predictable circle as the day drew on. Nupuru had told him long ago, "No man dies with trees about—he only changes into one." Would he be about to help him as he had helped Gara and the others flee from the Boomerang? Perhaps he ought to stay away; that white man was using him as a bait! Let's hope the wise dingo would not be lured so easily, he thought.

Trees are born from black men's spirits too; Nupuru had told Anawari that. The old man would lay his hand on the trunk of a gum and smooth the bark as he told proudly of the tree's vigor, its size, and its benign behavior. "Each of these trees has sprung from the spirit of one of us—there's *karan* inside," he told Anawari. Trees, growing far taller than men, can see much farther afield, and Anawari had been fascinated to hear that they chanted to old Nupuru and told him stories; that they waved their branches to tell of the wind sweeping across the desert, slanted their leaves to the sun to tell the time of day better than the white man's watch could do, and bent their branches to show as clearly as by singing aloud, how damp the earth was and so where water might easily be found.

Perhaps the whites had learned the secret that each tree hides a man, and they were so appalled at having a murmuring forest of black fellows about, none of whom they could either chase out or intimidate into silence, that they had brought a curse upon the whole grove. No, the bomb had wiped out the country. No excuse—the whites had made it; then the country had plummeted into a marathon drought.

A *wana*, a digging stick, had to be made before the ground could be broken in search of water. Anawari found a piece of wood about the size of a spade handle, struck the end of it against a rock until enough split off to give the tool a sharp point, and then plunged it into the mixture of stones and sand. He had gouged a hole about a foot deep before he noticed the pain from the blisters that had raised themselves on the skin of his palm; the *wana* had been left too rough. Anawari cracked a stone into several pieces, chose the one with the sharpest edge, and rubbed it repeatedly against the stick, smoothing away the roughness. Before plunging the *wana* into the ground again, Anawari slipped it through his fingers, trying to detect any rough spot that had escaped the smoothing stone, and was finally satisfied with his handiwork.

When setting him free to Pulkarin Valley the major told Anawari, "Nupuru should be able to perform that miracle again." So, they might not want him to die, not in the white man's usual way, but to be part of the traditional tribal oracle the country had known for generations and something that the whites do not have their thumb on. Nupuru, yes, he was the one they were after, not him. The man smeared with goanna fat came to Anawari's mind; he had seen him from his back veranda when in the settlement. He had not asked that man if one needed *nangari* around to depart. If you are to turn into a tree, the medicine man should be about to see you through.

Anawari looked down Pulkarin Valley. The lake was not visible, but he stared into the empty vastness still trying to determine the position of the Boomerang. The whites like to believe in the miracle of men walking across the lake, though they think no human could turn into a tree. It is because they have not seen *karan*. Nupuru would be the only one around to see that little speck of life, but he would successfully withhold the secrets of the rain. The major hopes to catch *karan* of rain, but you don't track that little thing with flying monsters and scanners—the machines are made to crush the country. Growing life belongs strictly to the tribal healer; he knows how to walk across the lake or turn man into a tree and let him grow again—no man's gadget could track that. Let's see if there is some water about; no new life could begin without it, Anawari told himself. He guessed that if there was any water to be found, it would be in the vicinity of a small sandy depression below the embankment piled against the tree trunk. At a depth of some feet a trace of moisture indeed appeared, but it was too little to be of use. Anawari began to burrow under the pile of debris, knowing that if any frogs existed, they would be lying buried in the coolest sand, and that with a bit of luck they might still have some water stored in their bellies; he had drunk such water once before, when on walkabout in the bush with Nupuru, and though its flavor was not the best—even the old man was not terribly impressed with it—the few drops of liquid had given them strength to go on.

After *karan* leaves Anawari's body, it will hang around for a while hiding in the river debris or under pebbles, too small to be noticed by the major or Ily if he comes around with his scanners. No soul is foolish enough to shoot into life from a pile of dry sand. *Karan* is like seed; it hangs on to the ground awaiting a good rain to spring out. Rain could be years away, Anawari warned himself, feeling unhappy that he might have to wait for so long. There ought to be some water about; even damp sand under the riverbed would help life spring into being again and get hold of the ground. Once they have taken root, young trees are like old ones—they can be dormant for years waiting for rain. Once the rain comes and the ground grows wet, the roots branch out and shoots bloom overnight aiming for the sky—that is the way to grow in the black man's world. The people of Ghost Gum, Blood Gum, River Gum, and Box Gum have all come from the trees and will turn into one when the time comes. Anawari enjoyed seeing himself grow as a huge *pipalia* tree, with large limbs tough enough to withstand the storms, and bark thick enough to shield his trunk from the sun. "Trees shed old bark when spring comes, just as the animals shed their fur." Anawari could not remember who told him that, but assumed it must have been in his dream that he had been taught the secrets of growing up.

Nothing came of his burrowing now, however, and Anawari was surprised not only at the absence of frogs but that while digging, he had come across several large roots of the trees and in none of them, though he had peeled the softer parts which had once been bark, had he found one single *maku*, the grub. Years ago the earth had been more generous—Anawari and Nupuru had once dug a single hole behind a *witjuti* bush and filled their dish to the brim with enough squirming *maku* to satisfy their bellies for two days. He would not let me down now, that wise old man?

227

When Anawari stopped to rest and lay flat on his back on the sand, he saw Nyinyi perched in the dead tree above; the bird had probably been watching him for some time, for it was settled on a branch with both its eyes closed as if snoozing and only opening one of them now and then, to glance at him.

"Tell me where to find water," Anawari assumed he was thinking, and was startled to suddenly hear his own words spoken aloud. Both of Nyinyi's eyes opened, but only for a second and then the eyelids folded down again.

"You know every single foot of this country. Tell me, where's the water? Without it a tree never grows. We are going to stay here, it is our country."

Nyinyi tucked its head under one wing as though deliberately ignoring Anawari and this behavior upset him, for it seemed he was to be cast out and punished for something he had not done. Anawari was tempted to speak in his own defense, but decided not to show any discontent, for there was a real fear in his mind of insulting the bird, and further weakening the already fragile cord between himself and that almost forgotten world of his *tjamu*. Anawari's self-respect—his very existence—depended on a delicate thread still binding him to the ways of his ancestors, and he could not risk snapping that thread through his own carelessness. A man would never be turned into a tree if he is mistrusted by his ancestors, he warned himself. It dawned on him, however, that *tjamu* are keeping away from the country because of the whites and not him. That monstrous metal bird would be perching on a dead tree not far away, its senses tuned up to catch the secrets that have kept the country, trees, and man alive ever since that mythical rain. No *nangari* would be foolish enough to let that be stolen, nor would Nupuru.

On the other hand, since the trees had died and the tribes had gone, it might never rain again, and perhaps Nyinyi knew that there was nothing that any spirit, bird or man, could do about it. Nupuru had said that long ago, in the time before the beginning, when the whole country was a plain of shimmering sand, Malu, the Kangaroo Man, was wandering about hoping to start a new

228

world. It never rained in that ancient mythical time, and to make the rain come one would have to dance *intichiuma,* raise a cloud of dust, and sing out the chant that would call the rain; but there were no people in the land to do that. Fortunately for Malu his *tjamu* sent a whole mob of tall, vigorous men to earth, to perform a rainmaking ceremony, and it was such an impassioned dance with such loud chanting that, the following night, an immense storm broke and, for the first time, soaked the dry sand. After the storm, however, very few plants sprang to life other than the spiny spinifex bush, and no more rain fell for many years.

According to the story that Anawari had been told, the group of dancing men was called again to help Malu, but after performing the *intichiuma* the second time, they were changed into *pipalia,* the huge river gum trees, and so had to stay in the country forever; and now after each long dry spell the trees chant, and sway their tall branches in the air to signal the clouds and bring the rain again.

Anawari found himself suddenly thinking of that night on the diggings when he was tracked by the monstrous bird, for he felt that now too the whites had a beam on him from some distance away. There should be a way of turning into a tree without them knowing about it. Without water about, one does not grow, however. On the left flank of the valley a ridge made a sharp incision in the horizon behind, and there was a hope that there might be water among the rocks there, or that life in the hills might have escaped the same fate as that in the plain below.

Halfway to the hills Anawari stopped to rest and saw at his feet a skeleton, lying partly buried in the earth; it was *malu,* the kangaroo, and pieces of scattered charcoal strewn around the bones suggested that those tribesmen who, years ago, had placed the animal in the hot ashes, had not been given enough time to consume their meal. A dozen steps away Anawari saw another heap of charcoal showing up clearly against the red soil, and another and another until he had counted altogether twenty-two piles set in a rough circle about the same distance apart, and each presumably marked the position of a *wiltja,* a tribal hut, in front of which they were lit long ago. Anawari guessed that they had lain un-

229

disturbed for twenty years or more and that the predominantly dry climate of the island had preserved the few pieces of sapling that had formed each primitive shelter, and that now lay tumbled on the ground. Anawari stepped on one length of wood, expecting it to disintegrate under the weight of his foot, but it was unyielding and stone-tough. Anawari saw the likeness between this strange, hard wood and the river trees, quite dead but upright still, and mused on the mystery. A round pad that a tribal woman had used when carrying a heavy load on her head, known as *manguri,* lay on the ground, reduced finally to a circular patch of fur, dry grass, and human hair, and no longer of any use in carrying the wooden bowl, the *piti,* full of water as it once had been.

Just forget about water for a while—you are being watched by the whites, Anawari told himself, and looked about for the debris of tribal life he felt around. He picked up the lower member of a pair of grinding stones the size of a frying pan but of an irregular shape. Its flat surface had been partly worn away leaving a shallow depression in the middle, and as Anawari ran his fingers gently over the smooth stone he whispered, "*Tjiwa.*" The other member of the grinding pair, the upper stone called *tjungari,* should have been somewhere about, and as Anawari searched for it, he stumbled on a light-colored stone of an odd pyramidal shape—a *kanti,* the woman's knife—one side of which had a very sharp edge for use as a cutting blade. Anawari, on closer inspection of the implement, found a layer of sooty material thick on its base, and when he scraped this with his nail, he recognized it as the remains of *kiti,* the resin made from porcupine grass with which a wooden handle was often fastened to a stone implement.

How far *kanti* must have traveled, for the implement was made of a flinty stone, very hard to come by and often passed from one tribe to another as trade goods or gifts and by which means some had traveled across half the continent. Nupuru had carried a flint blade with a wooden handle decorated with a dingo track design, his totem, which he kept in a paper sheath hanging from his *maranga,* the belt. On walkabout Anawari had seen Nupuru cut a pair of wooden fire-making sticks in a matter of minutes, for the stone knife, though now worn with age, was as efficient as when he first used it crossing the desert and traveling far up the coast, in flight from the white man, or in search of rain, perhaps. The desert crossing had often been on his mind since he had fled from the settlement, for he felt that Nupuru had been crossing the desert frequently and there should be a track made by him, stretching from one waterhole to another across the country. Anawari talked about the idea of crossing the desert to Ily when last with him, hoping the story might excite him and, as in their old school days, make him aware of the color of his skin. That was a mistake, perhaps. Ily quickly calculated the distance between the 27th and 15th parallels and, with the mind of an efficient surveyor, added some additional figures for deviations from the main course line, and grinned. "You have to be more than human to make it across." The old schoolmate mentioned, however, that he heard of a tribal ancestor who made such a trip with his pack of dingoes, but that would have been in mythical times, long before Pythagoras was born and set the course of science. In spite of his professional suspicion Ily stressed that Australia is different from the rest of the world, the bush, in particular, where tribal spirits tend to travel eternally and traverse the desert at will. "Do keep in touch. We might set off on that journey across the desert one day." Ily sounded formal.

Several spent rifle shells, with the shine of their brass long ago lost and their coat of tarnish now blending itself into the color of dust, lay scattered about, but Anawari stepped resolutely over them and headed toward the lower slopes of the ridge. About halfway between the abandoned camp site and the hills Anawari paused again; in a thicket of dry bushes that had once been *ili* (wild fig) the remains of a human skull could be seen, the back part of which was missing as though blown away by a shot from the back. Anawari hesitated a moment, out of respect, and then slowly, and softly for fear a noisy footstep might disturb the wandering spirit, walked on. Anawari, surprisingly, found no need to cast about looking for the right track; he felt as a man who knows his way around in his own home, and this place no longer seemed strange as it had done at first. Although no specific detail or scene rose from Anawari's memory, and the whole of his infant life was a world beyond recall, it appeared that yet there was an instinct that, like an unseen guide, directed his steps.

A shadow moved about. Anawari thought it was the major with that monstrous metal bird coming to pester him at a time when he was searching through the debris of his tribal childhood. No, it was her. Anawari watched the Skeleton Woman waiting for him in the shade of a dry tree. As he moved closer, she walked off heading toward the ridge. One of her bony arms swung for a moment. Was she trying to say something, perhaps just a signal to follow? Anawari wanted to call her to wait; they could sit down and talk. Later she could show him the country around the camp. If there is any water about, she will be the one to know. No, you don't speak to the spirits, not till you're spoken to, he reminded himself as he followed her slowly.

Anawari stooped under a rock shelter, to find ashes left from the last fire there, hardened but quite undisturbed; he felt sure that if there had been a single animal still alive, it would have left paw marks there, in the cool shadow of the overhanging stone. Stuck in a crack in the rock was a *kuntil,* a spinning frame made of crossed tecoma bush twigs mounted on a longer stick—*inti*—to serve as the rotating shaft; a handful of yarn, spun from animal fur and human hair, was still wound over and around the cross bars of the shaft. Anawari turned the spindle over his skin; he could not tell where he had seen a *kuntil* before, for certainly the spindle could not have been of use to the women in the settlement camps, where mangy dogs and nearly bald tribespeople could provide no material for spinning; and yet Anawari felt sure that he knew the correct tribal word for the operation and his fingers manipulated the device with some skill. Some power, not that of man alone but of the whole race from which he sprang, led him about—Anawari felt that every step, glance, and thought had been sucked into his mind from some unknown world into which he had been catapulted. Namir, too, must have gone through all this.

Anawari was drawn deep into the rock shelter to its darkest

232

corner, where he picked up a wooden object in the shape of a small, shallow trough, and before he could raise it to the light, his exploring fingers had identified it as a *kanilypa,* a cradle. Rough lines were left behind from the chipping out of the interior wood, and though later smoothed with a rubbing stone, they remained uneven and Anawari could feel them now under his fingers. Had he felt that roughness when he lay in the *kanilypa* to be breast-fed? Anawari thought not—the surface of the wood seemed, somehow, soft and still tenderly warm as though hardly a moment had passed since it had last cradled a baby. Anawari reflected that one of man's most poignant longings was to return to his cradle, yet how much greater was his despair when he would have given everything—the whole world—not to have been dragged from that *kanilypa.*

Had Namir come from that same cradle, and Ily also? Anawari waited for the answer, but suddenly realized the unimportance of it. He had followed the path, not only of his mate, but of many unknown brothers and sisters whose anguish and pain had been much greater than his. We're just grains of sand in the storm that had engulfed the desert. He looked back to Pulkarin Valley searching for that monstrous metal bird, which he felt was following him about, and added: Grains of sand could turn into trees if our spirits so decided. No white man's gadgets can detect that. As the day neared its end, he walked back to the river looking for a place to rest. Though the dusk brought with it a breeze, the country looked just as dead as during the afternoon. When Anawari walked back along the dry riverbed the following morning, however, and stopped at the dead gum tree, he saw that water had gathered in the bottom of the hole he had dug the previous day. As he knelt to scoop up a handful of liquid, Anawari glanced up and saw Nyinyi sitting on a branch, its flickering tail reflecting the red light of the morning sun in glowing sparks on each shining feather.

Anawari closed his eyes while his mind traveled through the desert. Somewhere in the unknown vastness, many skies away, Nupuru sat under a mulga tree with his pack of dogs. "Thank you for caring for me," Anawari whispered to the old man, feeling more sure now than ever before that the sacred word of his *tjamu* was behind him. Those wise elders would never let him suffer more than other tribal souls—for that, that alone, he felt grateful.

Fill in the hole, he told himself, throwing back some sand with his foot. With ground water about trees can grow now and reach for the sky. Anawari sat on the ground trying to keep still, just as that man rubbed with goanna fat did. "Thank you, *tjamu*, for seeing me through." The old man sat under the mulga tree with his pack of dingoes; next to him sat a tribal elder of lighter skin, worn off by sandstorms and the desert sun—Rotar, there he is at last. Both men had on *kadaitja* shoes and wore *yakiri* headbands decorated with parrot feathers and cockatoo down. They have put on their ceremonial fineries to see me off—thank you both. Nupuru held *maban,* rubbing the shell surface slowly with his fingers, while Rotar clapped a boomerang against the shaft of a spear and both chanted.

Grown tired of walking around the world, the trees settled down for good. Though they still hop about now and then, they have long passed on the secrets of wandering to man. Man was also told by the plants how to travel through waterless country and shield from the sun, just as leaves know how to protect themselves during the hot summer blaze.

When man journeys through unknown country, trees, like faithful dogs, follow him. They are often seen in sheltered valleys, and never fail to be about at a dry river crossing to give him a drink. Trees also hang around large boulders, for times when traveling man stops there to camp and hugs against the warm rocks during cold desert nights. No traveler who knows about trees will lose his way in the bush; the branches can always tell you which way to head on.

No man buries his foot in the ground and spreads roots, for he is on the move—the trees thought of that and gave him the spear to hunt for food and let him shape the boomerang from a bent branch. Trees let man chisel soft wood to make dishes to gather grass seeds in or carry water about. When you want a tree to turn hard, leave your wana, newly made digging stick, in the sun and it will become stone in no time.

Being taller than man and much wiser, trees can always tell of an approaching storm. They sight a cloud as soon as it rises beyond the horizon and rustle their leaves to tell the news. Later on as the willy-willy gallops across the country, whirling a column of dust, trees lash their branches to warn man of the oncoming storm. Cling to a large trunk and the branches will sway down to shield you. When old, trees grow even kinder, opening part of their trunk to let birds, animals, or men hide in the hollow.

Be kind to trees and they will bloom into flower for you, and attract a flock of honeysuckers and a swarm of bees. They repay you even further with crops of nuts and by making a home for grubs down in their roots. Remember, trees are relatives of man, after all.

CHAPTER 22

Not till Anawari grew up to the fifth notch and just before beginning to branch out did he see Nupuru. The old man sat still on the ground and only the top of *pukati,* the tall ceremonial headdress decorated with possum fur and parrot feathers that rose like an anthill, appeared. First, Anawari wished he could rise faster to see his ancestor's face to thank him for letting him grow safe in his country again, but no soul could suddenly rise sky high, and if it did, it would tip over. While growing up steadily, his roots had spread under the ground not only to nourish him, but to hold on against the onslaught of a sudden storm that might come about. As he paused to fork his first branch, Anawari left behind a dormant bud. Young trees do bend in the wind, but they often snap off, and if it happens, there is something left to shoot out from again.

Seen from above, the country looked bare except for the skeletons of dead trees along the river valley. The tide of sand is still rising, he warned himself, seeing that some of the trunks had been buried up to their forks. The sand was on the move because of the drought. Anawari assumed that there had been no rain ever since the tribes were rounded up. Farther down the river, the lake, long dry, had turned into a salty claypan blazing in the sun. Some water still remained in the ground under the salty crust, though no tree would grow on that. Anawari wondered for how long the moisture would remain in the ground to which he was rooted. "Trees die from drought, just as humans do," Nupuru had told him long ago. Growing further up with new shoots, Anawari saw the old man at last sitting with a pack of dingoes and with Rotar, both men ceremonially dressed. The clapping of the boomerang sounded much clearer though, and so did the chant:

Clumps of dry mulga grass
groomed with *maban*
magic
seashell
stored with rain

For a moment Anawari worried that the major might hear the sacred chant for rain and rob the old men of that too, but he remembered that trees see farther than humans could imagine, and so do they hear. The whites never sit still, he told himself. Growing up a space higher, Anawari saw a man with a tripod on his shoulder, as he struggled through the wilderness. Around him whirled a sandstorm; the man turned his back for a moment to catch his hat blown by the wind—Ily! Ahead of his old schoolmate and the storm, Anawari saw a lonely track that cut across the plain of smooth sand, heading toward the horizon and farther, toward the sea. On reaching a rise Ily set the tripod down and pointed his surveying instrument at the track. Anawari wondered how anyone could tell which way the traveler had gone from the prints of *kadaitja* shoes, when he heard, "Fantastic!" He looked for the major, but instead of him saw the monstrous eagle perched on a rock behind Ily. With its voice partly muffled by a metallic rattling, the monster explained that they were not far from cracking the rainmaking code and said, "Soon the drought will break and the war will end." It surprised Anawari to hear about the war going on, for there was no tree about to cut a spear or a boomerang from. Later he realized that the whites were fighting drought and not tribal warriors, and he felt jubilant when he remembered that no man had ever won against the tide of sand; but the spirits can. Ily must have thought of that too; he tried to reset his tripod. The tripod sank as though it had been placed on water; Ily complained,

"When on the march the sand can level the sea—engulf the whole world." The major told him not to panic and thought for a while, stretching out one of his wings to brush off the dust from its metal quills. "The water will hold the sand—let's get on with the rain." Ily wondered what good the sand could be, whether dry or wet, when nothing would grow on it, but he was told that some miracle would happen and the sand would turn into clay; that is how the world began according to the Bible—from clay. "We shall make a new start after the rain—man's made of clay." Excited by the prospect of going through a new period of creation, he fluttered his metal wings, raising a cloud of sand and dust. The disturbed dust quickly grew into a willy-willy sweeping the ground. Ily clung to the ground and tried to hold on to the tripod that trembled under the onslaught of the wind. He thought man was made of wood, not sand, and tried to explain that the first man had been made like a boomerang, carved out of a trunk, rough at first, but smoother later. The major still insisted that the world had come from the sand—the clay actually—but the clay came about after the sand had been processed and the minerals extracted. Ily objected, explaining that the black man had come from a different line, but he was ordered to think as expected of him, and to concentrate on his search and that *kadaitja* track ahead of them.

The rain was much on Nupuru's mind as well. The old man rubbed his *maban,* and filing off tiny fragments of shell and gathering them in his palm, raised his hand. Behind him Rotar hastened, clapping the boomerang and still muttering words of the sacred chant. They must have been calling for the rain often, for the shell in Nupuru's hand looked small, reduced to a disk hardly bigger than a button. Tiny as it looked, Anawari knew that *maban* is stored with *karanita,* essence of rain, enough of it to deluge the whole desert. The shell came from Tapidji, the sea on the northern shore of Australia; only Nupuru knew his way there, for to cross the drought-stricken country, one has to be *nangari* and more than human. Nupuru blew the specks of shell dust out from his palm. He then sucked the *maban* and spat toward the horizon.

Country engulfed by sand
waits for *karan*
   rain droplets
   out of shell
   fly to sky

Though *maban* held enough *karan* of rain to flood the whole
world, no tribal healer ever wanted to see his country turned into
a sea and would release only a few showers at a time—enough
to soak the desert. Anawari had been shown the magic shell in
his dream, when on that outing in the desert with Nupuru. The
old man wore a *pukati* headdress, just like the one seen on him
now, though he did not chant then, nor was Rotar with him to
clap the boomerang. However, he swung his hand about, touch-
ing tips of mulga grass clumps with *maban*—the grass, though
dry from long drought, still looked like patches of silvery clouds
scattered over the sky. Anawari hardly believed in dreams then,
but soon after he found himself expecting the rain, and even after
returning to the settlement to his job, had often kept glancing
through his office window, looking for the clouds to appear.
When that dry storm hit the settlement, blowing off the roofs
and breaking a pane in his window, he told himself, "Here it
comes!" The dust storm blew over without a single drop, but
during the night that followed, *nangari* appeared in Anawari's
dream again, explaining that his *maban* had been stolen by the
whites and that the drought would go on till a new shell had been
brought from Tapidji, and by then the whites, harassed by sand,
would hopefully leave the country. In his dream Anawari offered
to write to a friend living in the coastal area of Australia, to send
him a shell by mail, which could bring the drought to an end.
He was told that only a shell brought by *nangari* would make the
rain. After crossing the desert in search of that shell and on reaching Tapidji, the medicine man leaves his *kadaitja* shoes in a hollow
log before entering the shallow sea inlets inundated with immense
water lizards that eat humans and spirits alike. The medicine man
frightens them off with his spear and, walking through the shallow
water, looks for the shell that moves about like a fish. As soon

as he eyes one of them, the healer nails it down to the sandy floor of the pool. The hole made by the spear later becomes very handy for poking through a cord, so that the healer hangs *maban* around his neck and prevents the precious shell from being stolen.

Anawari remembered the story of the magic shell whenever he looked through the window of his office and saw the rising tide of sand and dust outside. He often turned to a map on the wall, after trying to measure the distance from the northern shore of Australia to the desert around him. "Thousands of miles," he had concluded. But however far the distance stretched, he knew that the medicine man had been crossing it for generations, and given time, he would do so again to bring the rain.

Now as he watched Nupuru sucking the ribbed fragments of the shell and spitting them out, Anawari saw *karan* of rain—tiny droplets flying from the healer's mouth toward the horizon. They flew out like a swarm of midges above the dry crounty. They faded from sight for a moment or two, and Anawari thought that they had been drawn into the heat haze hovering about the desert, but they soon appeared far on the horizon, each droplet turned into tiny fragments of cloud. "It'll rain," Anawari told himself, and rustled his leaves to spread the news, but realized that around him were only skeletons of trees—the rain would be of no help to them. Would one tree be able to make the whole bush grow again? He looked at the bare expanse of the salty claypan down the valley; when it comes, the rain will fill up the lake, though hardly anything will ever grow there again. Farther on the Boomerang—yes, there is a tree growing there with clumps of scrub poking from behind the rocks. He assumed that the tree was Namir and rustling his leaves tried to say, "We'll form a new tribe again—the other fellows should be around soon." The clumps of scrub rose higher to reveal that they were trees, too—scores of them. It pleased him to see that even the detainees had turned into trees, and it would not be long before the bush reclaimed the desert again. He would have been happier if Namir had been growing on the opposite bank of the river instead of the island. If close by, they could branch toward each other, or make their

240

roots meet halfway in the ground under the riverbed, but it was nice to be back in the tribal country and grow, even though half a lake apart. "The whites have gone for good!" Anawari tried to call toward the island.

As he grew higher, Anawari learned that the whites had not quite gone yet. The major, still struggling across the desert, kept muttering, "Man's made of clay," as he tried to fight his way out of the whirling dust storm. Ily, trying to drag his tripod buried by sand, still held that man is made of wood and supported his claim with the logic: "The whole earth was covered with forest. The plants were far ahead of humans, trees in particular. Being so numerous they stood a far better chance of creating the world than anyone else." Ily struggled to set his tripod on the drifting sand and beamed the instrument at the *kadaitja* track. The major explained that trees rot—in the rain forest one feels nothing but the pungent smell of decay. Rotting plants produce bacteria, too small to be seen by the naked eye, but microscopes do not lie. The Black Death rose from the forests, as did malaria, leprosy, smallpox, and bigger pox, which wiped out tribal Australia. "Man's made of clay, says the Bible." As the two men argued, the sandstorm swallowed both of them.

Much else sank into the sand. As he spread his leaves in anticipation of the rain and growing further, Anawari saw the settlement at last. The communication tower appeared first, leaning on one side with loose metal bars dangling in the wind. After that appeared the chimney of the William Wilberforce Hospital, though no fragment of smoke showed up now. For a moment Anawari thought that Dr. Tinto and his staff might be holidaying, but learned that the hospital had sunk into the sand as had everything else around. Instead of the settlement there now lay a plain of drifting sand. He looked for the tribal camps, but soon reminded himself that trees and men had gone long ago, and the country had descended into the Dry Age, looking more like a scene from the galactic world than a tribal country. Out of the sand stood a piece of wood looking as though someone had left behind a walking stick stuck in the ground. "It's old Kaltu's spear, poor fellow,"

Anawari reminded himself. However, that old man and his tribal relatives will be back growing sky high as the country becomes green again. He watched the shadow come spreading across the plain of sand. It rolled over the remains of the hospital, the communication tower, and the old spear shaft, and then moving farther engulfed the whole country. . . .

The droplets grown into clouds
turn into *walpa*
   downpour
   soaks sand
   greening desert

The chant accompanied by the clattering of the boomerang hastened; the sky grew darker and the clouds closed in. "Here it comes!" Anawari stretched his limbs and spread his leaves to catch the best of the downpour.

It rained and rained for days; coming out from the prolonged drought the world plummeted into a deluge. Thirsty for years, the earth drank far more than her belly could handle and then vomited. The water gushed out through old crevices, from holes left behind by roots of long-dead trees and the burrows of vanished marsupials. The trees handle water better than humans. Anawari spread his roots toward the riverbank, searching for higher ground less saturated. By now he had grown a trunk strong enough to withstand storms and floods alike. He had shed his lower branches, straightened his shape, so as not to be tipped over. The river next to him had turned into a torrent, rolling down the trunks of dead trees and rocks, elbowing constantly and burrowing into the banks. Anawari had to strengthen his crown root, anchoring deeper into the soft ground, and he let the river debris pile up against him to divert the current. He lowered his branches and held still, fearing that if he swayed his limb, it could tip him over. Farther down the valley the lake expanded rapidly, swallowing the country, though on Boomerang Island, Namir and all those growing around him stood far above the water mark.

A car canopy suddenly appeared floating down the river. Anawari thought to yell out to Namir that the whites were coming, but soon learned not to fear the old debris. Down under his branches, tumbled by the river, passed an old truck. The current had torn off most of the panels, except for one that dangled behind and poked out of the water now and then showing the fading sign PROJECT JANIZARY. It was followed by more wrecks that the whites had brought into the country and left behind. The river must have swept through the settlement, for Anawari sighted a huge *W* that had once stood on the facade of the hospital. It was followed by a briefcase like the one he had seen in the superintendent's office; then came along the machine Laura and Ann had used to work on when injecting the oranges with drugs. Stuck to the machine he saw a piece of paper; he thought it could be his missing photograph, but now that mattered little. Trees do not write letters applying for jobs that need photographs. Suddenly Anawari saw the computer from his office, stuck among the debris that had piled up against his trunk. Trees do not need machines to tell them how to grow; the tribal healer does far better, providing he has a boomerang and a magic seashell at hand.

Under Anawari's branches, tumbling down the river, passed the monstrous bird. When in the water the metal had sunk to the bottom, but pushed by the current, one wing poked out and driven on by the flow kept flapping about. Anawari dropped some leaves in respect, mourning his old enemy that had hunted him for so long. He thought of dropping his leaves again later on, when a panel from the helicopter came down tumbled by the torrent: Would that be the sergeant's machine or the one Ily had flown about in? That too mattered little now. When the wrecks reached the lake, the metal would rust just the same, no matter who had used them. Anawari looked for a while into the turbulent water below him, searching for Ily, and thought it would be nice to have *kurta,* a brother, growing next to him. One of them could always be on the lookout, while the other rested. The trees chat to each other on long windy nights; wild storms often happen and bushfires come about. Trees are like birds—they do not like to be caught by surprise. Anawari looked at the patch of ground on the bank high above the water mark. It would be just the right spot for Ily. There could be no better place to grow up than the bank of the Rotar River. The man must have been their father, tribal father only, for no child in the desert has ever come from man, but from *pulkarin* rock. Anawari assumed that wherever Ily might be, he would eventually find his way back to his tribal country to grow like a tree. "There's no room for all of us here."

Years later as the country greened, slowly healing the scars of red sand, and after Anawari had begun to grow hollows for cockatoos to nest in his trunk, he noticed a strange object that had slid from the eroded banks down to the river. It looked like a rusted part of one of the white man's machines, but after the water washed off the dirt, he saw a skeleton of a hand gripping a microscope. "Dr. Tinto, I presume," he told himself, and wondered what metal rusted down to—sand or dust. For an old tree, that now mattered little.

GLOSSARY

boong	- derogatory term for Aborigines
didjeridu	- immense, deep-note wind instrument made from up to eight feet of hollow tree
gabi	- waterhole
gabi-bulka	- large waterhole
gabi-wia	- dry waterhole
gabitjara	- moving water
gibber	- oval stone unique to Australian deserts
idi	- baby, child
igama	- club, fighting stick
ili	- wild fig
inma	- ceremony
inti	- rotating shaft of spindle
intichiuma	- ceremony, life-increasing rites
irama	- club
kadaitja	- ceremonial footwear
kali	- boomerang
kaltu-kaltu	- seed from wild grass (*Panicumm decompositum*)
kanilypa	- wooden dish, used also as cradle

kanti	– stone knife
karan	– soul, spirit double
karanita	– life essence
karupa	– digging tool
kiti	– resin extracted from the spinifex bush
kulata	– long hunting spear
kulpitji	– sacred totemic emblem or design
kuntil	– spinning frame of spindle
kuri	– wife, woman
kurta	– brother
maban	– magic seashell
magarada	– peace-making ceremony (term from North Australia)
maijada	– ceremony master
maku	– grub
malu	– kangaroo
mamu	– spirits
manguri	– woman's head pad for carrying a load
maramura	– rainmaking ceremony
maranga	– man's belt
mawulyari	– traditional woman's hair skirt or belt
milmilpa	– very sacred
miru	– spear-throwing device
mukulpa	– barb or peg on spear thrower, on which the spear is balanced
mullina	– age-grading ceremony
nalta	– kurrajong tree
nangari	– medicine man
nanpa	– man's belt

narngi	- frog
ngintaka	- goanna fat
ngura	- country
nyinyi	- finch, small bird
nyuma	- damper (unleavened loaf)
palka	- hollow recess on spear shaft
panya	- manhunt
para	- ghost gum tree
patupiri	- bat
pipalia	- river gum tree
piti	- smaller wooden dish
pukati	- headdress
pulkarin	- life-giving rock
takapiri	- emu
tjamu	- ancestor, ancestors
tjamu–ngura	- ancestrial country
tjiwa	- lower grinding stone
tjungari	- upper grinding stone
tjurunga	- sacred totemic object similar to *kulpitja*
tjuta	- blood gum tree
urtjanpa	- tecoma bush (*Pandorea doratoxylon*)
walpa or waralpa	- storms, downpour, wind
wana	- digging stick
wankar	- half man
waru	- fire
wata	- spearhead
wiltja	- hut, simple shelter; usually temporary, of propped saplings and branches

witchetty grubs	– large edible grubs found in roots of wattle tree
witjinti	– corkwood tree
witjuti	– wattle tree (*Acacia kempeana*)
wonambi	– mythical serpent
woomera	– spear thrower
yakiri	– headband
yalpiri	– box gum tree